THE NIGHT SEASON

THE NIGHT SEASON

CHELSEA CAIN

THORNDIKE
WINDSOR
PARAGON

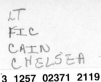

This Large Print edition is published by Thorndike Press, Waterville, Maine, USA and by AudioGO Ltd, Bath, England.
Thorndike Press, a part of Gale, Cengage Learning.
Copyright © 2011 by Verite Inc.
The moral right of the author has been asserted.

The text of this Large Print edition is unabridged.
Other aspects of the book may vary from the original edition.
Set in 16 pt. Plantin.

LIBRARY OF CONGRESS CATALOGING-IN-PUBLICATION DATA

Cain, Chelsea.
    The night season / by Chelsea Cain.
        p. cm. — (Thorndike Press large print crime scene)
    ISBN-13: 978-1-4104-3779-2 (hardcover)
    ISBN-10: 1-4104-3779-5 (hardcover)
    1. Sheridan, Archie (Fictitious character)—Fiction. 2. Ward, Susan (Fictitious character)—Fiction. 3. Police—Oregon—Portland—Fiction. 4. Women journalists—Fiction. 5. Serial murderers—Fiction. 6. Portland (Or.)—Fiction. 7. Large type books. I. Title.
PS3603.A385N54 2011b
813'.6—dc22   2011005183

BRITISH LIBRARY CATALOGUING-IN-PUBLICATION DATA AVAILABLE

Published in 2011 in the U.S. by arrangement with St. Martin's Press, LLC.
Published in 2011 in the U.K. by arrangement with Pan Macmillan Ltd.

U.K. Hardcover: 978 1 445 85822 7 (Windsor Large Print)
U.K. Softcover: 978 1 445 85823 4 (Paragon Large Print)

Printed in the United States of America
1 2 3 4 5 6 7 15 14 13 12 11

For my husband, Marc Mohan.
Go, Pack!

DOWNTOWN PORTLAND

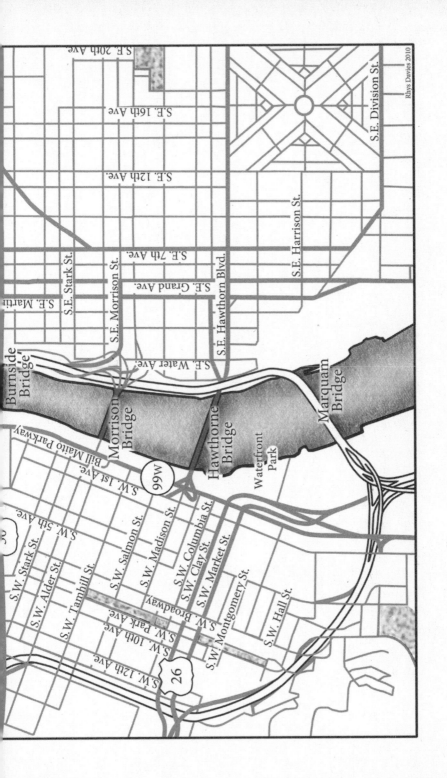

REMEMBER:
DIKES ARE SAFE AT PRESENT.
YOU WILL BE WARNED IF NECESSARY.
YOU WILL HAVE TIME TO LEAVE.
DON'T GET EXCITED.

*— Statement issued by the Housing
Authority of Portland to the people of
Vanport, Oregon, on May 30, 1948.*

PROLOGUE

Memorial Day, 1948

Floyd Wright came bursting into Williams's office, red-faced and out of breath, his clothes dusty from the speeder.

"It's bad," Floyd said.

Williams stood up at his desk. He took the news in stride. You didn't get to be president of the Portland Union Stockyards without having an iron stomach. He'd known this could happen. It's why he'd sent Floyd out on patrol. He was already calculating their losses, rerouting cattle cars on alternate lines. If the tracks were down for a few days, they could still get the butchers their meat.

Williams's secretary scrambled into the office after Floyd, but Williams didn't want her interrupting. He motioned for her to wait, and she stopped a few steps inside the door.

"What are we looking at?" Williams asked Floyd.

Floyd held his hat in his hands. "It's the west side," he said. "Complete collapse. Fifty feet, at least."

Fifty feet? They had expected that the dike might spring a few leaks. Those could be repaired. A fifty-foot breach was something else entirely. There weren't contingencies for that.

"Oh my lord," the secretary said.

She was staring out the window, her hand covering her mouth.

Williams had spent enough time at that window watching the cattle cars come in to know exactly what she was looking at.

He stepped around his desk and moved quickly to her side, motioning for Floyd to do the same. It was a clear sunny day, seventy-six degrees. There wasn't a cloud in the sky. The office was on the top floor. Beyond a hundred acres of wooden pens that held cattle waiting for slaughter, they had a good view of the city of Vanport, and to the east, the railroad tracks that formed the city's eastern boarder. Seventy-six two-story apartment buildings were arranged in groups of four around utility buildings. A movie theater. An elementary school.

The railroad bed functioned as a dike,

holding back Smith Lake from the Vanport floodplain. The breach was visible even from the window. Brown water gushed from where the gravel and dirt had given way to the lake's pressure, over the tracks and down toward the city.

Vanport was going to flood, and fast. Williams felt his stomach knot. The stockyards were above the floodplain. The cattle, the buildings, the water wouldn't reach them. But those people in Vanport. *All those people.*

"Call the Vanport city manager," Williams barked at his secretary. "Tell them there's a fifty-foot gap in the railroad fill near the northwest corner of the project."

The girl hesitated. Her eyes looked wild.

"Now," he said.

"Yes, sir," she said, turning and running to her desk outside the office.

Fifteen thousand people lived in Vanport. Working people. Families. Plenty less than lived there during the war. The apartments were cheap, but the walls were paper thin, and there wasn't hot water or heat at night.

"They don't have telephones," Floyd said. "Company decision."

As the minutes ticked by, the two men listened in silence for the emergency siren. Williams didn't hear anything. He lifted the

13

window. The smell of cattle and hay settled in the office. He could hear the moan of the cows, the tremble of their hooves on the bare beaten ground. But he still didn't hear a siren.

It was 4:35 P.M.

His secretary returned.

"Well?" Williams said.

"I told them," she said.

Several more minutes passed. Williams began to fume. He picked up the pair of binoculars that he kept on the windowsill and aimed them out the window. The breach had widened, and was now nearly a city block long. The water from Smith Lake spilled through the dike like a gleaming brown waterfall. It was coming with such force that Williams could see it moving, see it spreading on the west side of the dike, a new lake forming, widening by the second, the muddy water transforming as it advanced, reflecting the calm blue of the sky, deceptively tranquil. He followed the water west with the binoculars, toward Vanport. A boy riding his bike in the two feet of water that had already collected on North Portland Road. A car driving up Victory Avenue. A couple walking together across a park.

"What's taking them so long?" Floyd asked.

It was a good goddamn question.

Williams put down the binoculars, picked up the phone on his desk, and fumbled with it, his palm slick with sweat. But he didn't make calls. His girl did. He looked at her helplessly and she came around his desk and took the receiver and dialed, and then handed him the phone.

"Hello?" a man's voice asked.

"For God's sake," Williams hollered into the phone, "alert those people."

It was a few minutes after that that the sirens finally started.

Williams glanced at his watch. It was 4:47 P.M.

The entire railroad bed had given way now, and the lake flowed freely over it. The railroad tracks, snapped in half by the surging water, the ground washed away beneath them, now seemed to hang in midair.

The secretary began to cry quietly. Williams thought he should say something, but he didn't know what. Floyd coughed. No one spoke. The three of them stood together at the window, wordless, as the water continued to swell. The binoculars sat on the sill. Williams didn't want to look.

CHAPTER 1

Present day

Technically, the park was closed.

But Laura knew a place where the wire fence was split, and she had let the Aussies through and then climbed over behind them. It looked like a pond. There was, in fact, no place muddier in the winter in Portland, Oregon, than West Delta Dog Park, and that was saying something.

The dogs ran ahead of her in the standing water, splashing it behind them, already matted with wet dirt and dead grass. Occasionally they turned to look back at her, their warm breath condensing in the January air.

Laura wiped her nose with the back of her hand. It was a terrible day to be out. Her rain pants were slick with rain, her trail runners were soaked. She'd spent the early morning sandbagging downtown and her back ached. The stress fracture in her foot stung. Stay off it for six weeks, the doctors had said. As if.

The cloud cover hung so low that the tops of the trees seemed to brush it.

She loved this.

The worst weather, body aching. Nothing could keep her inside. Biking. Running. Walking the dogs. She was out there every day, no matter what. Not like all those poseurs who came out in the summer in their REI sun shirts and ran along the esplanade with their iPods and swinging elbows. Where were they in the dead of winter? At the gym, that's where.

God, Laura hated those people.

Franklin glanced back at her, wagged his stubby tail, barked once, flattened his ears, and took off across the old road to the slough. It was their usual route. Penny, the puppy, stuck closer to Laura, zipping ahead ten feet and then circling back.

Laura heard it then. She had heard it all along, but it had faded to white noise, an ambient sound, like a jet passing overhead.

The Columbia Slough.

She knew it would be high. They'd had a ton of snow in December. Then it had warmed up and started to rain. That meant snowmelt from the mountains. Lots of it. The storm drains were backed up. The Willamette was near flood stage. The local news was live with it day and night; they were considering evacuating downtown. But that was the Willamette. Miles away.

As Laura rounded the corner, past the trees, where the old concrete pavilion sat sinking into the slough bank, she was aware of her mouth opening.

In the summer, the slough was still and flat, blanketed by algae so thick it looked solid enough to walk on. That slough was so stagnant that Laura was surprised anything could survive in it. That slough looked like a bucket of water that had been left on the back porch all summer.

This slough was alive. It moved like something angry and afraid, churning fast and high. Whitewater swept along the bank, pulling up debris and washing it downriver. Laura saw a branch get sucked into the water and lost sight of it in an instant as it was swallowed by the seething froth.

Franklin was up ahead, nosing along the old concrete pavilion at the slough's bank. He whined and gave her a look.

She called his name and slapped her thigh. "Let's get out of here," she said.

He turned to come to her. He'd been a rescue dog. Her husband had found him on the Internet. He'd been kept in some barn in Idaho, given little food and no human comfort. It had taken them years to teach him to trust people. And it filled Laura with pride to know that he had turned into such a good dog.

Even with the noise of the slough, he'd heard her. He'd turned to come.

And that's when it happened.

Did he slip? Did the slough rise up suddenly and take him? She didn't know.

He was looking right at her, and in a second he was gone.

It took her a moment to move. And then she snapped into action.

Her dog was not going to die. Not like this. She ran. She didn't think about the stress fracture. The sore back. The raging river. She ran to the edge of the bank, scanning the water for him, as Penny barked fiercely at her heels.

Her heart leapt. She saw him. A glimpse — a wet mound of fur struggling in froth. He was already moving down the river, but he was alive, his black nose just above water.

She had several options.

Maybe if Franklin hadn't been looking her in the eye when it happened she would have considered more of them. She would have called for help, or run alongside the river, or tied a rope around her waist.

She knew what happened to people who went into water after pets.

They died.

But Laura had seen something in Franklin's brown eyes. He'd looked right at her.

"Stay," she said to Penny.

And she plunged into the cold water after him.

Laura's first sensation, in the rushing dirty sludge, was of not being able to breathe. She'd been hit by a car once, on her bike. It was like that. Like having all the air forced out of you by an impact of steel and concrete. Laura forced herself to take a deep breath, filling her lungs, and she tried to orient herself. Her head was above water, her wet braid around her neck. She was already turned around, already ten feet away from Penny, fifteen, twenty. The roar of the slough was unrelenting. Twigs and branches snapped against Laura's face in the current, stinging her skin. Penny stood barking at the shore, pawing at the ground. Until Laura couldn't hear her anymore.

Where was Franklin?

Laura struggled to see him, but at water level all she could see was more water. She was fifty feet away from Penny now. Sixty. She couldn't see. She couldn't see the shore. Just the sky, dark clouds, above her.

Float.

Cold water survival. You lost heat swimming.

Just float.

She took a deep breath and lifted her hands, already numb, foreign, like they belonged to someone else, and she spread her arms and bobbed on her back, and let the current take her.

The current had taken Franklin.

It would take her to him.

Cold water filled her ears. They ached. Her teeth chattered, the sound lost in the roar of the slough. Her clothes felt heavy, filled with water, dragging her down.

And then she heard him.

Laura rolled over and used the last of her strength to fight her way through the current toward the whimper. He was there, caught against the roots of a fallen tree, the water trapping him. He saw her and his ears perked up, and his paws paddled in vain toward her.

She got to him.

She didn't know how.

She got to him and wrapped her arms around his neck. He could have fought her. Animals did that. Panicked. But he didn't. He went limp. He went limp into her arms, and she was able to use the tree as leverage and push her heels into the silt at the bottom of the slough, and she managed to somehow inch them both to the muddy riverbank.

She collapsed beside him in the mud, still holding on to him, still not letting him go. Her heart was pounding. They were soaked. Franklin whined and licked her face.

They'd made it.

She rolled onto her back, almost giddy. They were alive. She'd like to see one of those fair-weather esplanade runners survive something like this.

Franklin shook the water from his mangy coat and Laura turned away, lifting a hand over her face. "Hey, boy," she said. "Easy."

He growled, his upper lip tightening. He was looking at something behind her.

"What?" she said.

Franklin's eyes narrowed, still focused over Laura's shoulder.

She shivered. Whether it was from cold or fear, she didn't know.

Laura turned around.

In the mud of the bank, partially exposed, was a human skeleton.

CHAPTER 2

Susan Ward was singing along to "Smells Like Teen Spirit" when she almost hit the seagull.

Portland, Oregon, was an hour from the ocean. But when it was windy at the coast, the seagulls were blown inland.

Since the storms started two weeks ago, the city had been infested with them. They got into open Dumpsters, and shat on decks, and stood around on the sidewalk arguing in small groups like first-grade girls at recess. They were angry, bossy birds. But Susan figured she'd be angry, too, if she'd just been blown fifty miles.

Susan laid on her horn, and the gull gave her an accusatory look and flapped off into the rain. He was a western gull — white with slate wings and a yellow bill. They were big birds, knee-high, and built like bouncers, not the scrawny gulls of the Atlantic. Susan didn't know for sure he was male. It was just a theory. Something about the look he gave her.

She spotted Archie's unmarked police car on the last dry patch of asphalt in the parking lot and managed to squeeze her old Saab in beside it, then put the hood of her slicker up and stepped outside into the rain.

It was early afternoon, but it looked like evening. That's how it was in Portland in the winter. Permanent twilight.

The rain on her hood sounded like grease popping in a skillet. It made her crave bacon.

She looked down the hillside to where Oaks Park nestled up against the flood-swollen Willamette River.

Susan felt about parks the way she felt about nature in general. She liked knowing it existed, but didn't feel the need to partake personally. This was not a popular point of view in Portland. Portlanders, in general, took great pride in their parks, and felt compelled to visit them regularly, even in the dead of winter when it was dark and the grass had gone to mud and no one bothered to pick up their dog poop. There were wilderness parks, rose gardens, rhododendron gardens, Japanese gardens, classical Chinese gardens, skate parks, public plazas, parks with fountains, public art, food carts, tennis courts, swimming pools, hiking trails, monuments, and amphitheaters. There was even the world's smallest park, Mill Ends Park, which was roughly two feet by two feet. Susan had always found that last one sort of ridiculous.

Then there was Oaks Park. ("Where the Fun Never Stops!") It had been around for as long as anyone could remember, which is to say about a hundred years. A couple dozen rides, a roller-skating rink, carnival games, picnic grounds. Wholesome good times for the whole family, punctuated by a few brief periods when it was the go-to place for drugs and a van quickie.

A dead body had been found on the carousel.

Susan smiled. Sometimes this stuff just wrote itself.

She finished slogging down the hill and made her way through the pretty white wooden archway to the fairway.

The cops standing around the carousel looked miserable. Hunched over, their black rain ponchos lifting in the wind, they reminded Susan of crows loitering around a carcass.

All but Detective Archie Sheridan.

He was standing away from the others, wearing one of those coats with fur-trimmed hoods that you get at army surplus stores before expeditions to the Arctic.

It was fifty degrees. Practically tropical for January, but he had his hood up. She only knew it was Archie because of how he was holding himself perfectly still, one hand in his pocket, the other around a huge paper cup of coffee, just watching. And because he was alone.

He looked over and saw her and held up the coffee cup in a sort of absentminded wave. His hangdog face was as creased as ever, crooked nose, heavy lids, but he had color to his skin again, and his eyes had more life. A green scarf covered up the horizontal scar on his neck. His brown curls poked in odd angles around his forehead.

"Is it her?" Susan asked him.

"Looks like it," he said. "Robbins will issue an official ID from the ME's office."

Stephanie Towner had been reported missing two days before. The cops had found her car in the parking lot at the Bishop's Close, an estate garden along thirteen acres of high river bluffs on the west side. Portlanders liked to take peaceful walks there when they weren't crouching to take pictures of plants with their iPhones. The cops had found Towner's purse at the top of a slick of mud where it appeared

27

someone had taken a header down the riverbank. You could blame Darwinism. Or you could blame the bottle of wine her husband had reported that she'd had before she left. Maybe a little of both.

"I thought she drowned," Susan said.

The corners of Archie's mouth went up slightly. It had taken Susan a year to recognize the expression as a smile. "I think she did," he said.

She followed his gaze to the carousel. It was housed in an octagonal-roofed pavilion that was open on all sides. Fifteen or twenty seagulls fought for space on the roof. They shifted their weight from one foot to another and squawked nervously. The iron fence that ringed the ride was open and Susan walked inside. One of the poncho-wearing cops put a hand out to stop her. "Not on the platform," he said, jerking his head toward the muddy footprints on the carousel's oak flooring.

She nodded and peered forward from the platform's edge. The corpse was positioned on an ostrich. The ostrich was beautiful, carved out of wood, brown with a red and gold saddle. His yellow legs stretched apart, as if frozen in a joyful skip. Stephanie Towner was posed as if riding the thing. But it wasn't convincing. She'd slumped down, her chin now pressed against the base of the ostrich's neck, her arms dangling on either side of its belly. Thankfully, her hair covered her face. Susan couldn't see well enough to make out many details. But it was clear that she'd been in the water. Or at least in mud.

Archie stepped up behind Susan. She could smell the coffee in his hand and the wet fur on his coat. The rain fell against the carousel roof. The seagulls squawked. "She was moved," he said. "There's mud and grass." He turned to face behind them and motioned across the park to the picnic area at the river's edge, where a chain-link fence lined the riverbank. "We found hair on the fence. Looks like the current washed her downstream and she got tangled up there. Then someone found her, got her over the fence, and dragged her here. Rain washed away any good footprints, but you can make out the drag marks in the mud."

Susan got out her damp notebook and wrote all that down.

Archie was throwing her a bone and she knew it. He'd done that a few times over the last six months. It wasn't his fault that she'd almost gotten herself killed a couple of times in his presence, but he didn't seem to know that. So he gave her a heads-up on the weird stuff. Scoops. She was sure everyone at the newspaper thought they were sleeping together.

"Who called it in?" she asked.

"Crew working on the rink," he said. "I think they're doing something to the floor."

Susan had grown up roller-skating at the Oaks Park Roller Rink. Everyone celebrated birthdays there. All the kids skated around under the disco ball until someone inevitably broke a bone and had to go to the emergency room. The rink was now the home of the Rose City Rollers roller derby team, a bunch of tattooed, big-thighed, bad-ass girls in short-shorts. "It floats," she said. "The rink floor. It's on pontoons. When the park floods they detach it from the foundation."

Archie shrugged and took a sip of coffee. "That's clever. I guess."

Susan craned her head toward the roller rink, which was at the other end of the park, and tried to catch sight of the workers. "You think one of them . . . ?"

"Doesn't look like it," Archie said.

She turned back to the carousel. It was ringed by three rows of animals on ascending circular platforms. Jumping horses. Standing horses. A cat. A deer. A dragon. Zebras. Mules. Pigs.

"Why the ostrich?" she said. Whoever had put the body there had gone through a lot of trouble. It couldn't be easy getting a corpse over a fence. "It's on the inner circle. Why carry her all the way in there?"

"What do they call that color?" Susan heard Henry Sobol ask. He stepped beside Archie, grinning.

Susan blushed and touched her hair, which she had recently dyed raspberry. "You are stealthy, for a large person," she told him, tucking her hair back under the hood of her slicker.

Henry was wearing a watch cap over his shaved head, and his salt-and-pepper mustache glistened with rain. "Professional training," he said with a grin. His black motorcycle boots were caked with mud, probably from the picnic area where the body had originally washed up.

"Let me guess," Susan said. "You were a Navy SEAL."

"Doorman," he said. "I learned how to lurk."

Susan never knew when he was kidding.

But she didn't let on.

"I liked it purple," he said. "What did you call that color?"

"Plum Passion," she said. "It's Manic

Panic. This one's called Deadly Night-shade."

"Whatever happened to Clairol?" Henry mused to Archie, and Susan saw Archie smile.

"Moving a body is a crime, right?" Susan asked.

"Abuse of a corpse," Archie said. "It's a Class C felony in Oregon. People who really like abusing corpses go to California. There it's only a misdemeanor."

"Figures," Susan said.

She'd already called the paper to get a photographer, but they were all out on assignment covering the flooding. The *Herald* would run a wire photo of the carousel, or a photo of Stephanie Towner in better days, if they ran a photo at all. Right now readers were more interested in whether their homeowner's insurance covered mudslides than in women who fell into the Willamette and drowned. Even when they ended up on ostriches.

"Third person who's drowned in the Willamette in two days," Archie said.

"The city's flooding," Henry said, noticing the mud on his boots with a frown. "And people are stupid around water."

"Yeah," Archie said.

Henry gave Archie a look and tapped his watch.

"You sure you can handle things?" Archie said to him.

"Go," Henry said. He pulled a handkerchief from somewhere in his coat, bent over, and dabbed it at his boots.

Archie turned to Susan. "I've got a thing across the river," he explained.

He tossed his coffee cup in a park trash can, which was immediately beset by gulls, and then headed off in the direction of the parking lot.

Susan watched him go. Past the Tilt-a-Whirl, past the children's train, and past Oaks Park's hottest new attraction: "The Beauty Killer House of Horrors." She remembered when it used to be your standard haunted house: glowing skull, hologram ghosts, scary dark hallways. Now it was all Beauty Killer crime scenes. Susan had heard they even had a mannequin made up to look like Archie, strapped to a gurney, with an animatronic Gretchen Lowell, like a giant Barbie, torturing him with a plastic scalpel. When Gretchen pressed the scalpel into the mannequin's chest, a stream of blood jetted out three feet.

WEAR GOGGLES, a sign at the entrance warned.

Everyone loved it.

"Saw your column about the skeleton they found at the slough," Henry said.

"I thought you only read German poetry," Susan said. But she was secretly pleased. She'd done a long story on the skeleton. In any other news cycle, it might have gotten more attention. She'd been disappointed when it hadn't.

Henry rubbed the back of his neck. "What do you know about Vanport?" he asked.

She should have known he'd be critical. "What I wrote. The whole town was washed away in 1948. People died. Some bodies were never found. And the dog park where the skeleton was found is right where the town used to be."

"The skeleton's been in the ground sixty years, so he must have died in the Vanport flood?"

"I didn't say he died at Vanport," Susan said evenly. She'd had the same argument with her editor. "I said he died about sixty years ago, and was found smack-dab in the middle of the area that used to be the city of Vanport, before Vanport was washed away by a flood sixty years ago."

"Just be careful what you stir up," Henry said.

"I exude caution," Susan said.

Henry snorted.

A hundred feet beyond the ride, the river churned chilly and brown, the current whipping debris by at a frenzied pace. A few seagulls circled above the water, but none dared to settle in it. The oaks at the bank were dead-looking, their tops disintegrating into the low wet mist that draped the city like muslin.

Susan had a sudden feeling of dread.

"What?" Henry said, looking up.

She shook it off. "Nothing," she said. "I just got cold."

CHAPTER 3

"Any nightmares?" Sarah Rosenberg asked.

A curtain of water fell outside her office window. Archie's socks were sodden, his pants damp almost to the knees. More coffee would have been good. But Rosenberg only had tea.

"I'm okay," he said. His gun pressed into his hip.

"Really?" she said. Her dark hair was knotted in back and held in place with a pencil, and she was wearing sweats. No makeup. She'd been thinking he wouldn't show.

"No nightmares," he said.

She raised a skeptical eyebrow.

After what he'd been through, he could see why she didn't believe him. "I know this is hard to fathom," he said, "but I've actually been doing pretty well."

It had been three months since his last appointment with Rosenberg, six months since Gretchen Lowell had gone to prison the second time. He was back at work. He'd stayed off painkillers. His physical wounds had healed.

"You haven't been in touch with her?" Rosenberg asked, leveling her gaze at him.

"No," Archie said. "From what I hear, she hasn't spoken a word since she was booked." He glanced away from Rosenberg, out the window, where a gnarled plum tree glistened dark and wet, its last handful of yellow leaves a miracle against the wind. "She just lies there."

"Is she trying for an insanity defense?" Rosenberg asked.

Archie shrugged, and returned his attention to the room. "She's not crazy. She just likes killing people. She'll get the death penalty this time."

A gust of wind shook the old house, and the windows rattled. Rosenberg's mouth tightened. She reached out and centered the tissue box on the coffee table. Archie was no psychiatrist, but he'd been a cop long enough to know the heebie-jeebies when he saw them.

"It's just the wind," he said.

Rosenberg's eyes flicked up. "What's it like out there?" she asked.

"Bad," Archie said. It was only going to

get worse.

"I was surprised you came."

He hadn't even considered canceling. He'd made a commitment. "We had an appointment."

He could see something shift in her shoulders, a glance at the clock on her desk. Their fifty minutes were up. "That's it," Archie said. Rosenberg nodded and followed him as he walked from the office to the front hall, where his rain boots sat dripping on the Oriental rug Rosenberg used as a front mat. He pulled them on, the rubber pressing the wet wool to his feet. They were useless anyway.

"How's Susan?"

Archie glanced up, startled. "Why ask about her?"

Rosenberg frowned innocently. "I read her column."

Archie knew Rosenberg never asked anything casually. He looked at her for a moment, then answered the question. "Working on her book, scrambling for stories. Same old thing."

"Uh-huh," she said.

Archie cleared his throat. "I'll see you in three months, Sarah."

She held out her hand and he shook it. "You can come sooner, if you like," she said.

"Stay off the roads."

Rosenberg opened the heavy front door for him. "Henry said you moved," she said.

So Henry was still checking in on him. "I did."

"Where to?"

Archie looked out at the rain and smiled. "Higher ground," he said.

CHAPTER 4

Susan's desk at the *Herald* was on the fifth floor and if she got up and walked thirty feet and really squinted she had a view of The Heathman Hotel across the street. It wasn't really worth the effort. Mostly Susan stayed in her seat, where she pounded out her quirky crime roundup column, in between searching for a new job on Monster .com and looking on eBay for the red velvet blazer that Tom Ford designed for Gucci in 1995. She'd agreed to write the column in a rare moment of job insecurity, and had been disheartened at how quickly it had taken off. It turned out that Oregonians loved themselves some gore, the weirder the better. Her first column was about a Ukrainian chemistry student who had a habit of dipping his gum in citric acid to make the flavor last longer, and then died after he accidentally dunked his bubble gum in the explosives he was using for his experiments.

He blew off half his face. You couldn't make this stuff up. She still got letters about that one.

It was an easy job. She got the international stories off the wire or the Internet, and turned up the local horror herself. An old skeleton in a slough, for instance.

Today's headline? THE DEAD GIRL ON THE OSTRICH.

She'd just e-mailed it to her editor when the flowers came.

Technically, the receptionists downstairs were supposed to call before they sent up a visitor. But they never did. Receptionists always hated Susan. She didn't know why.

Susan heard Derek Rogers cluck his disapproval from a few desks down before she even saw the flower shop guy.

The *Herald* was that quiet — it was like working in a museum. Especially since all the buyouts and layoffs started. The city was flooding and the newsroom was so quiet that Susan could hear the toilet flush in the men's room all the way over in editorial. Derek sat a few desks over from her, and she swore she could hear him when he swallowed. There was something about the acoustics of that place, that huge open floor plan, all that carpet. Miles of carpet. There were over a thousand chemicals used in the manufacture of carpet. Between the central nervous system damage from the fumes and the radiation from all the cell phones on that floor, Susan was waiting for the day they'd all start bleeding out their eyes.

She straightened up and spun her task chair around.

Don, the flower shop guy, looked like he'd just gotten off an Alaskan crab fishing boat: black fisherman bibs, rubber boots, and a yellow rain slicker. He had one of those full beards that all the men in Portland decided to grow about a year ago, and he was a giant, so he could sort of sell the fisherman thing. But Susan was still pretty sure he'd never been on a boat.

His boots squeaked on the carpet.

"It's getting bad out there," he said, wiping rain from a ruddy cheek. "No more deliveries."

"Your shop is across the street," Susan said.

He handed her the wet bouquet he was holding. There had been more ceremony the first few times he'd come.

Susan looked down at the bouquet. It was prettily arranged in a square glass vase. Purple calla lilies, red berries, surrounding a few fist-sized balls of leaves. For a guy with fingers like sausages, he had a way with floral design. "Is that cabbage?" she asked.

"Decorative winter kale," he said with a sigh.

"Oh."

"Seriously," he said. "Tell your admirer to take a break until after the rain stops. The governor declared a state of emergency today." He looked around at their sad, empty office. "Don't you watch TV?" he said.

"I read the *Herald*," Susan said pointedly. Someone had to.

He shook his head and trudged off toward the elevator, leaving a wet spot on the carpet where he'd been standing.

Derek rolled his task chair next to Susan's. The musk of his aftershave was overpowering. Stetson. He was the only guy in his twenties Susan knew who even used aftershave. "Leo Reynolds is bad news," he said, pumping a finger toward the flowers.

True, she thought. *But I bet he doesn't use Stetson.*

Leo Reynolds had sent Susan a bouquet at work every week for six months. The cards all said the same thing: *To Susan, From Leo.* A real formalist. The flower shop guy said that Leo placed the order by phone. He probably had an account at every flower shop in town. Leo's family money had been made importing massive amounts of drugs into the West Coast, but Susan had to admit she liked the attention.

"You never sent me flowers," she said to Derek.

"He's rich," Derek said. He lowered his voice and glanced around at the twenty or so people still in the office, all wearing headphones and staring blankly at their computer screens. "I make thirty-two thousand dollars a year," he said.

"Oh," Susan said.

"Oh?"

"Just, oh."

Derek squinted at her. "How much do you make?"

Susan made forty-two thousand. And the advance for her soon-to-be-released book about weird ways people die had been a hundred thousand. She shrugged. No point making him feel bad. "About that," she said.

"How's the Gretchen Lowell book?" he asked. Susan's skin prickled. He knew she'd given up on the Beauty Killer book. He was just being catty.

"I'm kicking a new idea around," she said.

"About?"

"Fighting crime in Portland, Oregon."

"So, true crime?"

Susan felt a twinge of embarrassment.

"More like a detective story."

He blinked at her. He'd played college football. And those concussions add up. "So, fiction?" he said.

"Creative nonfiction," she said.

He narrowed his eyes. "Who are the main characters?"

Susan smiled resplendently. "A plucky girl journalist with a chip on her shoulder and a recovering Vicodin-addicted cop with a dark secret who solve crimes together."

"You're writing a book about you and Archie Sheridan?"

"My agent says it's very marketable."

Derek lifted his hand and laughed into it until his eyes watered. "What does that make you?" He cackled some more, already pleased with what he was about to say. "Dr. Watson?"

Susan gave him a hard look.

His hand dropped and he cleared his throat. "Seriously. What if nothing exciting happens?"

Susan reached up and touched the pea-sized scar on her cheek where a crazy masked murderer had stabbed her with a piercing needle. When she didn't cover it with makeup, it looked like a huge zit.

"Something exciting always happens," she said.

And then, as if Susan had willed it, her phone rang.

CHAPTER 5

Stephanie Towner had been murdered. This was the only fact that Archie had been able to make out when Lorenzo Robbins had called him. It wasn't even a fact; it was conjecture. But Robbins liked to be dramatic. Once, he had announced that an eight-year-old boy had been murdered by his ten-year-old sister. When he got everyone's attention, he went on to explain that the sister had unwittingly passed along the parasite that had spread to the boy's brain and killed him. So when Robbins reported this news about Stephanie Towner, Archie knew to follow up.

"Define 'murdered,' " Archie said, holding his cell phone to his ear with his shoulder. He unlocked the door to his apartment, walked inside, tossed that day's mail in a pile of other unopened envelopes, and took off his coat. He'd left the lights on. It was something he did now. He hadn't mentioned it to Rosenberg.

There was noise on the phone line: voices, what sounded like furniture scraping. "I don't have time to talk on the phone," Robbins said, "just get down here as soon as you can."

The line went dead.

Archie's windows looked north, toward industrial Portland, where ships loaded with grain from the Midwest set off for Asia and then returned loaded with Toyotas. The port hadn't flooded yet. That was something.

Farther north was the Columbia River, and across it, Vancouver, Washington, where his family lived. "The 'Couve, as it was known, was one-third the size of Portland, and seemed even smaller. A lot of Portlanders had never been to Vancouver, except to drive through it on the way north to Seattle, or to chaperone a school field trip to historic Fort Vancouver. It was twenty minutes from Archie's apartment to Debbie's house, but it felt like another country.

His kids liked Debbie's new boyfriend. He worked in the wind industry. He'd gotten the kids composting. He probably recycled his used Q-tips.

Archie punched Henry's name on his autodialer.

It rang once.

"Yeah?" Henry said. There was always a trace of panic in his voice when Archie called, like it could only be bad news.

"Robbins thinks Stephanie Towner was murdered," Archie said.

"The girl on the ostrich? She drowned. They found the skid mark. Open-and-shut."

"Except for the ostrich thing," Archie said.

"I'll meet you down there."

Archie took off his sweater. It smelled like a wet dog. That's what happened when wool got wet. It stank. Some people thought it smelled like a drenched sheep, some people thought barnyard, urine, mold. Archie liked the smell. It reminded him of when he was a kid, when that's what Oregon had smelled like in the winter — one big wet dog. Now, with the advent of Polarfleece, everything had changed.

He had a button-down shirt on under the sweater. He'd put it on ten hours earlier and its smell was not as pleasant as the wet wool. He unbuttoned it and tossed it in the laundry hamper that Debbie had bought him when he'd moved out. Then he got another button-down out of the drawer and put it on. He didn't examine himself in the mirror anymore. His scars were as much a part of him as his eye color. The heart-shaped scar that Gretchen Lowell had left on his chest nearly three years before served only as a reminder of his failings. If he didn't look at it, he could pretend it wasn't there. He could avoid thinking about her. It was the only way he could function.

He buttoned the second shirt as quickly as he could and pulled the sweater back on. He hadn't eaten all day, but there was nothing to grab to go, and no time to make anything.

Rain splattered the window, causing rivulets of seagull shit to run like white threads down the glass.

Archie put his coat back on. He left the lights on when he went out.

CHAPTER 6

The Multnomah County morgue was downtown, just across the Willamette from Archie's apartment. Portland had a pretty downtown, with restored brick and sandstone storefronts, lots of public art, and bike racks and coffee shops on every corner. In the summer flower baskets were hung from the lampposts, in the winter the trees were strung with white lights.

Most of the inner west side was laid out on a grid, numerical avenues parallel to the river, and alphabetical streets perpendicular. The blocks were short — dollhouse blocks, they called them — so the city founders could sell plenty of corner lots. The morgue was on Fourth Avenue, which meant it was four doll house blocks west of the river, uphill, well above flood stage.

But it was also, as morgues tended to be, in a basement.

It had flooded.

Archie knew it the moment he arrived. The first-floor hallway was already filled with equipment and gurneys, boxes and computers. Two morgue employees, pathology assistants, red-faced and puffing, lugged a heavy steel device that looked like it had been stolen from a butcher shop. A bone saw sat next to a drinking fountain. An organ scale sat in front of an elevator. The hallway was tracked with wet footprints.

"Where's Robbins?" Archie asked the pathology assistants as they squeezed by him.

"Downstairs," one of them said. "Follow the screaming. And take the stairs, the elevator's shorted out."

Archie worked his way through the obstacle course of hallway debris and found the stairs, where a dozen people had formed a chain to pass up contents from the morgue. Archie couldn't help wondering what was sloshing around in the Tupperware containers that were being stacked at the top of the line. Someone's lunch? Or someone's stomach?

Robbins bellowed up at him from below. "Get down here!" he said.

Archie flashed his badge and ducked past the people on the stairs. Robbins was at the bottom, standing in a foot of water.

"Can you believe this shit?" Robbins said.

The lights must have shorted out, because the overhead emergency lights flickered, giving everything a sci-fi-green tint. Several alarms pulsed from various directions. Robbins was in his civilian clothes, no lab coat, his shirt unbuttoned to mid-chest. Sweat stained his pits. His pants were tucked into the tall black rubber boots that Archie had seen him wear at crime scenes. His dreadlocks, which he usually wore tied back with a rubber band, dangled loose against shoulders. The light made him look like he was vibrating.

"Where are the bodies?" Archie asked.

"I was thinking I'd stack them upstairs in the hall," Robbins said, wiping his dark brow with a latex-gloved hand, "and then I remembered that thing about decomposition I learned in medical examiner school. We've got to keep them refrigerated. Gets real stinky otherwise. Emanuel and OHSU have offered to take them. We're still figuring out the best way to transport them. Did you drive?"

Archie thought of his police-issue Cutlass upstairs, and wondered if he could fit a corpse in the backseat. "Could I use the carpool lane?" he asked.

Robbins smirked. Then his eyes flicked

down to Archie's feet, and he was all business. "Good, you're wearing boots. Don't touch the water." He headed off, beckoning for Archie to follow him. "C'mon." The water throbbed as Robbins plodded through it.

A young man in a lab coat walked past carrying an aluminum roasting pan with a human skull in it. The skull was stained with age, almost the color of tea.

Robbins took the pan out of his hands. "I'll take that," Robbins said. "Get the computers. The equipment. Biohazards. And make sure you get the TV out of my office." He leaned in to Archie. "Flatscreen," he explained.

They heard a splash and both turned to see Susan Ward appear at the bottom of the stairs. She was wearing rainbow-striped rubber boots tucked into jeans and a knee-length yellow rain slicker. It was unzipped, revealing a blue T-shirt with white bubbly writing that read CONSERVE WATER, SHOWER TOGETHER. She kicked at the water like a kid in a wading pool and grinned at them. Her lipstick was the same bright berry color as her hair. "Whoa," she said. "Cool."

Robbins lifted his fingertips to his temple. "This is still a secure area, people," he hollered up the stairs. He gave Archie a tired look. "You told her Stephanie Towner was murdered?"

"Stephanie Towner was murdered?" Susan said. There was a series of splashes as she sloshed over to them. Her face glowed pink under her freckles.

Archie hadn't told her anything. She just had a way of showing up. Sometimes Archie wondered if she ever went to the *Herald* offices at all.

Robbins stared at Archie, waiting for an answer, still holding the pan with the skull.

Archie shrugged. "I didn't tell her," he said.

"I came because I heard the morgue was flooding," Susan said. She leaned close to Archie and said out of the side of her berry-red mouth, "I got a tip from someone I know at Emanuel."

Then something seemed to occur to Susan and she glanced down at the water they were all standing in. "Are we going to get electrocuted?"

"Probably not," Robbins said.

"Electrocution is the second leading cause of fatalities during floods," Susan said.

"We're not going to get electrocuted," Robbins insisted. "Power's shorted out. The emergency lights run on batteries."

Archie wondered why so many alarms were going off, if there wasn't any power.

Robbins seemed to read his mind. "The alarms all are coming from very expensive equipment that doesn't like getting unplugged."

Susan opened her mouth to ask another question, but then Archie saw her eyes travel to the aluminum pan. She did a double take. "Is that a skull?"

"Some dog walker found it in West Delta Park," Robbins said.

"Oh," Susan cried in recognition. "I wrote about him." She bent her knees so her face was level with the skull. "I wrote about you," she said to the skull.

Archie had read that column. No, Archie remembered — Henry had read the column to him. Susan had come up with some theory that the dog park skeleton had something to do with the Vanport flood. Henry had been irritated by it.

But that was not why they were here.

"Talk to me about Stephanie Towner," Archie said.

Robbins jerked his head in Susan's direction. "You okay with her listening in?"

Susan had no business being there. If this was actually a homicide investigation, which Archie wasn't sure it was — if it was just

Robbins wanting to show off, then what did it matter? "It's off the record until I say it isn't," Archie told her.

Susan bounced her chin up and down.

"You trust her?" Robbins asked dubiously.

"I do," Archie said. He surprised himself at how easily he said it.

Susan beamed. The bleeping of alarms continued all around them. There was a vague smell of decomp in the air. Archie wondered bleakly if it was the water.

Robbins sighed and shook his head. "This way." He led them down the green shimmering hallway, past an office where two morgue employees were rescuing a flatscreen TV, and into the autopsy room.

The water was deeper in there, only a few inches below the top of Archie's boots. It bubbled and gurgled at four distinct points in the center of the room.

"Water's coming up through the floor drains," Robbins explained.

Archie had seen what went into those floor drains. He could only imagine what might come back up. "Along with what?"

"A whole host of biohazards," Robbins said. "I told you not to touch the water." He held the skull out in Susan's direction. "Here, hold this."

Susan took the pan. "Where's the rest of

him?" she asked.

"Around," Robbins said.

Susan lifted the skull so she could look him in the eye sockets. "I think I'll call him Ralph," she said.

"I'm glad you made a new friend," Archie said. "But could we get back to Stephanie Towner?"

Robbins adjusted his posture, straightening up like he was about to give a lecture. "What do you know about drowning?" he asked. *Here we go,* thought Archie. Water continued to gurgle up from below the floor.

"We're listening," Archie said.

Robbins crossed his arms and leaned one shoulder against the morgue cooler. "Stage one is fear. Most people, they don't flail around and holler. They're focused on breathing. Stage two, they go under. Take a lungful of water, choke on it, which makes them breathe in more water, which causes their larynx or vocal cords to constrict and seal the airway. That's called 'laryngospasm.' It's involuntary. Now they're underwater. Stage three. They're unconscious and in respiratory arrest.

"Stage four," he continued. "Hello, hypoxic convulsions. Some jerking. They start turning blue."

Robbins turned to Susan. "You getting all this?"

"Blue," she said. "Got it." She tossed Archie an amused glance. "This is really going to come in handy next time I'm at the pool."

She was clearly enjoying antagonizing him. "Continue," Archie said to Robbins.

"Stage five. My old friend, clinical death. Heart attack. Breathing and circulation stop."

"So what's stage six?" Susan asked dryly. "Heaven?"

This was all going somewhere, Archie told himself. It had to be going somewhere.

Robbins waved a gloved finger at her. "Aha. That's where it gets interesting. Stage six is biological death."

"What's the difference between clinical and biological death?" Susan asked.

"About four minutes," Robbins said. "That's how long you have to start CPR and defibrillation before your brain gets all mushy and there's no going back."

He cranked a lever on the morgue cooler drawer he'd been leaning on, and slid Stephanie Towner's corpse out on a conveyor tray.

As corpses go, she looked better than she had at the park that morning. Her hair was wet and combed back from her face; her flesh was clean of mud and debris. But she was still a disturbing sight. Her face, neck, and upper chest were blotchy with the telltale dusky bruising of lividity. She looked like she'd been punched around. But looks could be deceiving. Bodies floated face-down, the head lower than the rest of the body. What looked like bruising was most likely just where her blood had settled once her heart had stopped pumping. A slight trace of pink foam circled her nostrils. A brutal Y-incision, sealed with industrial-looking staples, marked where Robbins had opened her chest up for autopsy.

Archie checked in on Susan. She was staring at the corpse's thighs. The flesh was pimply. Goose-skin, Archie had heard coroners call it. That was fine. As long as she wasn't fixed on the face. As long as you didn't look at the face, you could pretend that what you were looking at wasn't human.

Archie knew she tried to seem tough. But the rattling skull in her hands told a different story.

"Here's the thing," Robbins continued. "Most people, once they're unconscious, their larynx relaxes and their lungs fill with water. Your vic? No water in her stomach.

No hemorrhages in the middle ears. No water in her lungs. This can happen. Some people keep that seal. Drowning is tricky when it comes to cause of death. But it got me thinking, and I took a real close look at her. And I found this."

He gestured to the woman like a waiter presenting the catch of the day. Then gently folded open her fingers to expose her palm. Her finger pads were blanched and wrinkled, like she'd been in the tub too long.

Archie and Susan both leaned forward from opposite sides of the conveyor tray, nearly bumping heads. Robbins indicated a tiny brown spot near the center of the palm. It looked like someone had marked her with the tip of a brown felt-tipped pen.

This was Robbins's big evidence? "What is it?" Archie asked.

"A freckle?" Susan guessed.

"It's a puncture wound," Robbins said.

Susan didn't seem convinced. "It looks like a freckle."

Archie had to admit, it did look like a freckle. Or a thousand other things. "She was in the water awhile, beaten up," Archie said. In fact, the body was covered with scratches and lesions where she'd run into who knows what on her way downriver. She'd been lucky she hadn't ended up in the propeller of a boat. Then there were the fish who'd been feasting on her.

Archie glanced down at the floor. The water was almost to the top of his boots. A sealed Tupperware container bobbed by.

"There was nothing under her fingernails when they brought her in," Robbins said. "No injuries to her fingertips. She would have grasped at something. If she slid down that bank, she would have clawed to save herself. There are scratches on the back of the hand. But not the palms."

Archie was still having trouble seeing how all this added up. "You think she was dead when she went in the water. That someone rolled her into the river." But he'd seen pink froth around her mouth and nose, both at the park and in the morgue, a common indication of drowning. "What about the frothing?" he said.

Robbins nodded. "Foam is a sign a person was alive when they went in the water, sure," he said. "But it can also be caused by a heart attack *before* a person went in the water." He leaned over the corpse's head and tenderly peeled back one eyelid, revealing a vacant, bloodshot eye, the white of it peppered with tiny scarlet dots. "Petechial hemorrhages," he said. "Rare in drowning. But common in other asphyxial deaths.

Respiratory paralysis, for instance. That would cause a heart attack."

"Stage five," Susan said. "Of *drowning.*"

"The order is important," Robbins said.

"Puncture wound," Archie said. "Heart attack. River."

Robbins nodded slowly.

"Something or someone punctured her," Archie said. He knew what Robbins was driving at. "You think she was poisoned? Based on a dot on her palm?"

"Based on these." He produced two printed digital photographs from his pants pocket and placed them on Stephanie Towner's pimpled thigh. "They're autopsy photos of Megan Parr and Zak Korber."

Two other people who'd drowned in Portland that week. Each had been swept away. No witnesses.

Both photographs featured a hand, palm up, a yellow arrow pointing to a small brown dot. It looked like a freckle.

"It's the same mark," Archie said.

"I missed it the first time around," Robbins said.

"What's going on?" Susan asked.

Someone was poisoning people and pushing them in the river.

Archie looked over at her. "Off the record," he reminded her. "Remember that."

She nodded, and the skull made a tinny noise as it slid an inch in the aluminum pan and settled against the rim.

Archie turned back to Robbins. "Tox screen?" he asked.

"My morgue is underwater," Robbins reminded him. "But I'll farm it out pronto."

There was a commotion and soon a parade of firefighters appeared, coming down the stairs.

"It took them long enough," Robbins said, and he went off to bark instructions at them.

Archie returned his gaze to the photographs.

The spots were all on their hands. It was an odd place for an injection point. Had they reached up to protect themselves, exposing their palms in the process? And then another scenario occurred to him. They had been holding it. That would explain the hand thing. They had been holding something that punctured them. Something booby-trapped? Something they had picked up?

Archie couldn't keep people away from the river. Not when half the city was down there, sandbagging to save downtown.

The alarms stopped. All at once, like someone had thrown a switch. Archie had almost gotten used to the noise.

What time was it?

Archie felt a sudden gnawing in the pit of his stomach.

Where was Henry? He should have been there by now.

Archie hit the autodial. It rang and rang. But Henry didn't pick up.

CHAPTER 7

There were fifteen hundred volunteers at Tom McCall Waterfront Park, filling and stacking sandbags in the rain. There were also a few hundred city employees, several dozen National Guard troops, and a few thousand people, give or take, just getting in the way. The goal was to build a four-foot-tall, mile-long temporary wall to keep the river from flooding downtown. This involved a lot of plywood, lumber, plastic, and concrete Jersey highway barriers. How it was going to hold, Susan had no idea.

But by the looks of the water level, they didn't have a lot of time.

Bright construction lights augmented the yellow glow of the old-fashioned streetlamps that lined the park's concrete promenade. The light illuminated the rain, which fell in a bleak drizzle.

A Coast Guard chopper thwapped by overhead.

Archie was on foot. The morgue was six short blocks away, and the streets were chaos. Susan hadn't bothered asking if she could come. She had just loped after him. She zipped up her slicker and dug her hands in her pockets, finding coins and gum and lint.

The sandbagging stations were set up at intermittent points along the length of the park bordering the Willamette. On the other side of the park, just a hundred yards from the river, Portland's downtown skyline stretched up into cloud cover.

"There's Claire," Archie said.

Detective Claire Masland, tiny to begin with, was dwarfed by a knee-length raincoat with the hood up over her short dark hair. Susan didn't know how Archie had recognized her. But then, when you spent ten years working on a task force tracking a serial killer, you probably got to know each other's silhouette. Henry and Claire had been an item for less than a year. But Henry, Archie, and Claire had worked together for ages.

"I found his car," Claire said.

Henry still hadn't answered his phone. Now it appeared he'd never left the waterfront.

"Something's happened to him," Claire

said. Only a small tremble in the corners of her mouth gave away that Henry was more than just a colleague to her.

Susan turned away from them and toward the river. There were too many people along the water, all of them moving around, everyone wearing soggy hats or hoods — Henry could be there and they wouldn't be able to see him. Maybe he'd gotten caught up in the seawall project and had decided to keep working. He could be filling sandbags thirty feet from them right now.

But Susan knew this wasn't true. Henry would do almost anything for Archie. If he'd said he'd meet him at the morgue, he would have been there. Henry didn't just not show up.

The rain-beaded plastic sheeting over the seawall flapped in the wind where it hadn't been secured. The people working on the wall were right on the edge of the river. Usually it was a twenty-foot drop from the promenade to the water, but now what was it? A foot? One misstep and you were in the water, in a fast-moving current. Stage one, Robbins had said. People didn't cry out. They didn't wave their arms and shout.

Susan shook the thought from her mind.

Henry was strong and stubborn and big.

He wouldn't drown. Unless he'd been poisoned.

Stephanie Towner. Megan Parr. Zak Korber. They had all been murdered near the river.

A sandbag brigade, made up of men and women in wet coats, their hair plastered to their heads, passed sandbags to the wall. They talked in the hushed, serious tones of people who were working on deadline and could not waste a minute. So many people had turned out to help, it made Susan feel proud of her city.

If there was a killer loose down there, even the possibility of it, shouldn't these people be warned?

She looked around at all of them. The slickers shiny in the construction lights. National Guard troops in black floppy rain hats. The old and the young. And that's when the transient caught Susan's eye. There were always transients at Waterfront Park. They sat on the benches at the north end by the Steel Bridge, and slept on the ribbon of grass in front of the Japanese American Historical Plaza.

This guy was sitting on a park bench, wrapped in a piece of wet plastic sheeting that looked like the stuff they were using for the seawall project. What caught Susan's attention was the brief pale blue glow of an LCD screen. She took a step toward him and squinted. She couldn't be sure. He was ensconced in plastic, like something out of the freezer. Maybe it was just a reflection?

She hurried back to Archie and Claire. Claire was just dropping her phone in her jacket pocket. "I just tried him again," Claire said. She gave Archie a steely look. "We need to call in backup. This isn't like him."

Susan grabbed Archie by the elbow and motioned for them to follow her. She led them around the crowd to the park bench. Then, to give them a reason to stand there, she pretended to throw something away in the trash bin between where they stood and the bench.

"Try Henry now," she said to Claire.

Claire looked confused, but pulled her phone out again, and, with a doubtful glance at Susan, tapped a button.

"Wait," Susan said.

And then they heard it. The sound of a phone ringing. Mere feet away.

CHAPTER 8

The man in the plastic wasn't talking. Archie had him by the shoulders, the plastic slippery and crinkling under his hands. The man just stared at him, lids peeled back, nostrils quivering, his few yellowed teeth exposed behind bared, chapped lips.

"Where did you get the phone?" Archie asked again.

Nothing.

Archie wanted to shake him, to wrestle the truth from him. Archie knew how to hurt someone. Gretchen had taught him a thousand ways to hurt someone.

The phone had fallen off the man's lap when Archie had lifted him from his seat, skidding along the concrete. Claire had scrambled after it and now was scrolling through the call log.

"The only recent activity is the conversation with you, and then when we all started phoning to find him," she said.

Archie bunched the plastic tightly in his fists and pulled his hands closer together, so that the plastic sheeting was wrapped firmly around the man's torso, squeezing him. The man's upper lip twitched but he still said nothing. Did he not speak English? What, then? They didn't have time to find a translator. Archie needed to get a reaction out of him.

"The phone belongs to a cop," Archie said. The man's eyes widened further, revealing two things. One, he spoke English. Two, he hadn't known Henry was a cop. The man glanced over Archie's shoulder, north. He was on the verge of breaking. "If anything has happened to him, you will be in a world of hurt."

"Mighty Willamette," the man said gruffly. "Beautiful friend. I am learning. I am practicing. To say your name."

"What the fuck?" said Claire.

"It's carved onto one of the stones at the Japanese American Plaza," Susan said. "At the north end of the park, by the Steel Bridge."

"The phone was on the sacred ground," the man said. "There was no one attached."

Archie heard Susan say his name.

He turned. Susan was standing, arms at her sides, staring at the crowd by the river.

The sandbag brigade had disbanded and joined a huddled group pressed against the seawall, straining to see over it into the river. The sandbags lay where they'd dropped them, getting splattered with rain. There were maybe twenty backsides, more joining by the moment.

"There's something going on," Susan said.

Archie let go of the plastic and the man slid out of his hands back onto the bench.

People were pointing now, hollering for help. There was something in the river.

Archie ran. He got out his badge as he did, raising it up to show people as he elbowed them aside.

"There's someone in the water," a woman shouted.

A National Guard soldier, probably just out of high school, was at the center of the crowd, frantically scanning the dark river. Archie could see the anxiety in his face, the panic in the angle of his shoulders. Uniforms had a way of fooling people into thinking the wearer had a plan. Never mind that the kid was nineteen. He was probably terrified.

Besides, they'd never spot anyone in the dark.

Archie took control. He made his way to the soldier. "I'm a cop," he said. "What's your name?"

"Carter, sir," the soldier said.

Archie pointed out a nearby construction light. "Get that light over here."

Carter nodded quickly and moved to reposition the light.

"Who saw this person?" Archie asked the crowd.

A woman in a nylon ski jacket raised her hand.

Archie could feel Susan at his shoulder. He wondered where Claire was, and hoped that she had secured the man in plastic. Archie didn't want him to run.

"I saw someone," the woman said. She pointed out at a spot ten yards from the edge of the river. "There." Archie saw only blackness.

"Are you sure?" Archie asked. How anyone could see anything out there, he didn't know.

"It was a person. I know it was a person." Her voice was reedy with hysteria. Whatever she'd seen out there, she believed it was human.

Carter had rolled the light closer to the river's edge.

Archie tried to calculate the speed of the current. If there was a person out there, he or she was probably under the Burnside

Bridge by now. "Swing it over there," he said.

In the sudden silence, the rain seemed to get louder. It pelted the slickers and nylon jackets. It bounced on the concrete. It ran down the back of Archie's neck. It fell into the river, more and more water — the Willamette seemed to rise even as he looked at it. Archie squinted. The river surged north, a blur of dark, roiling current.

The Willamette in January was about forty-five degrees. In water that cold, you'd have maybe thirty minutes until you lost consciousness. An hour if you were strong and lucky.

Had the woman really seen something?

And then someone shouted:

"There!"

Archie snapped his head to follow her finger, and Carter swung the light to center on it.

Something in the water. A bird? No, a buoy? No. A person. A child. Jesus Christ. *A child.*

A child, moving north. Fast.

Archie started to run along the seawall. You were never supposed to approach a drowning victim without a flotation device, a rope around your waist, something. Drowning victims panicked. They flailed.

They took people down with them. The kid was alive. Conscious. If he weren't, he'd have gone under. There was no time for flotation devices or ropes.

Susan was right behind him, along with the growing crowd, everyone pointing and shouting. Archie looked for Claire but didn't see her. He took his coat off and stuffed the pockets with his badge, wallet, and phone. Then he unclipped the gun from his belt, put it in the coat's inside pocket, zipped the pocket, and handed the coat to Susan. "Call nine-one-one," he told her. "And don't lose my gun."

Then he looked for the light. Good. Carter had kept his cool, kept the light trained on the kid in the water.

Archie climbed over the wall, got a bead on the kid, took a deep breath, and jumped into the dark, frigid river. His breath left his body as soon as he hit.

CHAPTER 9

Susan had lost sight of Archie.

She'd hung up with 911, and now she couldn't find him in the water. It had only been a minute. But it seemed like longer. She realized she was hugging Archie's coat to her chest.

People who drowned in the Willamette were usually never seen again.

There were more lights now. More National Guard soldiers. The mob was growing as they moved along the promenade, everyone at a slow jog, eyes on the water where the lights all met. A small head bobbed. Rubber boots smacked against the pavement. Wet slickers squeaked. Puddles splattered. The seawall was higher in some places, where the construction process was further along, and they all had to strain to see over it, their heads bobbing up and down at the wall's edge like paparazzi.

People already had their camera phones

out, taking low-res video of the dancing light on the dark water. These days, everyone was a reporter.

"Got 'em," someone snapped.

Susan's throat swelled as she saw Archie in the light.

The throng burst into spontaneous applause.

"He's still gotta get him out," the Guard soldier named Carter said under his breath.

It was true. They all watched, riveted, as the shape that was Archie circled the shape that was the kid, two heads in the water. Susan couldn't look, and at the same time she couldn't look away. Archie was still an arm's length from the kid, who seemed to be shrinking in the water, so much so that it was difficult to keep sight of him in the rough current.

"Why doesn't he just grab him?" Susan asked.

"He's trying to get him from behind, under the arms," Carter said. And then, as if to explain his sudden authority, he added, "Lifeguard, all four years of high school."

Suddenly, the two forms joined. Archie had him. He had the boy.

There was more applause and another soldier joined Carter and Susan. "They're slowing down," the new soldier said.

Susan hadn't noticed until he said it, but he was right. They weren't moving nearly as fast. That was good, wasn't it?

"He's swimming against the current, Captain," Carter said.

That didn't make sense. He couldn't fight it, couldn't get back to them, couldn't get to the seawall. And even if he did, what then? There were rusty metal ladders that led up the concrete from the water, but they were only every hundred feet or so. What were the odds he'd be able to get to one?

"What's he thinking?" the captain asked. "He's going to exhaust himself."

Susan knew what that meant. If Archie lost strength, they'd go under. They'd drown.

She saw Carter glance away from the light, upriver, then back at Archie and the kid. "The bridge," he said. "Captain, I can get them from the bridge."

The captain hesitated.

"I won the fifty-yard freestyle at State," Carter said. "I'm six-foot-two. If someone holds on to me, I can reach them. We can pull them out of there. I can do this. Sir." He bent his head toward Archie and the kid, who were now nearly holding ground. "He's buying us time."

The Steel Bridge, built in 1912, was one

of Portland's oldest. It was a double-lift bridge, which meant that the whole middle of the structure could be lifted straight up to allow vessels to pass underneath. It was also a double-decker bridge, cars and light rail on the top deck, trains and pedestrians below, and the lower deck was only twenty-five feet from the river, at normal levels.

But the river was not at normal levels. The river was high. Very high. So high that the lower deck was probably only five feet above the water. They could reach him.

"Let's go, soldier." Carter passed the light to someone else and followed the captain. They ran, tapping other soldiers on the shoulders, until there were a half dozen of them sprinting for the bridge. Susan splashed along the pavement after them, still clutching Archie's coat, like it was a part of him, like if she held it tightly enough she might be able to will him out of the water.

The center of the bridge was up. It had been up since that morning, when the city had ordered it raised indefinitely so that it wouldn't short out and get stuck in the down position. It would be hard to get to him from there. If Archie didn't get to the side, he'd wash right under the bridge and there'd be no way to get him. North of the Steel Bridge the river widened and the park gave way to condos and the port.

Susan chased the soldiers as they dashed down the promenade and onto the bridge's concrete pedestrian walkway. They ran to the drop-off, where the rest of the bridge had been lifted, and climbed over the safety gate. Carter knelt down on the edge of the walkway. "All you have to do is hold on to my ankles, and when I have them, pull us up," he said to the others, as if it were that simple.

Susan strained to see Archie and the kid fighting the current in the light. They were close. Maybe thirty feet away, maybe fifty. "They're almost here," she said.

Carter handed her a black flashlight off his belt. "Turn this on and hold it so he can see us."

She would be his light, so he knew they were there, so he'd come to them.

Suddenly calm with purpose, Susan tied Archie's coat around her waist, turned the flashlight on, and lay flat on the wet bridge so she could get as close to Carter as possible. Then she hooked her feet through the safety gate, extended the flashlight off the end of the walkway, and pointed it south. She turned the flashlight on and off, hoping to catch Archie's attention. Unlike most of Portland's other bridges, the Steel Bridge was not festooned with lights. It was an old girl: functional, practical. Just streetlights on the upper-deck roadway, and a few lights along the length of the bottom deck.

See me, Susan willed Archie. *See me.*

She could feel the weight of Archie's gun in his coat, like a fist. The wet concrete and metal was cold but Susan pressed the side of her face into it, trying to get her arm even lower. She could feel tears hot on her cheeks, or rain, or both.

"He's coming this way," she heard someone say from above.

"Lower me," Carter said.

Susan could hear them just behind her scrambling to hold on to his legs, the grunts as they dangled him off the edge. She couldn't turn her head. Couldn't see if he was low enough, if he could even reach them. Instead she concentrated on the flashlight. On, off. On, off. She had a task. She could do this right. She would not fuck this up.

The lights were almost under her now, and she could see the back of Archie's wet head.

Carter started hollering. "Here, here. I've got you. Over here."

It happened fast. Carter lurched. He lurched so hard that Susan could feel the walkway shudder under her chest. The other soldiers struggled to hold on to him, and then everyone was there, pulling, shouting, groaning. Susan let the flashlight fall out of her hand into the river and grabbed on to someone, she didn't even know who, pulling with all her strength.

They got Carter up, and with him, Archie and the kid. A boy. A little boy. Carter sat on his haunches, shoulders heaving. Archie was on his side, sopped and visibly shivering. The boy, who appeared to be about eight, was nearly cyanotic. He wasn't shivering. Susan knew that was a bad sign.

The soldiers had to pry him out of Archie's arms.

Two of the soldiers started peeling off the boy's wet clothes, a hooded sweatshirt, a long-sleeved shirt, jeans. He complied limply, eyes open, but unresponsive. As they tossed away his wet clothes, they wrapped him in their own coats. Susan crawled on her knees to Archie. The captain was next to him, struggling to pull a sodden wool sweater over Archie's head. Archie was trying to help, but his fingers fumbled uselessly. Susan helped pull the sweater off.

"You did it," she said to him. "You got him."

She could hear sirens now, and shouting. She hadn't noticed it until then, but the crowd had followed them onto the bridge. They parted in the middle to make way for the EMTs, who came running forward with rolling gurneys. Claire was with them, in the lead, showing them where to go. Somehow she got the safety gate open.

Archie was still shaking badly. Susan and the captain unbuttoned his drenched shirt and got it off of him. He crossed his arms across his chest. He was reflexively hiding his scars, Susan thought, even though it was too dark for anyone to see them. The captain took off his own jacket and put it around Archie's shoulders.

Susan could hear Archie's teeth chattering. She untied his sodden coat from her waist and draped it over his shoulders on top of the other.

"Hey," he said. "You didn't lose it."

The EMTs were upon them. Black rain pants. Red jackets. Billed caps. There were four of them, and they moved quickly and quietly.

Claire took charge, answering their questions. What happened? How long had they been in the water? Susan was glad they were talking to Claire. She didn't think she could talk without crying.

An EMT took the jackets off Archie and wrapped him in a Mylar survival blanket. It looked like it was made out of aluminum foil, like something an astronaut would sleep under. Archie tried to wave the EMT away. "Take care of the boy first," he said. He tried to pull himself to his feet, but faltered, and the EMT took him by the shoulders and guided Archie back down. Susan put her arm around him, taking his weight as the EMT got him seated.

The EMT sat on his heels and looked Archie in the eye, making sure he had his attention. "You're hypothermic," the EMT said. "We need to get you warm. No sudden movements. You move around, you send all that cold blood in your extremities to your heart. You want to have a heart attack?"

Next to them one of the gurneys was raised, and the boy, wrapped in another space blanket, was wheeled away through the hushed crowd.

"Is he okay?" Archie asked.

"He will be," the EMT said.

Susan and Claire stepped aside as two EMTs gingerly positioned Archie on the remaining gurney and strapped him in. Susan's father had been wheeled from the house strapped to a gurney just like it when she was fourteen years old. He never came home.

Archie seemed to sense what she was thinking. "I'll see you soon," he told her.

She picked his coat up from where it lay on the concrete and laid it over his lap.

The EMTs raised the gurney and its legs extended.

"Wait," Archie said. He lifted his head and looked around, his eyes settling on Susan. "The guy who grabbed us. It was Carter, wasn't it?"

Susan nodded.

"I want to talk to him," he said.

Susan looked around and quickly spotted Carter and motioned him over. "Hey," Archie said to him. Archie smiled weakly. "You did good, kid."

Carter straightened. "Yes, sir."

They were moving then. The EMTs pushed Archie through the crowd, one on either end of the gurney. Some people applauded, some took pictures. Susan and Claire tried to shield Archie from the flashes. Susan knew it was no use. His picture would be everywhere online by midnight. She wondered if these people recognized him — Archie Sheridan, hero cop, the one who'd been tortured by Gretchen Lowell, the one who'd caught her, twice. They probably didn't. But eventually someone would.

They cleared the bridge. Susan could see the rotating red and blue lights of two ambulances. They'd parked on the promenade.

"Do you want me to call anyone?" Claire asked Archie gently.

Archie was looking around, taking in his surroundings. Susan thought she could see his brain clearing. He wasn't shaking as hard anymore. "This is the Steel Bridge?" he said.

Claire nodded.

"Henry," Archie said. "Find Henry."

CHAPTER 10

The two women were alone.

The *Herald* reporter he recognized. Her photograph ran next to her column. The hair was a different color, but it was definitely Susan Ward. He would not have known her a week before, but he had studied her face since then, his fingertips tracing over the column he'd clipped until the newsprint smeared.

The other woman wore a gold badge around her neck.

He'd watched them move from the light into the dark of the plaza after the ambulance left.

They made him curious.

The organism of the crowd was reconfiguring itself, volunteers finding their way back to their stations at the seawall. Everyone was interested in something else — the cops in the edge of the bridge where the boy and man had been brought up; the TV crews in the witnesses; the National Guard soldiers in dispersing bystanders. No one noticed the two women in the dark.

Except for him.

The cop had a flashlight. He watched, didn't move. He could see Susan Ward's profile in the edge of the flashlight beam, and she reminded him of a squirrel in the road, equal parts focus and terror. The cop handed her something and Susan fiddled with it and then a slender beam of light appeared. A penlight. Its uselessness made him smile.

"What rock was it?" the cop asked.

" 'Mighty Willamette. Beautiful friend,' " Susan said. Her hair was a wet helmet around her head. She had a hood on her coat, but it was back, either forgotten or neglected. He could almost feel her shiver.

He knew the quote.

The plaza was centered on a cobblestone path that traveled beside a slanted stone wall. Rising out of the wall was a collection of carefully arranged stones in the style of a Japanese rock garden. A haiku was carved into each stone, like a collection of graves. A cherry orchard, as jagged and black as any nightmare, stretched the length of the path.

The women walked, and he followed. He

stayed five feet behind, creeping along the grass at the edge of the path, the sound of his footsteps lost in the splatter of rain.

He was drawn to them.

"Search the ground," the cop said. "In a grid pattern, like this." He watched as she demonstrated, moving the circle of the flashlight's beam up and down and then across on the path in front of them, and then on the stone embankment to the left and the grass to the right. Neither of the women saw him. The waterfront was noisy, and he moved slowly. He was used to the dark. Besides, they were focused on the ground, and the surrounding night was filled with shadows.

"I'll start over there," the cop added. "We'll meet in the middle."

He could not believe his luck as the cop trotted away into the darkness, leaving him with Susan.

The trill in his chest started.

"So I bet that homeless guy is long gone by now," Susan said.

The cop was gone, the only sign of her a bobbing flashlight beam.

He moved forward, catching up to Susan, pressing his feet, heel to toe, oh so gently on the grass. His blood pulsed in rhythm with the river.

"I handcuffed him to the bench," the cop said from the other end of the plaza.

"Should we go back for him?" Susan asked.

"Let him get wet," the cop said.

He was just two steps behind the reporter now — they were completely in sync. Susan moved the penlight in a grid pattern on the ground in front of her. Each search pattern took eons and he reveled in their secret closeness.

He could kill her. In a heartbeat. He would not even break a sweat doing it.

"You know, the plaza was dedicated in 1990, dedicated to the memory of those who were deported to internment camps during World War II," she said. She seemed nervous now, busying herself with chatter. He wanted to believe that she sensed he was there, that animal instinct kicking in, the peripheral anxiety of prey. "There was a thriving Japantown in Portland before the war," she said. "But then residents were sent to camps and most of them lost everything. Their businesses were closed. When they got out, there weren't very many reasons to stick around."

The cop didn't answer.

"Did you know that the original state constitution made it illegal for a black

91

person to step foot into Oregon?" Susan asked. Her head turned down, another grid pattern. "It's no wonder people thought the Vanport flood was some sort of conspiracy."

He stiffened at the word.

Vanport.

Susan stopped and her head lifted. He could see her breathing quicken and her shoulders draw back.

"Keep looking, Susan," said the cop from the darkness.

"I am," groaned Susan, shining her penlight on the stone embankment to her left. "What are we looking for exactly?"

"A clue," the cop said. "Signs of a struggle. That sort of thing."

Vanport.

Her leather purse was open, and she wore it across her shoulder so the purse itself rested against her hip.

He cupped his hand over the edge of it and let the item drop from his fingers.

Then he took a step back, and then another.

CHAPTER 11

Susan paused at the stone. It was about four feet tall, jagged and flat, and flecked with minerals.

She shone the penlight that Claire had given her over the last two lines of the poem carved on its surface:

Why complain when it rains?
This is what it means to be free.

She ran the light down the length of the stone, tracing the ground around it.

She almost missed the hand. The brain has a way of making explanations for things, and for ignoring those that don't make sense.

By the time she'd processed what she'd seen, she'd already moved on with the penlight, and had to go back.

A hand, palm up, fingers curled.

"Claire?" Susan yelled.

Claire came running.

Susan's penlight was still trained on the thick fingers peeking out from behind the stone. A man's fingers.

"Hello?" Susan called tentatively to the fingers. She was frozen with fear, afraid to get closer, of what she'd see.

Claire wasted no time. She scrambled up the bank and knelt behind the stone. "It's Henry," she said. "He's not breathing."

Susan could hear Claire on the phone, calling for an ambulance, but she couldn't move. She didn't want to go up there. She didn't want to see Henry like that. He was a strong man.

Not breathing.

What had Robbins called it?

Respiratory paralysis.

"Help me," Claire said. "Susan, now."

Susan snapped to, and hurried up the rock embankment. Henry was slumped against the back of the stone, head bent forward. Clothing drenched. Rainwater beading his face. From a distance it probably looked like he was sleeping. Up close, it looked more permanent.

"I need to get him flat," Claire said. She was crying, wiping snot from her nose with her sleeve.

"What do I do?" Susan asked.

"Get his feet."

Claire got her arms behind Henry, under his armpits, and Susan pulled his legs out and they managed to work him into a prone position.

"Do you know CPR?" Claire asked.

Susan had taken CPR for her babysitter certification in high school, but right now she was drawing a complete blank. "Not really," she said.

Claire unzipped Henry's jacket and grabbed Susan's hands, putting the heel of one on Henry's chest between his nipples and over his sternum, and then placing Susan's other hand on top of the first.

"Push," Claire said quickly. "Like this." She pushed Susan's hands down. "Two inches. "You should be pumping at a rate of a hundred times a minute, so do it fast. Faster than once per second. Count. And when you get to thirty, stop, so I can breathe for him." She bent over Henry's face, plugged his nose, put her lips to his, and exhaled. Then she turned her head and listened at his mouth for a moment. Then she put her lips to his again and repeated it. "Now go," she said to Susan.

Susan started to pump. Two inches. "One," she counted. "Two, three, four . . ."

She was on the ground, the cold mud

seeping into the knees of her jeans. She kept pumping. She didn't look up. She didn't want to see Henry's face.

CHAPTER 12

Archie was covered with rubber heating blankets that looked like extra big bathtub mats. The feeling in his hands and feet had returned. His body was stiff, but his head had cleared.

He was in his own room in the Emanuel ER. The boy had been worse off than he was. They'd taken him somewhere to pump warm blood into him or something. There was no clock in his room, a clever way to keep patients in the dark about how long they'd been kept waiting. But Archie was the last person on earth with a watch. Assuming that, after a prolonged dip in the Willamette, the watch still worked, it was nine o'clock. He'd been in the ER for over an hour.

They had already announced their intention to keep him overnight. Every so often someone came in and checked his vitals and the temperature of his blankets. Once they got a look at his medical records they started giving him concerned looks. Gretchen had carved out his spleen. His liver was bad from pills. He'd seen the nurse's eyes widen when she'd opened up the blanket and seen his scars. And that was just the tip of the iceberg.

He was alone. More alone than usual. He still had Debbie listed as his emergency contact, but he'd told the hospital not to call. She'd want to come, and it was dangerous on the roads. He would have called Henry if he could have. Henry would have come and berated him for jumping into the river without a plan. Then he would have put his cowboy boots up on Archie's bed and turned on a cooking show.

The door to Archie's room was open, so he passed the time listening to the sounds of the hospital. A woman sobbed softly in the room next to him. A frail white-haired man who'd arrived holding a bloody shirt to his head was getting stitches. Orderlies and nurses cracked wise at the desk.

There's a rhythm to a hospital. Archie was amazed at how it came back to him. The sound of clogs on linoleum, curtain rings sliding on metal rods, distant TV chatter. Shapes moved by in the hallway at the same pace. It was self-contained — its own ecosystem. There was a labeled compartment for everything; every action was recorded in a chart; life moved at a predictable pace.

Until it didn't.

Archie could feel the shift. The building's pulse quickened. The tone of conversation outside his door darkened. The ambient hum of unnecessary movement ceased.

An orderly rushed a crash cart by Archie's door.

The boy, Archie thought. He still had no idea how the boy had ended up in the river, how long he'd been in the water, or how he'd even managed to stay afloat. He was barely responsive when Archie had gotten to him. As soon as Archie had hooked his arms under the boy's, the kid had gone limp. If he'd fought Archie at all they would probably both have drowned out there. Archie had saved that boy's life, sure. But the boy had also saved Archie.

They couldn't let him die.

Archie pushed the rubber blankets off, sat up, and swung his legs off the bed. He was cocooned in even more blankets, these white flannel, and it took him a minute to unwrap himself. Then he pushed himself off the bed and padded out of his room in his gown and hospital socks.

"What's going on?" he said.

A nurse trotted toward him, arm out-stretched. "You need to get back in your room, sir," she said. There was a whooshing sound of hydraulic doors opening and both Archie and the nurse looked to their right as a gurney was rushed in.

Not the boy.

The boy was fine.

This was someone else.

Someone who was really hurt.

Even from twenty feet down the hall, Archie could see that they had an oxygen mask on him, and someone was squeezing a bag. An EMT was running beside the gurney doing chest compressions, headed Archie's way.

The person on the gurney wasn't breathing.

Archie didn't move.

The EMTs had been met by two doctors and two nurses, who now joined in resuscitation efforts.

Archie saw the top of his head as the gurney raced closer. A big head. Shaved.

He reached behind, found the doorjamb he'd just stepped through, and steadied himself.

They rolled Henry right by him.

The medical staff working to save him

spoke in clipped, urgent medical jargon, but Archie could make out words he knew. Respiratory arrest. Intubate.

Archie stumbled from the doorway after them.

They were moving fast — five feet away, then ten. Archie couldn't make out what they were saying anymore.

"Sir," he heard someone say. "Step back, please."

"I need to see his hand," Archie said. A nurse stepped in front of him, blocking him from continuing down the hall and reaching the corner room directly ahead where they'd parked Henry. Archie tried to get around her, but someone was gently pulling him away from behind.

"Please," he said, trying not to sound like a madman, "I'm his partner. He's a detective. He might have been poisoned. I need to see if there's a brown spot on his hand."

"There is," said a voice behind him.

Archie turned to see Susan Ward. "It's there," she said. "On his left palm. I told them everything. They're going to run tox screens."

Archie looked back down the hall through the open door a dozen feet away where Henry lay dying. They were jamming a metal shoehorn into his mouth, and then guiding a tube down his throat. The oxygen flowed. Henry's chest rose and then fell as the machine on the other end of the tube began to breathe for him. It almost made him look like he was alive.

CHAPTER 13

Susan, Claire, Archie, Robbins, and Portland's chief of police, Robert Eaton, were hunkered down in Archie's ER room, where Archie had been ordered back under his heating blanket.

Every time the nurse came in to check on Archie they all had to shift their position to make room.

Susan was eating a packet of saltines that she'd found in one of the supply drawers under the sink. It was maybe the best food she'd ever had.

Robbins and Archie had just briefed the chief on their theory, which, when said aloud, didn't amount to much, and created more questions than answers.

Susan liked Chief Eaton. He was small, maybe five-four, but didn't seem that bothered by it. And he'd let Archie go back to work after his two-month stay at the psych ward, which must have required cutting through some red tape.

He rubbed his face with his hand. Looked at Archie. Looked at Robbins. And then rubbed his face again.

"Six houses just slid down the West Hills," he said. "Eleven dead. The river is still rising. I-5 is closed at Chehalis. Oregon City and Tillamook are flooding. You do not breathe a word of this. You get your team on it. Bring in whomever you need. But try to do it quietly. And keep me posted."

He started for the door and stopped in front of Claire, who was sitting in a plastic chair next to Susan.

"I'm sorry about Henry," he said to her.

"He's a good cop," Claire said.

"Cut the crap, Claire," Eaton said. "Everyone knows about you two."

"Yes, sir."

He put his hat on. It was covered with clear plastic to protect it from the rain. "Take care of yourself, everyone," he said, and went out the door.

Claire brought her hands to her face. "Shit," she said through her fingers. "I left that guy handcuffed to the bench." She dropped her hands and stood up. "I need to make a call," she announced, stepping out of the room.

Archie raised his eyebrows at Susan.

She knew when to change the subject. "How long will Henry's tox screen take?" she asked Robbins.

"Depends. They have to run a lot of tests. I brought them a sample from Stephanie Towner. That might help." He took a step toward Archie and clapped his hand on Archie's shoulder. "Look," he said, "I've got to get back to the morgue. We've got a lot we still need to get out of there. I'll check in later."

"Thanks," Archie said.

As Robbins passed Susan, he glanced down at her feet. "You've washed those boots since you were at the morgue, right? Before you came to a hospital and tracked biohazards all over the ER?"

She hadn't washed them. "Absolutely," she said.

When he was gone, it was just Archie and Susan. She didn't know what to say to him. He and Henry had been partners for fifteen years. They'd worked the Beauty Killer case together. Henry had been there for Archie's wife and children the ten days he was missing, and then sat vigil with her all those weeks in the hospital after Gretchen had let Archie go, barely alive. When Archie had gone off the rails, it had been Henry who'd protected him, and who'd finally convinced him to get help.

Archie had only recently begun resembling a sane person. He was eight months clean of painkillers. Six months out of inpatient treatment. Susan had no idea what would happen to him if Henry died.

"I'm okay," Archie said.

Susan looked up. She could feel tears on her cheeks.

"Really," Archie said.

Susan wiped the tears away and smiled. "Why does one of us always end up in the hospital?" she said.

The door opened and one of the nurses popped her head in.

Susan's heart dropped. Henry.

But the nurse wasn't bringing news about their friend. "Where's Robbins?" she asked.

Susan let out the breath she'd been holding. "He just left," she said.

The nurse was carrying a long piece of Tupperware sealed with a blue lid. "I have his ulna," she said.

"His what?" Archie asked.

"His ulna." She indicated her forearm. "Arm bone," she explained. "Apparently he sent some bodies to our morgue, and they found this ulna on one of the cadaver trays tucked next to a corpse. Robbins was supposed to pick it up."

Through the milky plastic, Susan could make out the bone, brown and cracked from so many years underground.

Ralph, she thought.

"Give it to me," Susan said. "I'll catch up with him."

The nurse hesitated for only a second. She had work to do, and Susan knew it. Susan grabbed the Tupperware out of her hands and took off out of the ER.

She knew Emanuel Hospital. Her father had died there. Like all hospitals, it was a labyrinth of hallways and exits and entrances. She headed for an interior arterial corridor in the hopes of catching sight of Robbins. Ralph's ulna rattled in the Tupperware as she ran.

As soon as she got to the corridor, she spotted Robbins's dreadlocks swinging down the hallway to the main entrance.

"Hey!" she shouted. "Robbins!"

He stopped and turned.

A woman pushing a kid in a wheelchair gave her a dirty look.

Robbins walked toward Susan. The hallway was entirely glass on one side, looking out onto the children's garden. It was still raining.

Susan lifted the Tupperware. "You forgot Ralph's ulna," she said.

Robbins dropped his head. "Shit."

"Crack team you've got there," Susan said.

He reached her and took the plastic tub. "It's a sixty-year-old skeleton," he said. "Not a top priority. Want to know what's going to happen to Ralph? He's going to end up in a box somewhere. Until someone accidentally throws him away." He said it matter-of-factly, and not without regret.

Susan, deflated, left Robbins and started trudging back to the ER. She hadn't made it far when her phone rang.

She recognized the ringtone and her stomach clenched — it was Ian, her editor.

She picked it up anyway. "Yeah?" she answered.

"Tell me you're in the building," he said.

She was pretty sure she wasn't in the building he hoped she was. "I'm at Emanuel," she said.

"What the fuck is wrong with you? Channel Six had a photograph of you standing next to Archie Sheridan on a gurney, and I just read a wire report that you were one of the two people who found Henry Sobol."

"I was going to report it," Susan said. "I've been busy."

"Are you dead? Are you mentally incapacitated?"

"No."

"Then get your ass into the office."

He hung up on her.

"I don't have a car here," she said to no one in particular. She had ridden to the hospital in Henry's ambulance. Ian hadn't even asked how Henry was, how Archie was. Nothing. He didn't care.

She dropped the phone back in her purse.

She could call a taxi. If she could get one in this weather.

Then she gave it some thought. Rain slid in sheets down the huge glass windows.

Screw Ian.

It wasn't even ten P.M. He could hold the presses for hours on the next day's edition.

Let him stew a little.

She turned a corner and took the elevator up to the fifth floor. The elevator opened onto a hallway overlooking the atrium. Susan took a right turn and headed down a hallway that led to the physicians' offices.

The photographs were still there, framed and hung on the light blue wall, one every third door. The black-and-white images were part of a permanent exhibit sponsored by the Oregon Historical Society. A black man in a fedora carrying a blond little boy through waist-deep water, past cars flooded to their roofs. An aerial view of dozens of apartment buildings that had been lifted off their foundations and clumped together, water up to the top floor. Rescuers holding hands, forming a chain, reaching out to save people.

She'd first seen the photographs when she was a teenager with a dying father and a lot of time to kill in the hospital. That was the first she'd heard of Vanport. You could grow up in Portland and never hear the name. It had been wiped out. Not a trace left behind. Even her teachers didn't know much. The death toll was murky. The official count was fifteen. Some said thousands. There were rumors of a conspiracy to cover up the real numbers.

Maybe she'd stretched it in her column, looking for connections where there weren't any. Ralph probably hadn't died at Vanport. But other people had.

Susan had visited those photographs again and again that year when she was fourteen.

It was something to do, when she wasn't sneaking cigarettes in the children's cancer garden.

An announcement crackled over the intercom, pulling Susan back to the present.

Emergency room. Code Blue.

Henry.

Susan ran for the elevator.

CHAPTER 14

Crash carts, up close, looked like Craftsman auto supply tool chests. Take away the IV pole, the green oxygen tank, and that's what you were left with — a sturdy, waist-high red metal chest of drawers, each drawer tidily labeled. But instead of SOCKET WRENCHES and HEX BOLTS, these drawers were labeled BREATHING and CIRCULATION.

Susan wasn't crying. It surprised her. She would probably cry later. But right now she just felt a shattering sense of dread.

The door to Henry's room was wide open, but Claire wasn't looking. She was outside the door, in the hallway, her back against the wall, turned away from Henry, both hands over her mouth. Why did people do that? Susan wondered. Were they trying to keep their emotions in, or keep the world out?

Archie was in the hall, next to Claire. He

had his hand on her upper arm. He was just standing there with her, in his blue-and-white gown and white robe, his bare calves and hospital slippers. Susan envied their closeness. They looked like they were holding each other up. She hugged her own arms across her chest.

Claire. Henry. Archie. They had known each other so long, been through so much. Susan felt like an interloper, like maybe she should go. Who was she to them, anyway? She still couldn't figure out exactly what Archie thought of her.

But while Claire didn't seem to be able to bring herself to look, Susan couldn't bring herself to look away.

There were things that Susan wished she didn't know. Details she'd picked up through the years of writing stories that haunted her still. The ingredients in movie theater popcorn butter, for instance. The amounts of fecal matter that can be found in most bowling ball finger holes. And how long a bedbug can live between feedings (one year).

Right now Susan was wishing that she hadn't done the story about defibrillation. Because she knew that patients rarely survived if they needed more than three shocks.

And Henry had already had two.

She looked over at Archie and Claire again. They were sharing some private moment, heads close. Were they praying? Susan had never asked Archie about religion. She figured that if he had any, he'd given it up in that basement with Gretchen Lowell.

Susan didn't know how to pray. She couldn't think of a single prayer. She wondered, if she Googled one on her phone, if it would count. Probably not. She should have taken that theology class in college. Most of her religious education came from playing Mary Magdalene in a high school production of *Jesus Christ Superstar.* That's where growing up with hippies got you.

When her father died, her mother read from *The Tibetan Book of the Dead:*

Remember the clear light, the pure clear white light from which everything in the universe comes, to which everything in the universe returns; the original nature of your own mind. The natural state of the universe unmanifest.

Susan still didn't know what it meant.

Henry's mouth opened and closed, like a fish gasping for water on dry land. His tongue pushed past his lips, then retracted.

His elbows were bent and his arms writhed slowly at his sides.

But he wasn't alive.

It was muscle spasms, from the first two shocks.

It was better that Claire and Archie didn't see this.

"Stand clear," the automated external defibrillator said. "Do not touch the patient. Analyzing rhythm." The computerized female voice sounded like one of those GPS navigation ladies. Calm. Competent. Bossy.

Defibrillators had come a long way since they'd tried to revive Susan's father with panels that looked like a pair of travel irons.

Henry's hospital gown was open and his gray-haired chest was bare except for two white adhesive pads, one on his right shoulder above the nipple, the other on his left flank at the bottom of his rib cage. White wires stretched from the pads to the machine on the crash cart. He looked ashen and sunken, like an old man.

They'd used a dummy the day that Susan had seen the new AEDs demonstrated. The machines saved time. In the old days, there'd been crash teams — someone from cardiology, respiration. It took a village to read the ECG, interpret it, and operate the machine. With the AEDs, the nearest medical staff could begin defib immediately.

This was what they'd said at the press conference when the hospital had switched to the new technology.

"Stand clear," the AED said again. "Do not touch the patient. Analyzing rhythm."

It was so quiet then that Susan could hear her pulse beating in her ears. Her throat swelled.

The five medical personnel in the room stood in suspended animation around Henry's bed, waiting for the shock.

People didn't arch their backs and jerk off the table the way they did on hospital shows. They just sort of flinched. No one had talked about that at the press conference.

"Come on," one of the doctors said, like he was in his car and the engine wouldn't turn over.

Susan felt Archie looking at her and glanced over at him. She knew that he could hear the quiet, too. He was watching her, waiting for the slump of her shoulders, the tremble of her jaw — some clue that it was over. Claire had sunk down to the floor and was resting her head on her knees. It had been too long. You didn't need a press conference on defibrillation to know that.

Susan turned her gaze back into the room,

just in time to see the AED administer the third shock.

Remember the clear light, the pure clear white light from which everything in the universe comes, to which everything in the universe returns; the original nature of your own mind. The natural state of the universe unmanifest.

She saw Henry wince. Like someone startled by a distant sound.

She held her breath. The pulse in her ears thrummed.

"Check pulse," the AED said calmly. "If no pulse, give CPR."

Susan couldn't see the heart monitor, not that she could have made anything of it. It had the attention of everyone in the room, though. They watched it without blinking, without moving a muscle, like they were at mission control waiting for Neil Armstrong to announce that he'd landed on the moon.

One small step for man, one giant leap for mankind.

Susan had always gotten in Henry's way. She'd annoyed him from the start. He'd been trying to protect Archie, and she came along intent on making Archie relive his nightmare. Henry had tried to protect her, too, to keep her safe. But she'd ignored every warning he'd ever tossed her way, nearly getting herself killed in the process. That was how she was with men in authority. She either rebelled against them with all her might, or fell in love. Never anything in between.

Wait.

Henry's jaw moved.

Not a muscle spasm. Susan didn't know how, but she knew it to be true without hesitation. This was something different. Something intentional. His jaw opened. His chest — which had seemed so sunken and pale, so decrepit — expanded and lifted. His skin flushed.

"He's breathing," someone said.

Susan felt hot tears running down her cheeks. If Henry lived through this, she would listen to him, she wouldn't get in the way, she'd be less annoying.

Please, God. I promise.

"We've got a heartbeat," someone else said. "It's getting stronger."

Susan turned toward Archie and Claire and grinned, wiping her face with her sleeve. They had heard. Archie was already helping Claire to her feet.

Susan's phone rang. She knew who it was.

CHAPTER 15

Archie was used to pain. There was the physical pain — the ribs that still ached where Gretchen had broken them, the acid that burned deep in his throat where the poison Gretchen had fed him had eaten through his esophagus. He'd mostly learned to live with it. He'd taught himself not to take deep breaths, to sit up when he ate, to sleep on his back. The emotional pain had taken longer. But he could look at himself in the mirror now, scars and all. He could spend time with his children without the crushing weight of guilt that clung to him like a smell.

There was always pain.

The trick was to make it part of you.

The machine inhaling and exhaling for Henry made breathing sound easy. Steady, strong. Each breath exactly the same as the last. You could trick yourself into taking that kind of breathing for granted.

It was eleven P.M., and the hospital was quiet. They'd moved Henry to the ICU, a land without doors, where all the patient rooms had three walls and were open to a central area, like a hospital doll house or a TV sitcom set. Everything in there was made out of molded tan plastic that reminded Archie of school cafeteria trays. Speckled linoleum floors; a soap pump and paper towel dispenser on the wall above a sink. The effect was part cheap motel, part public restroom.

Archie was sitting there in sweatpants and a sweatshirt borrowed from some hospital storeroom, his own clothes a wet bundle in a plastic bag at his feet, next to his coat.

The ecosystem had been restored, everything was in order.

Henry was alive for now, heart beating, blood pumping. But the tox screens hadn't turned up anything yet, so there was nothing the doctors could do but try to keep Henry breathing until his body fought off what ever was shutting it down. Archie wasn't about to sit around and wait for Henry's heart to stop again.

There were plenty of things that Archie wasn't good at. He knew that. He could tick them off like the names of family members. He hadn't been a good husband. He'd been

120

weak, self-indulgent, and careless. He'd given in to temptation, and lied. He'd disappointed the people who depended on him. But he was a good detective, always a good detective — always that. He could find killers. He could save lives.

The front of his head throbbed. He pushed a thumb and forefinger against his sinuses. He could taste the river water at the back of his throat, rusty and dank like flat cola. It was the middle of the night, but sleep was still far off. He was vaguely aware that Claire had gone downstairs to meet her sister. He hadn't known that Claire had a sister. But she was here now. That was good. The sister would be here for Claire, Claire for Henry. That meant that Archie could go and do the thing he was good at — his job.

They had to get back to the park. They had to re-create Henry's last steps. Archie's team was already down there. They had to stay ahead of the flood.

He'd apparently lost his boots in the river. The sweats and hospital booties would get him out the door. But he had to go back to his apartment to change before he could work.

But first Archie had to talk to the boy.

The boy had to have gone in the river at least a half mile from where Henry had been found. There had been thousands of people between them. But Gretchen had taught Archie not to believe in coincidence, and he wondered now if the attack on Henry and the boy going into the Willamette were related somehow. Had Henry seen something? Had he tried to help?

Archie leaned forward and cupped a hand on Henry's arm. It was cooler than it should have been, like something not quite alive. Henry's eyes were closed, and a faint sheen of sweat glazed his forehead. A vein zigzagged across his temple.

"Keep an eye on things here for me," Archie said. His voice sounded rough and loud in the silence.

He stepped out of the room and nearly ran into Susan, who had her hands filled with individually wrapped packets of saltines and was carrying a tower of foil-topped plastic containers of orange juice pinned between her chin and fist.

"I've got food," she said. Her raspberry-colored hair looked especially wild, electric from the rain and hospital lights. She seemed to see him notice it, and blew at a piece that had flopped over one eye. It fluttered up, and then fell back exactly where it had been. She'd taken off her yellow raincoat and tied it around her waist.

A nurse scrambled out from behind a desk. Her scrubs were pink and fitted, with cargo pockets on the pants. Her blond hair was pulled back into a ponytail. At first Archie thought she was going to admonish him for having left the ER, but she was glaring at Susan's armload of snacks. "You can't just take all that," she said to Susan.

Susan rotated a half step and shielded the food. "It was in unlocked cabinets."

Archie stepped between them. "I need to talk to the boy I came in with," he said to the nurse. He used his best voice-of-authority, though the sweat suit probably worked against him. The elastic waistband barely stayed up over his hips.

The nurse pulled at her ponytail. "He's resting."

"It's police business," Archie said, a little more firmly.

Her upper lip tightened. She had the telltale fine lines of a smoker around her mouth. "I'll have to check with my supervisor." She turned and hurried off. Her white sneakers didn't make a sound on the linoleum.

Archie held on to his bag of clothes and waited. If they wouldn't let him talk to the kid, there wasn't much he could do about it. He looked back toward Henry's room, but he could only see Henry's feet from here. A pair of lumps under a tan blanket. Archie thought he could still hear the machine, though: inhaling, exhaling . . .

Susan cleared her throat.

Archie glanced over at her. She was still balancing that ridiculous column of juice. The hair was still in her face.

"Room eleven," she said in a stage whisper.

It took him a second.

She jerked her head in the direction of the nurses' station, and Archie followed her gaze until he noticed the giant whiteboard hung on the wall. On it were the names and room numbers of every patient on the ward. JOHN DOE, HYPOTHERMIA, ROOM 11.

The kid was still listed as John Doe. It had been two hours since they'd been brought in. It had to be all over the news. But if they didn't have a name, it meant that the boy hadn't been claimed.

How does a kid disappear during a flood and nobody notice?

Henry was in room three.

The ICU was horseshoe-shaped. For luck, Archie would have joked, if he'd been feeling lighter-hearted.

He started walking, counting down the doll house rooms as he went, Susan on his heels, still with the snacks. There wasn't a hallway, just a variation in linoleum tile color, a thick black path on the floor where a hallway might have been. Archie glanced in at each bed they passed, finding only slack, unconscious faces. No balloons. No flowers. Unanimated like that, even the people looked the same.

"Next one," Susan said.

Room eleven.

Three walls. A sink. A wood-grain-veneer cabinet. Same colors and bathroom aesthetic. Except the tan molded plastic bed in this room was empty. Someone had been there, and recently. The white sheets were thrown back, the pillow dented. But there was no one in the room now.

Archie checked the number above the bed.

It was the right room. Archie recognized what looked to be heating blankets cast aside on the floor.

"Maybe he checked out," Susan said.

Had his parents come and gotten him after all?

The nurse in pink scrubs silently jogged up in her white sneakers. Another woman, older and sturdier, followed behind her.

The pink nurse squinted at Archie and gave him a disapproving frown. "You can't . . ." she started to say, but trailed off when she saw the empty bed. Her eyes widened. She was wearing blue mascara.

"Where is he?" Archie asked.

She looked over at the other nurse, who was wearing green scrubs — old-school, no cargo pants for her — and glasses around her neck on a practical-looking gold chain. A tiny silver angel was pinned above her heart. Pink's supervisor, Archie guessed.

The pink nurse hesitated and fluttered a hand in the air. "He should be here," she said.

Susan was still holding the snacks, though no one seemed that concerned about it anymore.

They all stood staring at the empty bed like it might get up and walk off, too.

"Marcie," the supervisor called calmly to someone back at the desk, "did eleven get taken somewhere for tests?"

"No," Marcie called back.

"Then where is he?" Archie said again between gritted teeth.

"Check the bathroom," the supervisor said, and the pink nurse scrambled to a nearby door and opened it.

"Empty," she reported.

They all looked helplessly at one another.

How could a kid just disappear from an ICU? A kid nobody reports missing, and nobody notices walk away from his hospital bed in the dead of night.

"Call security," Archie said. "Maybe he's still in the hospital."

"We never got his name," the supervisor said, almost to herself. "He never said a word."

Susan moved forward, and Archie almost told her to stop, to stay out of the boy's room, but there was something about her sudden purpose that made him wait. He watched as she walked up to the bed and opened her arms and let the juice containers and saltine packets tumble onto the mattress.

"She can't just take all those snacks," the pink nurse said again.

"No one cares about the snacks, Heather," her supervisor snapped.

Susan dropped to her hands and knees and reached under the bed. No one moved. Susan withdrew her hand from under the bed. There was something in it. She rocked back on her heels and held her hand out toward Archie, palm up, like a street kid looking for a buck.

Archie shuffled forward and stared down at the object on Susan's palm. It was rusted metal and looked like a key, but it was tiny — the size of a tack. Like something that would open a very small door.

"What is it?" Archie asked.

"Search me," Susan said.

CHAPTER 16

The drizzle was relentless. It was the kind of rain that got in your eyes and streamed down your cheeks, so everyone always looked like they were crying. Archie had gone home and changed into corduroys. That was one of the things you learned living in Portland — avoid wet denim. The wicking action of the cotton carried the water upward so wet cuffs would bleed up to your knees. The denim leeched heat from your body like a cold bath. When they found missing people dead from hypothermia in the snow, and they were wearing jeans, they weren't hikers. They were walkers. Tourists. Snow hikers didn't wear jeans. They wore wool hats and thermal underwear and polypropylene.

It was two in the morning, and the crowd was still working on the seawall at Waterfront Park. The mild weather that had been causing the snowmelt had chilled, but only to the low forties, far above freezing. Gravity was pulling the runoff from every mountain stream straight down into the valley.

Archie was wearing brown leather shoes. He imagined his boots out in the river somewhere, floating next to the incongruous glut of crap that the flooding had knotted together: empty beer bottles, logs, lighters, condoms, plastic bottle caps, water jugs, and the occasional lost Croc. The leather shoes laced up to his ankles. Clarks. Debbie had told him once that they had gone out of style around 1980, but Archie had a soft spot for them.

The entire Japanese American Plaza was cordoned off with crime tape. Judging by the flashlight beams, there were fifty cops down there at least. Some of them knew Henry. Most probably didn't. But that's how it was. If one of your own was hurt, you showed up. Never mind that it was the middle of the night and a state of emergency had been declared. Fifty cops. *Too many,* Archie thought.

They all knew Archie. He tried not to think about that now. Gretchen Lowell had brought him more than his share of infamy. Within the ranks of the Portland Police Department, he was a ghost or a prophet. The ones who thought he was a phantom back from the dead avoided eye contact. The ones who thought he was some super cop, brimming with serial-killer know-how — they wouldn't leave him alone. They thought he was smart and brave and lucky.

He was none of those things.

Not lucky, anyway. Certainly not that. Everyone around him suffered, one way or another.

Now Archie had to make up for that, had to find a way to save Henry. He couldn't do it standing there alone in the rain.

Detective Jeff Heil trotted up. Archie recognized him from his stride. The sky was a thick frosting of clouds that blotted out the moon and stars and seemed to have its own vast unnatural glow. It wasn't enough to see by. And even the buildings that lined the waterfront were dark — lights normally left on at night had been turned off, electrical box switches thrown to prevent short circuits.

Heil lifted his flashlight beam, illuminating his long face. His dark blond hair was so wet it looked painted on, and the shadows of the beam made his chiseled cheekbones look even more hollow than usual. Heil had joined Archie's task force a year and a half ago, when Archie had come off his two-year post-Gretchen medical leave. Archie had been popping Vicodin all day long back then. Heil had to have known it. But as far as Archie knew, he'd never said anything.

"So?" Archie said, wiping rain from under his eyes.

Heil lowered the light. "We've searched it all," he said. "There was nothing there. Bird shit. Mud." He held something up. "And this."

Archie swung his own flashlight up to see that Heil was holding a plastic evidence bag.

It was empty.

"Is it an invisible clue?" asked Archie.

"It's a plastic bag," Heil said. He caught himself. "I mean, inside the plastic bag."

Heil focused his light on the bag, too, and gave it a little shake.

Archie took it and gave it a closer look. There was something plastic inside, almost exactly the same size as the evidence bag itself. From the looks of it, it was a plastic Ziploc freezer bag.

It looked clean. No drug residue. No crumbs from a sandwich. "Dog walker might have dropped it," Archie said.

Portlanders were zealots about scooping up their dogs' poop. The bags of choice were biodegradable store-bought ones designed for waste retrieval, or the blue plastic sleeves that *The New York Times* came in. Somewhere there was a landfill brimming with knotted blue plastic shit-filled *NYT* bags.

"Sure," Heil said. "But I wanted to show you something, and it's all we've got."

An empty Ziploc bag. If that was a metaphor, they were screwed.

"Where's the guy who had Henry's phone?" Archie asked.

"Under the bridge."

Heil led Archie up the promenade, shifting to get between the volunteers and guardsmen still hoisting sandbags into place in their race against time. Archie was grateful for the crowd. There were still local news teams around, and he didn't want to get spotted. They would have been on him in an instant, cameras rolling, wanting details of the rescue.

By now the department would have gone public about the missing boy. The hospital security cameras had captured his grainy image leaving through an exit door, alone. It was a lousy shot — three-quarters profile, still in a hospital gown, barefoot, fleeing into the midnight rain. That was Archie to a tee — save someone and then immediately lose him. Classic.

It took looking at the photograph to make Archie realize how much the kid looked like his son.

He wondered if it was even a top story. Probably no one cared. Probably the news was all flood watch, all the time. The kid's parents hadn't even noticed he was gone, why would anyone else?

Archie could still feel the cold of the river in his bones.

"There," Heil said.

They were under the Burnside Bridge. Archie felt himself exhale, suddenly lighter on his feet, and it took him a moment to realize it was the foreign sensation of being outside without being rained on. The concrete slab of bridge above them was supported by massive concrete pillars. This bridge had been built in the nineteenth century and then rebuilt in the 1920s. It wasn't bad, with its Italian Renaissance towers and pretty metal railings. But that was up top. Down here it was dank and dirty. Much of the year, weekends brought Saturday Market booths, with their utensil mobiles and hemp necklaces. But in the winter there was no market, and the gap under the bridge became a shelter for homeless people trying to get out of the rain.

It was crowded down there now, but not with the homeless. National Guard trucks, volunteers handing out coffee, Parks and Recreation vehicles — it was a regular tailgate party. At the center of the action — dwarfing all but the largest National Guard vehicles — was the Portland PD's massive new mobile command center. The only sign of the usual tenants was an abandoned shopping cart. Archie spotted two of his detectives, Mike Flannigan and Martin Ngyun, one on either side of the man who'd had Henry's phone. Only he wasn't wrapped in plastic anymore — he was cloaked in a gray wool blanket. There was a woman with them. She worked in social services. Archie wasn't sure how he knew — something about how she stood, chest wide, feet apart, unintimidated by the ambient chaos.

The lights under the bridge were different than the construction lights illuminating the seawall project; these rotated, white and orange, so that everything shifted color at five-second intervals. The effect was part disaster zone, part nightclub.

Flannigan gave the woman a soft push forward. She gave him a dirty look.

"This is Mary Riley," Flannigan said to Archie. "From the Mission."

The Portland Rescue Mission ran a soup kitchen and shelter on Burnside, among other charitable activities. The soup kitchen fed so many that sometimes the line of homeless people out front would stretch for blocks along the sidewalk of the Burnside Bridge directly above them.

"I need to get back," Riley said. Her brown hair was tucked up into a fleece cap and she was wearing a Columbia Sportswear jacket with a corduroy skirt and tights.

"She identified him for us," Flannigan continued. "His name's Dan Schmidt, but he goes by" — he lifted his fingers and made air quotes — "Otter. He's schizophrenic. Off his meds. From what we can interpret, he found the phone on the path of the Japanese American Plaza. Picked it up. Didn't see anything. He keeps mentioning this person Nick. Also, something about a spaceship and Ronald Reagan. We ran his prints. He's in the system, but nothing violent."

Archie could see how Dan Schmidt got his nickname. With his wet brown hair and bushy beard, wide flat nose and overbite, he did look like an otter.

"He's harmless," Riley said matter-of-factly. "Now can I get him out of the cold?"

Otter didn't even look at them, eyes glued to a spot on the ground. Who knew what was in his rattled brain? With the right pills he might have a whole different story, might be able to describe exactly what had happened to Henry. But they couldn't force meds on him, not without getting a court order, and they couldn't prove he'd done anything wrong. There wasn't a law against picking up a dropped cell phone. If he hadn't picked it up, they never would have found Henry in time. He'd be dead.

"Who's Nick?" Archie asked Otter.

Otter shuffled his feet. "River people," he muttered. His eyes flicked up and looked out across the Willamette to the Eastbank Esplanade. It was a popular camping spot for the down-and-out.

"You know this guy Nick?" Archie asked Mary Riley.

"He's kind of their leader," Riley said. "Lives under the Hawthorne, I think. But I haven't seen him all week."

The street people who lived around the river were their own tribe. The city had long ago stopped fighting their presence. As long as they didn't sell heroin to stroller moms or drink in public, they were left alone. Most of them stuck to the east side, where much of the esplanade was inaccessible to cars and there were plenty of places to hide.

If Otter couldn't tell them anything about what had happened to Henry, maybe Nick could. It was a place to start.

"You've got room for him?" Archie asked Riley, with a nod at Otter. "If I need to find him later?"

"I'll make room," Riley said.

Archie glanced back at all the activity behind them, the trucks and equipment and people. The place stank with exhaustion and anxiety. All that work, and they were still at the mercy of the river's whims.

Mary Riley handed him her card. "I'm taking him now, and getting some sleep. You can call me in the morning if you want to agitate him more."

Archie was just tucking the card away when he heard his name. He could tell by the looks on his detectives' faces that it was important. He turned to see Chief Eaton standing outside his command trailer, hailing Archie with an arm. Lorenzo Robbins stood next to him, towering over him a good foot.

There was good news and there was bad news, and Archie mostly dealt with the latter. He could recognize it at a distance — a reluctance around the mouth, a slope of the shoulders — and he could tell with one look that Lorenzo Robbins had bad news, and that the chief didn't yet know what it was.

Archie hung his head and jogged over to them.

Chief Eaton was in full-dress rain gear, fancy cap and everything. But he got points for not being in bed. "You wanted him. There he is," Eaton said to Robbins. "Now tell us what you've got."

Robbins took a deep breath and looked at Archie. Somewhere under the bridge, the beeps of a backing truck sounded. "We've identified the toxin," Robbins said. "But you're not going to like it."

CHAPTER 17

He saw the picture of the boy on the news. He was alive. Wanted for questioning. The detective from the plaza was in critical condition. Poisoned, they said.

The other three were still listed as drowning victims. Flood-related tragedies. It happened. Eighteen people had died across the state since the flooding had begun. He had read about them all. Mudslides. Boating accidents. Cars swept off rural roads. The *Herald* always seemed to turn up breathless accounts from some witnesses or survivor. He had seen one story about an elderly man who had been swept away trying to rescue his wife after the creek surged on their farm. The neighbors saw him dive in after her. Heard her cry for him. Then she was gone. They said they could see his head above water for a while, looking at the spot where she had been. Maybe he was waiting for her to come up for air. But she never did. And then he went under, too. His three, they didn't seem that special compared to that. To have a good story, you needed someone to tell it.

He thought about that as he prepared the tank.

It was only twenty gallons, small for an aquarium, but things got heavy quickly when you figured ten pounds for every gallon of water. He gently washed the rectangular tank out with warm water from the tap. Detergents and soaps were pollutants to such an otherwise pristine environment. He poured a blue aquarium gravel mix from the bag into a small clean bucket he had waiting on the bottom of the sink, and ran the tap over the gravel until the water ran clear. He rolled the pebbles under his fingertips. The blue was the color of the ocean from a travel postcard. It was why he had chosen such a pretty backdrop to Scotch-tape behind the glass — an image of a Greek island, white stucco houses and red roofs, alabaster cliffsides descending into that blue, blue water. He lowered the under-gravel filter plate into place at the bottom of the tank, and then carefully poured the clean gravel into the tank, making a bright azure floor three-quarters of an inch deep.

He positioned the filters and heater, and

then lowered the tank into the sink under the faucet. He put a small plate on the bottom of the tank directly under the faucet stream, to keep the gravel from getting unsettled. And he turned the tap back on.

It took some time to fill the tank three-quarters full.

But he didn't allow himself to get distracted. Instead he arranged his plants and decorations. Small plants in the front, taller in the back. He'd chosen a nice castle for this one, and a diving helmet and an arched bridge. When the water reached the three-quarters mark, he added these in, careful to press them securely into the gravel. He stepped back and admired the marine landscape.

Then he filled the tank to the top.

He unfolded the top of a small cardboard box and lifted the creature inside by the scruff of its neck.

The hamster had tiny black eyes and a quivering pink nose. Her belly was white, her head and back and ears apricot. Her little pink hands were clenched in panicked fists at her chest.

He dropped her into the tank and sealed the cover into place.

Wet, she looked like an entirely different animal. Tiny and slick, those pink feet uncurled, paws churning at the water. Her whiskers glanced against the surface, ears flat back, eyelids fluttering.

She would hold on for a while. They all did.

When she finally gave in, he'd let her rest for some time at the bottom of the tank, apricot fur feathering dreamily against the blue gravel.

And then he'd take apart the tank, wash it all, and start again.

He heard the back door open, and the rain get loud.

"There you are," he said.

The boy streaked by behind him. His wet hospital gown clung to his scrawny knees.

The hamster swam and swam.

The man glanced up next to the window over the sink where he'd taped the column that Susan Ward had written, and wondered if she'd found what he'd left in her purse.

CHAPTER 18

Susan hunched over her computer at the *Herald,* yawned, and tried to focus on her monitor. Never take Chinese uppers on an empty stomach. This was what Susan's mother, Bliss, had told her. It wasn't even real speed. It was just some herb in gel caps in a bottle with Chinese characters on it. Bliss had gotten it from her acupuncturist, and given it to Susan before she'd gone on her yoga cruise. It was just like Bliss to head off on a three-week yoga cruise through the Caribbean days before the flood of the century. She was lucky that way. The ship had a media blackout policy, for "cleansing" purposes. Bliss had no idea what was going on back in Portland. This left Susan in charge of the goat and the compost pile and the leaky basement.

Susan had moved back into her childhood home eight months before. It was supposed to be temporary. Then it was supposed to be just until she saved up enough for a down payment on a loft in one of those redeveloped warehouses in the Pearl District.

Living with Bliss had its pros and cons. Susan's mother wore her hair bleached and dreadlocked, boycotted anything plastic, and had recently gotten a medical marijuana card for unspecified "anxiety." But Susan could live there for free. And if you liked brown rice, a lot, Bliss made a pretty good meal. What Susan didn't like to admit was that, after what she'd been through over the last year, as crazy as it was, home felt safe.

She shouldn't have taken the Chinese uppers. But it was two in the morning. And Ian was demanding copy. He'd already gone ballistic on her for staying at the hospital with Henry and Archie rather than hightailing it back to the paper. She had really pissed him off this time. He wouldn't even pay for the cab.

"That's it?" Ian blustered. He'd been eating sour-cream-and-onion potato chips from the vending machine. Susan could smell them on his breath. He sat down on the edge of her desk, nearly knocking her purse onto the floor. She emphatically moved the purse to the other side of her keyboard. "You write a two-thousand-word column on some old skeleton they found at a dog park, and I get three hundred words on a half-murdered cop?" Ian said.

"Derek already wrote the news story."

"You were there when he was found. I want to know what he looked like. I want to feel him dying on the page."

"He's my friend," Susan said.

"You're a journalist. Act like one. I want a rewrite in twenty minutes."

"No."

"I can fire you."

Susan ignored him.

Ian threw his hands in the air. "You know what?" He sputtered for a few seconds and then pointed at her. "You're fired."

Susan looked at him sideways. Was he kidding? "You can't do that."

"Ian," Derek said.

Ian jabbed his thumb at Derek. "I can buy two of him to replace one of you," Ian said to Susan. "You're not that special." He smoothed his ponytail back into place. "Pack a box," he said. "I'm calling HR." And he walked away.

He was serious.

This wasn't happening. This was all a Chinese-speed-induced hallucination. This was why people shouldn't do drugs.

She moved her purse onto her lap and

held it there.

"Do you want me to help you find a box?" Derek asked.

CHAPTER 19

"Tetrodotoxin," Robbins said.

Archie had no idea what that was, but Robbins had been right — he didn't like the sound of it. Chief Eaton evidently didn't, either, because he immediately put a hand on Robbins's shoulder, motioned for Archie with the other, and steered them both away from the others, back toward the mobile command center. Up close it looked even bigger and newer, not a scratch on its shiny black paint job. Eaton led them around the back of the vehicle. Archie had never been inside. But he imagined rows of flat-screen monitors and red telephones. Lights surrounded the trailer, like it was for sale as part of some showroom display. But at least they could see each other.

Eaton lowered his voice: "Tetro-what?" he asked Robbins.

The truck was idling and diesel fumes were thick in the air. Eaton coughed and loosened his tie.

Bioterrorism. Archie knew that's what the chief was thinking. It's where the mind went these days. Archie didn't know what tetrodotoxin was, and he didn't care. They'd identified it. They'd found what was poisoning Henry. Now they could help him.

"Tetrodotoxin," Robbins said. "It's a neurotoxin produced by a bacteria. TTX for short."

Neurotoxin. That didn't sound good.

"What are we talking about here?" Archie asked.

Robbins hesitated, then reached inside his jacket, retrieved a folded piece of paper, unfolded it, and handed it to Archie. Archie recognized the format. It was a Wikipedia page.

Archie scanned the headers: Classification, Behavior, Feeding, Breeding, Venom. An image to the right showed a fleshy spade-shaped creature with soft tentacles. It was beige, and spotted with incredibly bright blue rings. Eaton leaned close, squinting to see the page over Archie's shoulder.

"What is it?" Eaton asked.

Archie looked up at Robbins. Was this a joke? Robbins met Archie's gaze without a trace of levity.

"A blue-ringed octopus," Robbins said.

"An octopus," Archie repeated. It sounded as ridiculous said aloud as it did when he said it in his head.

No one spoke for a moment. There was noise. Voices around them, idling diesel engines, radios crackling, orders being barked, the constant hum of the rain, the rushing river — but it was also oddly silent, the noises that were supposed to surround them absent. The Burnside Bridge was up, so there were no cars driving overhead. Naito Parkway, which ran parallel to the park, was closed to all but emergency personnel. No squawk of birds or kids laughing or dogs barking.

"Detective Sobol was attacked by an octopus?" Eaton said. There was no judgment to it; just a man in charge repeating information he'd been given by an expert. Archie could see why the guy had been promoted.

Robbins leaned close to them, his face tense. "Not just Henry — the three other victims, too. All tested positive for TTX."

It made one thing make sense. "The puncture wounds on the palms," Archie said. "But couldn't someone have isolated the poison? Be injecting it with a syringe?"

"The point of entry on the palms is from

a beak, not a needle," Robbins said. "A blue-ring delivers venom by puncturing its prey with its beak. But let me be clear, this isn't accidental. This thing is being used as a weapon."

"So what's the antivenom?" Archie asked.

"There is no antivenom."

Which meant there was no cure. Which meant that Henry was still dying. Archie felt a wave of nausea rush over him, and he reached out and steadied himself on the back of the trailer.

"The treatment is palliative care," Robbins said quickly. "Keeping him breathing. Keeping his heart beating. He's lucky Claire and Susan found him when they did. If he can make it twenty-four hours, odds are he'll recover."

Eaton pulled some more at his tie, and looked around them at the National Guard, the cops, the massive sandbag effort that had drawn thousands of volunteers to the river's edge. He didn't look so calm anymore. "Wait a minute, son," he said to Robbins. "You're saying that there's some sort of deadly octopi in the water?"

Archie could see Robbins bristle at "son."

"Octopuses," Robbins said. " 'Octopi' would only be correct for a second-declension Latin noun. 'Octopus' is a Greek third-declension masculine. And no, that's not what I'm saying."

Archie was doing math. He had last talked to Henry at six. It was now nearly three A.M. Nine hours had passed. That left fifteen to go. Fifteen hours between life and death. It didn't used to seem like such a long time. You could drive from Portland to Los Angeles in fifteen hours. Now it seemed like a lifetime. For Henry, it might be.

Three people had been murdered.

Archie coughed, the taste of diesel a paste in his mouth.

"The water's rising," Eaton said. "If there's something deadly in there, we need to warn people."

They weren't in the water. The chief hadn't made the leap yet.

"Octopuses live in the ocean," Archie said. He scanned the Wikipedia paragraph on habitat, the page already soft and damp in his hand. "These blue-ringed octopuses, their habitat is temperate salt water. They wouldn't last more than a few minutes in the Willamette."

Eaton's phone rang. He didn't pick it up. He put his hand to his upper belly, like it hurt. "So where are these people picking them up?" he asked. "Off the sidewalk?"

Archie thought about it. "Maybe someone

hands the thing to them."

"What?" Robbins said dryly. "Like, 'Here, hold my octopus.' "

Archie's mind was working now. He didn't feel cold anymore. It was like everything else fell away and the world narrowed to this one task, this one job — find the answer. It's what made him good at being a detective, and bad at being a husband. "Where do you get these things? Besides Australia?"

"You can buy them on eBay," Robbins said. "I checked."

Eaton shook his head slowly. "Some nut is using a goddamn fish to kill people?"

"Not a fish," Robbins said. "A cephalopod."

Archie remembered the empty plastic bag they'd found at the Japanese American Plaza.

"How big are these things?" Archie asked Robbins.

"Roughly?" Robbins said with a shrug. "The size of a golf ball, maybe."

Archie stepped away from the back of the idling command center and peered around to where Heil, Ngyun, and Flannigan were standing, waiting for news of Henry and the toxin. All three rolled up on the balls of their feet when they saw Archie look their way.

"Heil," Archie called. "Get that bag tested for traces of salt water."

Archie gazed past the chief, past Robbins, past the sandbaggers and the National Guard, past the seawall, and over the river. The Eastbank Esplanade was made up of a series of promenades and floating docks, metal-grated overpasses and dark underpasses — it had already started to flood. The lights that usually lit the walkway at night had shorted out. Parts of the esplanade were reportedly already underwater. It was dark and wet and cold.

Someone had to have seen something.

"What are you thinking?" Robbins asked.

Archie looked down at his wrong shoes, and wrong jacket, and wrong pants. He sneezed. Then he looked back across the dark Willamette.

It wasn't like he was going to get any sleep anyway.

"That I want to move to the desert," Archie said.

CHAPTER 20

Susan had taken her flowers with her. It had taken six trips. Seven, including the box with all her desk crap in it. A Hooters mug. A ceramic phrenology head. *The Dictionary of American Slang.* Two bottles of unopened red wine. These things took up room.

What kind of person fires someone in the middle of the night? In the rain?

She couldn't sleep. Too many Chinese uppers. So she poured herself her fourth glass of red wine, leaned back on the couch, and wondered at what point drinking late at night became drinking in the morning. If she went to bed, she'd just lie there obsessing anyway. She'd been fired. Terminated. Axed. Canned. Told to take a long walk off a short pier.

It was for the best, she decided. Getting the pink slip. Getting shown the door. This whole thing. She had money saved up. And it wasn't like she had to pay rent. Now she was free to write what she wanted. She was free of carpet off-gassing and fluorescent lights and people who rode the elevator one floor instead of taking the stairs. She was free of the lobby receptionists who always pretended to never remember who she was. She was free of Ian.

There were too many bouquets in the living room. What had she been thinking? It smelled like the bathroom of a fancy restaurant in there — all orchidy and oppressively sweet.

She got up and sniffed around the room until she found the most egregious offenders. Easter lilies. She'd always thought that lilies kind of stank. Who wanted a flower you could smell from upstairs? The Romans believed that lilies were created when Juno was nursing Hercules, and milk fell from the sky. Old breast milk. That's what lilies were.

Susan grabbed the lilies out of the earthenware vase she'd put them in and, holding them at arm's length, headed for the back door. It was still raining. It was going to rain for the rest of her life. She could hear it out there, falling in torrents off the overflowing gutters of her mother's crumbling Victorian house. Susan put on her rubber boots and the Mexican poncho Bliss kept on a hook by the back door, flipped on the back porch light, and headed out into the backyard with the bouquet.

The compost pile was in the back corner of the yard. Her mother had not upgraded to the big black plastic-lidded barrels that everyone else in Portland seemed to have. People in Portland were increasingly obsessed with composting. Even fast-food joints did it, at least the locally owned ones. You went to bus your tray and it took ten minutes to figure out which of the five categories your trash fit into. But Bliss was old school. She still had the giant wood-and-chicken-wire corral that Susan's father had built before he'd started dying. You had to pull bricks off the tarp that covered it, stuff in what you wanted to compost, and then stir the compost with a rusty pitchfork that would send most people running for a tetanus shot.

Susan tromped through the mud, chin down against the rain. The bricks were wet and the tarp was slimy, but she managed to jam the lilies into the bin and then replace the cover.

It felt good.

Not as good as having a job.

But good.

She was headed back into the house when

she heard the goat. It made a little goat sound.

"Oh, come on," Susan said.

The goat was standing in the rain, looking at her. It whined again.

"Go into your house," Susan said, pointing to the big wooden dog house that Bliss had painted to look like a psychedelic Tudor cottage. The goat was tethered to a stake, but it had plenty of room to get around.

The goat just stood there getting wet.

Maybe it was the wine, but Susan suddenly found herself feeling very bad for the goat. Out there all alone in the pitch-black. Trapped in an urban backyard. Did that goat dream of farms? Of green pastures and kids?

"You're lonely, aren't you?" Susan asked.

The goat bayed.

Susan walked over and unclipped the goat's tether, and led it by the collar up the back porch steps and into the kitchen. The goat did a little dance on the wood floor. Susan thought it looked happy.

She slipped off her muddy boots, took off the wet poncho, and opened another bottle of wine. Then she dried the goat off with a dish towel and led it into the living room.

The goat walked around in a circle a couple of times like a cat, and then fell asleep on the carpet. It smelled a little, but it was better than the lilies.

CHAPTER 21

The Eastbank Esplanade had been finished
in 2001 — one and a half miles of concrete
trail shoehorned between the interstate and
the east side of the river, and connected to
the west side with pedestrian walkways on
the Steel and Hawthorne bridges.

Archie parked in the esplanade's public
lot, which had been tucked under a knot of
freeway overpasses near the Hawthorne
Bridge, and looked over at Heil. He would
have come alone if he could have gotten
away with it. Heil was a good cop. But he
wasn't Henry. And he talked too much.

"You know two feet of water is enough to
wash away a car," Heil said.

"Good to know," Archie said.

Heil peered up at the dark sky. "Sun will
be up in four hours," he said.

Not soon enough, thought Archie.

They got out of the car. The freeways
overhead blocked the rain, but water fell in

sheets along every edge. The streetlights were still working. The water that flowed across the surface of the parking lot reflected their white glow.

"Four inches of moving water can knock someone off their feet," Heil said.

An empty shopping cart sat alone in the parking lot. A few more, loaded with bundles, were pushed behind a concrete pillar. A blue tarp lay nearby.

There didn't appear to be anyone around.

No sandbagging here. There wasn't as much at stake. The firehouse at the river's edge had been evacuated hours before. The water would continue to rise, to flood east-side streets and warehouses, but the potential property damage was nothing compared to what it was on the west side.

The water under their feet seeped east, away from the river. It wasn't deep — only a few centimeters — but it was definitely traveling. Whether it was the river's current or just the wind, Archie couldn't say.

"There," Heil said, and Archie turned in time to see a flash of light, like someone flicking a lighter on and then extinguishing it. It had come from a crevice where the elevated northbound lanes of I-5 met a concrete incline. They headed for it, passing eight blue plastic portable toilets that stood back-to-back, four on each side, one twisted slightly out of alignment.

Sound echoed down there, bouncing off the concrete that surrounded them, only to be almost simultaneously muted by the layer of water beneath their feet.

Archie was ahead when they heard the snarl coming from the dark crevice of the underpass. He froze and swung his flashlight just in time to see the brown shape barreling at him. The dog was all muscle, its gums peeled back around vibrating teeth.

"Pit bull," he heard Heil say in a low, urgent voice.

No shit, thought Archie.

The dog had stopped two feet in front of him, head level, eyes trained on Archie. He could feel its growl in the center of his spine.

Archie found a spot forty-five degrees to the left and looked at it, keeping the dog in his peripheral vision, avoiding direct eye contact.

Just don't move, he told himself.

The dog inched forward. Archie could feel all the hair on his arms stand up.

"Do you want me to shoot it?" Heil asked from somewhere behind him.

Dogs had short attention spans. As long as Archie didn't give it a reason to attack, the dog would get bored and move on.

Archie tried to keep his tone low and calm and casual. "If it attacks me, then yes," he said, his voice almost singsong. *Everything's fine! No worries here!*

"I don't think I can hit it if it's moving." Heil paused. "I mean, not without hitting you."

Great.

The dog growled and sniffed at the knees of Archie's pants. Archie could smell it, wet dog, like his wool sweater. Archie closed his eyes and waited.

"Gigi," a voice said.

Archie opened his eyes and looked back at the dog, ninety pounds of snarling, rippling killing machine.

Gigi?

The dog lowered her head, spun around, and barked once into the dark crevice at the crook of the underpass.

A young man stepped forward into the light and the dog ran to him and turned around and sat at his master's feet, facing Archie.

"We're not leaving," the man said.

He looked to be in his twenties, Latino, clean-shaven, dressed in jeans and cowboy boots and a dirty denim jacket buttoned up to the neck. He was short, but he held himself with an easy authority. He was used to being in charge.

"You must be Nick," Archie said.

The dog looked up at the man, thumped her tail against the pavement, and whined. Any hint of aggression had vanished. He rubbed her head. "She's not usually like that," he said. "The weather has her freaked out."

Heil stepped forward, and Archie caught a flash of his gun, still drawn, held against his leg. Archie could hear Heil breathing, short and fast.

"You can put your weapon away," Archie said to Heil. "The dog's okay now, right, Nick?"

"Yeah," Nick said.

Heil hesitated, his eyes still fixed on the dog.

"Put your gun away," Archie repeated calmly. He didn't look at Heil. He kept his focus on the man and the dog. No sudden movements. Calm and casual. Dog attack. Man with a gun. The rules for de-escalation were pretty much the same.

A minute ticked by. Archie counted. A minute, with a pit bull and a gun, is a very long time.

Then, after a slow glance around, as if he were pocketing something he'd shoplifted, Heil holstered his weapon.

Archie released the breath he'd been holding.

Nick hadn't flinched. If he'd had any idea his dog had almost gotten shot, he didn't show it.

"What are you doing here?" Archie asked him.

"We live here," he answered, the obvious implication being: *What are you doing here?*

"Maybe you haven't heard the news," Heil said, "but the river is flooding. That seawall they're building over there? That may keep the west side dry. But you don't see them building a seawall over here, do you?"

It was a fair point.

"I said we're not leaving." Nick's voice was weighty with determination, but under that Archie could detect a thread of anxiety. "Now, maybe you guys don't like to sleep, but we do. It's been a long day. So why don't you just move on, okay?"

"How many of you are there?" Archie asked.

Nick looked back into the darkness from which he'd come. "It's okay," he said.

Four people shuffled forward, circled by two more dogs. Two men and two women, each wrapped in a tarp or blanket. Their eyelids were heavy and their faces puffy from sleep. Archie could make out shapes behind them, and it took him a moment to realize that it was stuff — Hefty bags teeming with clothes, bicycles, folded-up tents, shopping carts holding all of someone's worldly possessions.

All that stuff, you couldn't take it to a shelter.

These four and Nick were staying put to keep an eye on what had been left behind.

They were all young. The four who had just appeared wore hooded sweatshirts layered under other clothing. The men had beards, one shaggy, one that had been divided into tiny braids. The women were small, the quilts they were wrapped in muddy and dragging on the ground.

"That's everyone," Nick said. He said it with confidence, like a captain who'd evacuated a boat, then walked every deck to make sure no hands were left behind.

He felt responsible for these people. Archie recognized the impulse.

It wasn't about the stuff.

There had to be another reason. Archie tried to put himself in Nick's shoes. What would keep him there? And then it occurred to Archie. "Are you waiting for someone?" he asked.

Something in Nick's posture changed, and Archie knew that he was right. "This is where we're supposed to meet," Nick said. "We have this plan, for emergencies. If we get raided, whatever. We meet here. We wait for everyone." He paused and his shoulders slumped. "I didn't think about the river flooding when I was making the plan."

"Otter's not coming," Archie said. "He's safe. He's at the Mission."

Nick straightened up. "You've seen Otter?" he said. The other four exchanged looks.

"We had to question him," Archie said. "A police detective was hurt earlier tonight. Otter had his cell phone."

One of the young women protested. "Otter didn't hurt him," she said.

"No," Archie said. "I don't think he did. But we had to talk to him, to see if he'd seen anything. He's at the Mission. He's safe. We can take you over there."

Nick glanced at his charges, and then gently placed his hand on the top of his dog's head. "I'm not leaving Gigi or the other two," he said.

"Other two what?" Heil said.

Archie wished Heil would stop talking. "Dogs," Archie said.

He saw Heil look down at the dogs with the four river people, and then back at Nick and Gigi. "Oh," he said.

167

"What if I can make arrangements for you and your friends and your dogs?" Archie said.

"What about the stuff?" one of the women asked.

Nick ignored her. "You think you can make that happen?" he asked Archie.

Archie beckoned Heil over and found Mary Riley's card and handed it to him. "Call her," Archie said. "Explain the situation."

"And what if she says no?" Heil said.

"Then they all stay at your house," Archie said.

"I'm on it," Heil said, and he took a few steps away to make the call.

"I need to ask all of you some questions," Archie said to Nick. Nick and his friends looked at Archie. Archie tried to figure out a way to phrase what he needed to know without sounding like a lunatic, and then decided that there wasn't one.

"This is going to sound a little crazy," Archie said, "but that cop I mentioned earlier? He was poisoned by an octopus."

The man with the bushy beard said, "Octopuses live in the ocean, dude."

Great. A marine biologist. "That is true," Archie said. "We think someone was carrying an octopus, maybe in a plastic bag. This isn't the first poisoning. And they've all happened by the river."

"So," Nick said slowly, "you want to know if we've seen anyone with an octopus?"

"Pretty much."

One of the women frowned. "There's that guy who always fishes down on the dock. He has a bucket."

"He's there every day," the other woman said. "Has been for years. I've never seen him catch anything."

"Like you'd want to eat anything out of this stinking river," Bushy Beard said.

"What's his name?" Archie asked.

"We don't talk to him," Bushy Beard said.

"I don't think he speaks English," the first woman said.

"Is he Mexican?" Archie asked.

"No, like Estonian or something," the other bearded man said. He fiddled with one of the braids that sprouted from his chin.

"Estonian?" Archie said.

"I knew a guy whose family was Estonian," the man explained. "He sounds the same."

This wasn't really going anywhere. "Anyone else?" Archie could hear Heil on the phone, his voice plaintive.

"This time of year," Nick said, "unless the weather's weirdly nice, it's mostly the hardcore outdoorsy types. They run, you know. They don't carry extra stuff. Maybe an iPod. And their clothes are skintight, so we'd see anything they had on them. Some of the dog walkers are still out. They've got pockets full of plastic bags to pick up after their dogs."

"You get the lunch people," the second woman said.

"The lunch people?"

"The people who work downtown," she said. "Some of them walk at lunchtime instead of eating. You can always pick them out because they have on the stupidest sneakers."

The others nodded in agreement.

"You haven't seen anyone acting strangely?" Archie asked.

"People who walk instead of eating lunch are strange," the woman said.

"Besides that," Archie said.

"Esplanade's been closed for two days," Nick said. "Only people we've seen since are utility workers and social workers. We haven't been to the west side since they raised the bridges this morning. Otter must have gotten trapped over there."

Heil was still on the phone. Archie had one more angle. He got out the picture from the hospital security camera and handed it to Nick. "What about this kid? Does he look familiar to anyone?"

Nick glanced down at it and handed it to one of the women, who looked it and passed it along. No one's hand shot up.

"Was he alone?" the bearded man with the braids asked, looking at the picture.

"Probably," Archie said.

Heil returned, phone back in his pocket.

The man stepped forward and handed the image of the kid back to Archie. "We would have noticed a kid alone," he said.

That was it. Archie took the photo and folded it into quarters, half to fit it back in his coat, half to hide his disappointment. "So?" Archie said to Heil.

"She said she knows some people," Heil said. "They take in rescue dogs. Specialize in pit bulls. They can take all three dogs until the flood danger has passed. They're good people. The woman volunteers at the Mission. Her name's Violet."

"I know her," Nick said. "She works at the soup kitchen." He turned to the others. "The one with the weird eyebrows." They all seemed to know who he was talking about.

"So you okay with that?" Archie said.

Nick looked down at his dog, and then up in the direction of the river. "Yeah," he said.

"What about us?" one of the women asked.

"The Mission's full," Heil said. He grinned, pleased with himself. "But she said she could find room for five more."

"Sorry we weren't more help," Nick said to Archie.

"Do me a favor," Archie said. "Ask around about the kid. Or about anyone down by the river who might have seemed suspicious."

"You got it," Nick said.

Gigi thumped her tail again.

"See?" Nick said. "She's a good dog."

CHAPTER 22

Susan had just decided to close her eyes for only a second on the couch when the phone rang. If she hadn't been so disoriented, she would have let it go to voice mail. But she'd had a bottle and a half of wine and wasn't thinking straight. Her purse was beside her on the floor. She reached into it and felt around for the slippery surface of her phone, found it, pulled it to her face, and mumbled something that sounded like "Hello."

"Is this Susan Ward?" a voice asked hesitantly. A woman's voice. Elderly.

Susan blinked, trying to clear her head. "Yes."

"From the *Herald*?"

Susan felt something pulling at her pant leg, and looked down to see the goat nibbling on the dirty hem of her jeans. The goat. Christ. How long had she been asleep? She could feel a sore welt on her face where her cheek had been pressed against the seam of the cushion. "Who is this?" she asked.

"My name is Mrs. Gloria Larson. I don't sleep well."

Susan waited.

The line was silent.

"So?" Susan said.

"I like to read the Internet," the old woman explained. "They have a computer room set up for us here. I go down there at night when I can't sleep and I read the news. I saw your column on the computer. About the skeleton."

She was a reader. One of the *Herald*'s many elderly busybodies. Old people were the only ones who read newspapers anymore — the dead tree kind. At least this one was shuffling into the digital age. "How did you get this number?" Susan asked.

"I called the paper and pressed the numbers for your answering machine and a recording had this number."

Ian had changed her outgoing voice-mail message. And left her personal cell phone number on it. Dick.

"Mrs. Larson, if you want to write a letter to the editor —"

"You said they found an old skeleton near the slough." Gloria Larson paused. Something caught in her voice. "A man."

"Yeah."

"I was at Vanport," the woman said. "In 1948. I was there for the flood."

The photographs from the hospital flashed in Susan's mind. "Really? I mean, wow. Sorry."

"That skeleton? That man they found? I think his name was McBee." She took a breath. "I have to go. Someone's coming."

The phone went dead.

"Wait!" Susan said quickly. "Vanport? You think he really died at Vanport?"

But she was talking to herself.

Susan dialed star sixty-nine and got the voice mail for the Mississippi Magnolia Assisted Living Facility.

She looked at the clock. It was four-thirty in the morning. There were bits of plant material scattered all over the living room. Shredded leaves. Petals. Broken pieces of earthenware and glass.

The surviving vases were empty.

The goat had eaten all her flowers.

CHAPTER 23

When Susan woke up again, she had a headache and was in her bed. The goat had been banished to the back yard. The sun was up, or at least what passed for it these days. Behind the curtains, her bedroom window was a rectangle of gray light. She rolled over and turned on the radio to check on the flooding. They were in for more rain. It was warming up. Snowmelt was fierce. There'd been three more mudslides in the West Hills. Two houses destroyed. Susan switched the station to alternative rock.

Her head hurt.

McBee.

She wasn't even a journalist anymore, at least not for the *Herald.* Identifying Ralph was not her problem. The old woman was probably just another one of the *Herald's* kooks. Then again, if she did know something, and Susan had been on to something when she'd brought up Vanport in her column — that would be a vindication.

That would make her right. And Ian wrong.

She got up, took six ibuprofen, made coffee, and put on black jeans and a black sweater. (With the rainbow boots, raspberry hair, and yellow slicker, a neutral foundation was crucial.) She vacuumed up the smaller ceramic shards in the living room. Then she sat down and Googled "Mississippi Magnolia Assisted Living Facility." They accepted guests from ten A.M. until seven P.M. And they were located on North Mississippi Avenue, not far from Emanuel Hospital.

It wasn't Ian she wanted to prove something to. It was Henry.

She sat at the keyboard for a moment, gathering her courage, before she typed in the URL for the *Herald*'s Web site. If Henry had died while she was asleep, there would be a headline.

No update.

He was still alive.

Who was she kidding? Identifying Ralph wasn't going to do anything for him. There was nothing that Susan could do for him of any real value. Unless she discovered some latent gift for toxicology, she was useless.

It was too bad Henry didn't have a goat

she could offer to take care of.

Then she had an idea. She couldn't whip up an antivenom, but maybe there was something she could do to help. Her headache immediately lifted, and she found herself humming happily.

Good Samaritans lived longer. There'd been a study.

She tossed a couple of apples off the back porch to the goat, slammed her coffee, and headed out the door to the hospital.

Susan found Archie and Claire in Henry's ICU room, one on either side of his bed. Claire was asleep in one, curled up like a child, knees to her chest. Archie was out cold in the other, head back, body planked at a forty-degree angle, legs straight out, crossed at the ankles. A copy of that morning's *Herald* was on his lap, folded open to Susan's column, THE DEAD GIRL ON THE OSTRICH. Her last column, she realized.

Susan always felt a faint stirring of delight when she saw Archie reading her work. It made her feel a little ridiculous — like a kid seeking approval. He was only forty-one, just thirteen years older than her. So why did she feel like such a teenager?

She had already second-guessed this whole idea of hers. She'd had plenty of time on the way to the hospital to feel like an idiot. Half the streetlights were out, and a whole portion of the main one-way north on the east side was closed, forcing her to wind her way north taking side streets.

She'd had the radio on. The river had risen another four inches overnight.

Now she looked down at the white paper bag in her hand. She'd stopped at the coffee shop in the atrium and bought Archie a muffin. She hadn't thought to get Claire anything. How could she have forgotten about Claire? Of course Claire would be there. And now here was Susan, with a huge muffin for Archie and nothing else. The muffin was the size of a cat's head. It weighed like two pounds. Maybe they could split it. Crap. She should just go. Should she leave the muffin? With a note?

Archie stirred and opened an eye.

For a half second, Susan considered bolting.

"Hey," Archie said, his voice still rough from sleep.

Susan searched for something to say. He looked so sad and rumpled, his clothes wrinkled, his face creased, eyelids swollen from lack of sleep.

He ran a hand through his curly brown hair. If the intent was to smooth it, it didn't work. One side was still plastered against his scalp where he'd rested his head against his shoulder as he slept.

"I thought Henry might need someone to feed his cats," Susan said. She said this quietly, so as not to wake Claire.

Archie's eyes widened and he sat up in the chair.

"I mean, I know Claire's busy," Susan said quickly. "And you are, too. And I know where he lives. So if you give me the keys, I can stop by." She took a small step toward the foot of the bed. Henry was still hooked up to the respirator, the machine inhaling and exhaling for him. IV tubes threaded into his veins, wires monitored his heart rate. The blood vessels in his face, the ones that bulged bright and red when Henry was angry at what ever idiotic thing Susan had done, had vanished — replaced by a blood-less ceramic sheen. There were women who'd eat glass to have skin like that.

She didn't know the first thing about cats.

"That's nice," Archie said. "But I can do it."

Right. Now she was embarrassed. It had been presumptuous of her. It wasn't her place to feed Henry's cats. That was some-thing a friend would do. She should have listened to her rational side when it had tried to talk to her in the car.

"How is he?" Susan asked.

"Holding on," Archie said. He lifted the newspaper off his lap. "I bought the paper," he said.

Susan had seen it. The story of Archie rescuing the kid had made the front page, below the fold, with a big photograph of Archie in his Beauty Killer Task Force days. BEAUTY KILLER COP SAVES BOY, the headline read.

"The paper had already gone to press by the time he went missing," Susan said. "It's online. But won't be in the print edition until tomorrow. I didn't write that headline."

"I read the story about Henry."

Henry hadn't even made the front page. He'd been relegated to Metro.

"You didn't write it."

He'd noticed.

"It's Derek's beat."

"He doesn't even quote you. You were there. You and Claire found him. You were at the hospital. No quote."

Susan didn't want to go into it. She held the paper bag out stiffly. "I brought you a muffin." She might as well give it to him. It had cost three bucks. He looked hungry. "I don't know what kind of muffins you like, so I just grabbed one." In fact, she'd spent

181

ten minutes debating whether to get lemon poppy seed or banana nut, but she wasn't going to tell him that.

He opened the bag and peered inside. She thought she saw him smile. "This looks great," he said.

The machine breathing for Henry heaved in and out. Claire mumbled something unintelligible in her sleep and then was quiet.

"Any news on the tox screen?" Susan asked.

Archie hesitated. He reached into the bag and pulled out a chunk of banana nut muffin and put it in his mouth and chewed. He looked away from her, his eyes heavy on Henry. "Nothing yet."

They lapsed into silence again. Susan felt big and loud in that place, like when Bliss signed her up for ballet class and Susan had been tall and clumsy and had worn the wrong color leotard, a terrible pea-green turtleneck leotard that zipped up the back and snapped at the crotch and was made out of a thick ribbed fabric that made Susan flop-sweat.

"I was fired," Susan blurted out. She wasn't planning on saying it. It just bubbled up. She could feel her eyes burn with tears. She'd been fired before. There was the time at the coffee shop in high school when the owner found out that she had been routinely closing a half hour early. In college she'd gotten a job as a checkout clerk at a grocery store, only to get fired her first day when, on her lunch break, she'd joined a bunch of migrant workers picketing the store. She didn't remember what they were protesting, but she was sure they had a valid point.

She'd been fired before. But those times she had deserved it. This time, she wasn't so sure.

"Why?" Archie asked.

Susan looked at Henry, half dead in his hospital bed. Archie had already noticed that Derek, not Susan, had written the story about Henry. He'd have to know that had cost her. But she didn't want him to know how much. He'd feel responsible somehow. "Ian didn't like my Vanport story. I wanted to follow up on it. He thought it was bad timing." It was partially true. Ian hadn't liked her Vanport story. It was the wrong flood. Old news. Just like Ralph. No one cared. Not when their riverside condos were flooding.

"It would have been a great story," Susan said. And she believed it, too. "Identifying the skeleton. Especially if it turns out that he died in the flood. You know, some people think thousands died at Vanport? That the government covered it up. Stacked the bodies in the ice-storage building downtown. Buried them in school buses. Some people even thought they shipped them to Japan to be returned as dead soldiers."

Archie looked skeptical. "But the official count was, what, fifteen?"

"Yeah. They only *found* fifteen. But there were so many people in Vanport who were there for work, didn't have families, didn't have anyone to report them missing. I mean, the river swept away the whole town. Everything. There were fifteen thousand people there. They found fifteen bodies. How many more were washed out to sea? Or ended up in the mud of the slough?"

Susan was getting excited, her voice rising.

"Ian acted like no one cares," she continued. "Like it was so long ago. But it's this amazing story. This entire town built for shipworkers during the war, integrated, working-class. Snowmelt. Unseasonable warmth. Rain. Sound familiar? They were told they were safe. The morning the levy broke, they were told they were safe, that it would hold, that there was nothing to worry about. Then fifteen feet of water washed away houses, cars, everything. It was chaos.

But a lot of them managed to save each other. To get the children out. They formed human chains to pull people to safety. Black and white, working together. And people in Portland now? They know nothing about it. It's been expunged from our history. Imagine if I could identify that skeleton. It could be some small bit of closure. Someone knew him. If nothing else, it will show that we still care."

Archie put some muffin in his mouth, chewed slowly, and shook his head. "Cold cases like this, they hardly ever get solved. Witnesses are dead. Paperwork gets lost. There's no physical evidence. You don't even know if this guy died at Vanport. Maybe he was fishing and died of a heart attack years before Vanport was even built?"

Susan could barely contain herself. "I have a lead."

She told Archie about Gloria Larson, McBee, and the Mississippi Magnolia Assisted Living Facility. "Anyway," she said, "it's probably nothing, but I thought I'd stop by after here and check her story out."

Claire opened her eyes. "Good morning."

"Sorry," Susan said, whispering belatedly. "Did we wake you?"

Claire shifted her position in the chair and stretched. "When you walked in the door.

185

God, you're loud. Sorry you got fired."

"I didn't get you a muffin," Susan confessed.

"Okay."

"I'm so sorry," Susan said.

"Did you say this old woman lives up on Mississippi?"

Susan nodded.

Claire jabbed in the air at Archie with her elbow. "You should go with her. Check it out."

Archie hesitated.

"I will call you if anything changes," Claire said. "You shouldn't be in the ICU anyway with that cold." She turned to Susan. "He needs to work," she said. "Or he'll go crazy."

It had an extra weight, given Archie's stay in the psych ward. Crazy was not such a faraway place for him. Crazy lived just up the road.

"There's nothing you can do until Anne gets in anyway," Claire added.

"Anne?" Susan said.

She saw Archie shoot Claire a look. It had to be Anne Boyd. She was an FBI profiler. They were bringing her in to profile the river killer. Which meant they had to have more than Archie was telling. They knew what poisoned him. But Henry was still lying there like Snow White, which meant that what ever the poison was, there wasn't an antidote.

"It's okay. I get it. You can't compromise the case. But Claire's right, you can't just sit here. Come with me. It'll be fun. Old people. There might be Jell-O."

Archie coughed and looked unconvinced.

"I'm not a member of the press anymore," Susan said. "This woman, she has no reason to tell me anything if I'm not writing a story." Susan held up a strand of her raspberry hair. "I'm not exactly catnip to old people." Old people crossed the street sometimes when they saw her coming. "But a cop? She'd talk to you."

"McBee, huh?" Archie said.

"Stop and feed the cats," Claire said to Susan.

"Really?" Susan asked.

Claire got up and opened a white Formica wardrobe. Susan couldn't see what was inside, but she assumed it was Henry's clothes, because it looked like she was digging in the pockets. She closed the wardrobe and tossed something through the air at Susan.

Susan resisted the urge to dodge it, and instead got a hand up in time to catch the key ring. She looked at it with surprise. She'd caught it! She almost never caught anything.

It was a heavy key ring. Henry was a man with many locks. She glanced down at them all, a great fist of silver and brass. Big keys. Medium keys. Keys with colorful plastic collars around the bows. Dirty keys. Clean keys. And on top of all those keys, one other.

A tiny black key.

Like something that might open the front door to a doll house.

Susan stared down at the key for a long second. There were lots of keys in the world. Lots of locks.

She lifted the key ring by the little key and held it up toward Archie.

She didn't have to say anything.

He reached out slowly and took it, and his eyebrows drew together.

"What?" Claire said, standing up.

"It looks like the key the kid left behind," Archie said softly.

Claire gazed down at the key. Her face was seven kinds of stillness. "That key wasn't on there yesterday," she said.

Archie fumbled with his wallet, opened it, and slipped out the key that the kid had left behind under his hospital bed.

The keys looked identical.

Archie got out his phone and hit a number. "It's me," he said. "I need to know what was found in the pockets of the three other TTX victims." He listened for a moment. Then lowered his forehead onto a hand and rubbed his temples. "What do the keys look like?"

Susan's stomach turned. The killer had left that key with Henry. Just as he'd apparently left keys with his other victims. The killer had touched it, and she had held it in her hand.

Claire reached into her purse, got out her own key chain, twisted off a key, and handed it to Susan. Susan understood. It was Claire's copy of Henry's house key.

"He'll be a while," Claire said. "I guess you're on your own with the old people."

Susan looked down at the house key. She was being dismissed. At least she still got to feed the cats.

Claire closed her eyes and settled back into the chair. "Leave the muffin," she said.

Archie was still on the phone when Susan left.

CHAPTER 24

Archie watched as Robbins propped the three photographs side by side against Henry's motionless calf.

When a body ended up at the morgue, all the personal items were removed, bagged, and catalogued. Clothing. Jewelry. Nipple rings. A morgue tech took it all. Sometimes it went back to the family, sometimes it got tagged as evidence, sometimes it got lost in the chaos of a flood evacuation. Sometimes it got photographed.

Three photographs. Three key rings. All different. Stephanie Towner's keys were on a silver *S*. Megan Parr's keys were on a Honda fob. Zak Korber's keys were at the end of a silver chain that had once been clipped to his belt loop. Different keys. With one exception. Each ring had the same small black key.

It was there, in every photograph, clear as day. Removed. Bagged. Catalogued. But no one had made the connection.

The key from Henry's pocket and the key from the kid were each in an evidence bag. Claire studied them now, and then sighed and tossed the two bags onto the bed next to the photographs.

Robbins scooted forward on his stool and adjusted one of the photographs on Henry's leg. "Are you sure he doesn't mind that?" he asked Claire, raising an eyebrow.

"It makes him feel like he's helping," Claire said.

"How did we miss this?" Archie asked.

"They all had keys," Robbins said. "If I shot you in the head right now and dragged your ass down to the morgue, I bet I'd find keys on your body, too."

"We didn't know they were murders until last night," Claire said.

Archie cracked his neck. His body ached from sleeping in the chair. He tried to stretch but there wasn't enough space in the room. "The killer waited until after they were paralyzed, and then took the time to add a key to their key chains," he said. The keys obviously meant something. He was sending a message.

Claire poked at the evidence bags. "The keys look the same," she said. "But they open different locks. Look at the edges.

They're different."

"I want these fingerprinted," Archie said, waving a hand at the photographs of the keys.

Robbins picked up the evidence bags. "I can drop these two off at the lab," he said. He glanced at the photographs. "The other three might take some turning up."

The morgue, thought Archie, his head throbbing. Its contents had been transported all over the city.

"It's not like they're lost," Robbins said. "They're just packed away somewhere."

"And the kid?" Claire asked, finally putting what they were all thinking into words. "Where did he get one?"

"I'll make another media push," Archie said. "See if we can identify him."

Now there was no question that the kid was wrapped up in this.

But how?

Archie picked up one of the photographs and held it a few inches from his nose. Claire was right. The blades of the keys were different. But the bows of the keys were the same — round, the size of a thumbnail. They were all black. And they all appeared to be covered with a fine patina of crud and rust.

Whatever locks those keys had once opened hadn't been opened in a long time.

CHAPTER 25

The Mississippi Magnolia Assisted Living Facility was on Mississippi Avenue, which explained the Mississippi thing, but not the Magnolia part. As far as Susan could tell, there was not a magnolia tree in sight.

She picked a piece of cat hair off of her black sweater — or was it goat hair? — and flicked it out her car window while she smoked a cigarette. Henry's cats had met her at his front door and had led her right to where their food was kept in the kitchen. A dirty coffee cup sat out next to the sink where Henry had left it. Susan fed the cats, gave them a big bowl of water, and locked up. She thought about rinsing out the coffee cup and putting it away, but decided against it. Henry would want to do that himself, when he got home.

She finished the cigarette and watched the street. Mississippi Avenue had been redeveloped over the past ten years. Boarded-up storefronts had transformed into coffee shops and record stores. Then a video store, a bar. A couple of restaurants went in after that. Some retail boutiques. More bars. The coffee shop and record store people hated the boutiques for attracting moneyed suburban types to the neighborhood for $300 pants. The boutiques hated the bars for attracting patrons who vomited on their flower boxes. Everyone complained about the new condo developments, but secretly hoped a Whole Foods would go in.

Susan liked Mississippi. It was a good place to go if you were looking for a bike helmet, a taxidermied hyena head, some sweet potato fries, and *The Prisoner* on DVD.

No one was doing much business today. Stores were closed. Traffic lights were out. The corner of Mississippi and Shaver had so much standing water it was impassable, and the only people around looked like they were triaging flooded basements.

Susan had parked directly in front of the Mississippi Magnolia Assisted Living Facility. This was one of the unsung pleasures of dangerous weather — it presented excellent parking opportunities. The building was rectangular and brick, and built right up against the sidewalk. It looked like someplace you'd go to file for unemployment.

It wasn't raining at the moment, but Susan ran from her car to the front door out of instinct.

She paused inside to wipe her feet.

There was a lounge area to the right. Nothing fancy. Someone had definitely gotten a deal on used hotel room love seats. But there was a piano, and shelves were stacked three deep with books.

The reception desk was on the left.

The woman behind the desk had a sweep of officious-looking hair and was wearing a purple turtleneck and blazer. She already had her arms crossed. Susan recognized the pose. She'd seen it a lot as a teenager after she'd bleached her hair, wore all black, and carried her backpack into stores.

"I'm looking for Gloria Larson," Susan said.

The woman's expression didn't flicker. She had that sort of impeccable Avon lady makeup that involved all kinds of pencils and shading. "And you are?" she said.

"I'm a journalist," Susan said. "Mrs. Larson has information on a story I'm working on."

The woman's brow furrowed in disbelief. "Gloria Larson?" she repeated. *"Our*

196

Gloria?" She still hadn't uncrossed her arms.

Susan smiled at her and tried to look like someone who wore lip liner, just not today, because she had forgotten.

"It's very important I talk to her," Susan explained. "She called me. She wants to help."

"What did you do to your hair?" the woman asked.

"It's a shade of Manic Panic," Susan said with a sigh. "Deadly Nightshade."

Susan's hair seemed to light a match in the woman's imagination and she looked hard at Susan's head, like she was inspecting the fat content of a candy bar she was considering buying, and then her painted eyebrows shot up, her arms dropped, and she beamed. "Susan Ward," she said. "I recognize you now. I read your column. Remember the one about the blind guy who stole the car?"

Why did people always feel the need to remind her about stuff she herself had written about? "I do remember that, yes," Susan said.

The woman clapped her hands, delighted. "He made it a half mile before he crashed into a tree and they arrested him."

It wasn't even a good story. Susan had

written that column in ten minutes. She'd been late to a movie. "That was a funny one," she said.

The woman leaned forward conspiratorially. "I cut it out and sent it to my niece in Florida."

"So, about Gloria," Susan said.

"I'm getting to it."

Ten minutes later Susan was riding the elevator with the director of the Mississippi Magnolia Assisted Living Facility. Fiftyish, he introduced himself as Barry. He had on tan pants and a blue button-down, no tie. An array of phones and beepers were arranged on his belt.

"She phoned you in the middle of the night?" he asked.

"Yes," Susan said.

"That makes sense. It's when she's most lucid."

"Alzheimer's?" Susan asked.

"Dementia, bundled with Parkinson's-like symptoms. She's never gotten a firm diagnosis." The elevator stopped and they followed him into a dimly lit hall. "At her age, the docs aren't very aggressive."

"How old is she?" Susan asked.

"Eighty-five," Barry said. He stopped at a door where a plastic Christmas wreath still hung, and knocked. "She came to us two years ago," he continued, "when her daughter could no longer take care of her. She's a lovely woman." He lowered his voice. "But she's in and out."

The door opened and a wizened face appeared. She was tall, for an old person, maybe five-eight. Her white hair was clipped back at the base of her neck, and she was dressed nicely in a pair of slacks, a blouse, and a cardigan. She looked at them with questioning blue eyes.

"Mrs. Larson?" Susan said. "My name's Susan Ward. I write for the *Herald.*" A tiny lie. "You called me last night?"

Gloria Larson smiled. "Hello, dear," she said. She turned and headed back into the apartment, leaving the door open for Susan and Barry the administrator to follow her. They did. A TV was on, turned to the local news. Gloria perched in a striped armchair that looked like it had been bought before *Gunsmoke* went off the air. She sat down easily, like someone half her age. Susan and Barry took seats on the matching striped couch.

The apartment consisted of a living room, small kitchen, bedroom, and bathroom. It smelled like talcum powder and the stale tang of Palmolive dish soap.

Gloria reached to the coffee table, picked

up the remote, and turned down the volume, but not all the way. "They say the flooding has killed twelve hundred cows in Tillamook County," she said. She said it conversationally, the way you might mention that asparagus season had started, oh, and squirrels were falling dead from the sky.

Barry shifted uncomfortably in his seat. "This woman," he said, with a head tilt at Susan, "is here because of the remains that were found in the Columbia Slough last week. The skeleton."

"All right," Gloria said.

"I'm a journalist," Susan said.

Gloria gave Susan a chipper nod. "I understand. You're here to question me."

She seemed coherent enough. "Yes," Susan said.

Gloria's clear blue gaze wandered around the room and then landed again on Susan. "Do you work here?" she asked.

So much for coherent.

"My name is Susan Ward," Susan said. "I wrote a story for the *Herald* about the skeleton they found at the slough. You said you might know who it is."

Barry adjusted his posture again. All those phones and beepers must have been uncomfortable. "Does any of this sound familiar, Mrs. Larson?"

Her eyes darted between them and she looked uncertain, like she was watching a table tennis game and didn't know the score.

"You mentioned a name," Susan said. "McBee?"

Gloria cocked her head at Susan. "Where did you hear that name?"

"From you."

"I don't remember," Gloria said, squinting. She turned her attention back to the TV. "They're talking about the flood. The dike's burst. Water's pouring through. Why aren't they evacuating?"

"Were you at Vanport, Mrs. Larson?" Susan asked.

"Memorial Day, 1948."

"You remember," Susan said.

The old woman looked off past the TV at nothing in particular. "I had a black 1939 Chrysler in those days. Beautiful car. Paid for it myself. I still took the trolleys, though. That was back when the trolleys went all the way down to Oaks Park."

Susan remembered all the upturned cars in the photographs she'd seen at the hospital. "Did you lose the car in the flood?" she asked.

Gloria smiled to herself. "I haven't seen that car in some time," she said. She reached for the remote and increased the volume. "They've evacuated six hundred people from Vernonia."

Charlene Wood from KGW was reporting from Tillamook. A dead cow floated past behind her. The scroll at the bottom of the screen promised more snowmelt, more rain, more flooding. U.S. 26, I-84, and U.S. 30 had all been closed due to mudslides. Amtrak was shut down.

Barry clapped his hands on his knees and sat forward. "I think we're done here," he said.

"Can I leave my card?" Susan asked. Gloria's gaze remained fixed on the television screen. Susan rifled through her purse, emptying items onto the coffee table — an Altoid tin, a box of tampons, an empty water bottle, used Kleenex, a pack of yellow American Spirits, a glittery pink Hello Kitty pen. She was looking for something to write on. She didn't want to leave a *Herald* card. But she didn't want to write her number down on the back of a Burgerville receipt, either. She settled on one of Archie's business cards. She'd grabbed a handful at some point, and kept them in her wallet, jammed behind the gym membership card she never used. You never knew when that kind of thing would come in handy. She was sure she could use one to get out of a traffic stop one day. She crossed out Archie's name and rank and the Portland city seal, and wrote her name and cell phone number on the back with the Hello Kitty pen. Then she added the word *McBee,* followed by a question mark.

"Call me if you remember anything," she said to Gloria. She set the card on the coffee table. Next to the remote, so Gloria would be sure to see it.

Gloria glanced back at her and smiled. "Of course, dear," she said.

Barry was already standing up, scrolling through text messages like he had something important to do.

Susan held the mouth of her purse open next to the table, and swept all the stuff she'd taken out of her purse back inside it. The tampon box top opened as she did, and all the tampons slid out loose into her purse. Ordinarily she wouldn't have minded. But Barry was acting all anxious to go, and it made Susan want to take her time. There was a study about that once. When people in parking lots saw that a car was waiting for their spot, they always took longer to pull out of it. It was a statistical fact.

She felt around the bottom of her bag and scooped them back up, the white paper wrappers already soiled with detritus from the depths of her bag — an old Jolly Rancher, lint, tobacco, a fingernail clipping.

Susan flicked the fingernail clipping back into her purse.

Barry looked a little terrified.

"Sorry," Susan said, stuffing the tampons back in the box.

She sifted her hand through her purse again and came up with a few more tampons, some change, a flattened Hershey's Kiss, and a few loose Chinese uppers.

There was something else in her hand, too, something she had scooped up along with the tampons. She caught the black glint of metal against the white of the tampon wrappers.

A hot acidity rose in Susan's throat.

She knew what it was. How could she not? She had held one just like it in her hand an hour ago.

This didn't make sense. She wasn't supposed to have this. Was it Henry's? Had she accidentally put it in her purse?

No. Henry's was still on his key chain. Archie had been holding it when she'd left.

This was another key.

Small. Black. Round bow. Just like the others.

Susan's face felt hot.

How long had it been in her bag?

"They found a dead horse floating in John Day River," Gloria said.

It could still have fingerprints on it.

Susan looked up. It was not like the big scene in the movie where the scary organ music plays and everyone in the room gasps with shock. Gloria's eyes were glued to the TV. Barry had his head bent over one of his phones.

Susan let the key fall from her hand into the tampon box and rose to her feet, clutching her purse to her chest.

There were a thousand explanations. All of them creepy.

"I have to go," she said.

She left Archie's card on the table, along with a half-melted watermelon Jolly Rancher and thirty-seven cents.

CHAPTER 26

Archie had enlarged the photographs of the keys and tacked them to the bulletin board in the task force conference room. The key from Henry and the one from the kid had been taken for testing. That left three. He held up his pinkie finger and pointed to the middle knuckle. "The keys are half the size of my little finger," he said. "What do they open?"

Heil, Flannigan, and Ngyun sat around the conference table, each on their third or fourth cup of coffee. Archie stood. The fridge in the room was dying, and its failing motor made a low grinding noise. The clock on the wall ticked. The rain fell. Two chairs at the table sat empty. One Henry's, one Claire's.

The major case squad was headquartered in a defunct bank that the city had bought years ago to use as office overflow space. Archie and his team had moved into the building after they'd reunited to track a serial killer murdering teenage girls. It had been the case that had brought Archie back from medical leave, and he'd assembled a group of detectives, many of whom he'd worked with at various times during the ten years of the Beauty Killer case. Ten cops. Most came and went, reassigned as needed from other units.

The bank was a square, one-story, flat-roofed structure surrounded by a parking lot. The drive-up ATM still worked. They'd ripped out the bank clerk counter, but inside it still screamed 1980s Wells Fargo, from the mauve task chairs to the gray carpeting.

The conference room had been the bank's break room. The fridge still had magnets boasting low-interest home equity line rates.

Archie sneezed.

"Gesundheit," Heil said.

"Diaries?" Flannigan said.

Ngyun rolled his eyes.

"What?" Flannigan said.

Archie wrote the word *diaries* on the dry-erase board next to the bulletin board. "Next?" he said.

"Golf cart keys?" Ngyun said.

Flannigan snorted. "And you think *diaries* was lame?"

"More," Archie said. He wrote down some of his own. Lockbox keys. Cabinet keys. Padlock keys.

"Could be keys to old trunks, or jewelry boxes," Ngyun said.

"Good," Archie said, adding them to the list.

"Maybe they're not keys to anything," Heil said. "I mean, maybe they're reproductions or fakes, you know? Dime-store stuff."

Archie's phone vibrated and he glanced down at it. Susan again. She'd called him four times in the last twenty minutes. He hadn't had a chance to check the messages.

Fakes.

They had been assuming the keys were old, but what if they weren't? The crime lab would be able to tell, but until they tested them, it was worth keeping an open mind.

Flannigan leaned back in his chair and crossed his arms. "How'd the kid get one?" he said.

That was the million-dollar question.

"He's a victim?" Heil said.

Archie looked at the pictures, the small black key lined up carefully next to the other keys found in each of the victims' possession. "He wasn't poisoned."

Heil shrugged. "Maybe Henry interrupted it."

It made sense. Henry gets attacked and they find a key on him. The kid ends up in the river within two hours of Archie's last contact with Henry, and he also has a key. There were too many coincidences for there not to be a connection.

"We need to find the kid," Archie said. He took the photographs off the board and slapped them down on the table in front of Flannigan. "Take these to a locksmith and see what you can find out about them," he said. "Heil, you keep contacting aquarium supply stores to see if anyone's been lurking around asking about blue-ringed octo-puses."

"Besides me," Heil said.

"Besides you," Archie said.

"And Ngyun, you troll cephalopod chat rooms and see if any homicidal fiends turn up."

"Cephalopod chat rooms?" Ngyun said.

"It's the Internet," Archie said. "They exist."

Heil pushed forward a four-inch-tall stack of paper. "These are all tips that came in online and by phone overnight alone," he said. "People who think they've seen the kid, or have had a vision about Henry, or just want to talk."

"The chief assigned us four patrol cops,"

Archie said. "That's an inch for each of them."

Ngyun raised his hand. "Um, are we going to talk about the octopus?" he said.

The door flung open and Susan stalked in. She looked as if she'd taken a shower fully clothed. Her bright berry hair fell in frizzy strips. Eye makeup was smeared across one cheekbone. Her black sweater hung wet and limp.

She stood for a moment, catching her breath. Then she said, "I have a problem."

They all looked at her, waiting.

She opened her purse and got out a blue rectangular cardboard box of tampons and tossed it on the table. It slid a foot and came to a stop in front of Heil.

"I found this in my purse," she said.

No one moved.

"Oh, for Christ's sake," Susan said. "Not the tampons. Look inside."

Archie picked up the box and tipped it. Several tampons slid out, along with a small black key. The key bounced on the table and then lay still.

Archie looked at the photographs in front of Flannigan and then back at the key.

It was a match.

"Where did you get that?" Archie asked softly.

CHAPTER 27

Archie turned Susan's palms up and held them in his hands, scanning for the telltale mark. He was amazed at how steady he was, how neutral his face felt. It was something all parents learned. Don't show panic. Don't show the terror welling up in your gut. That projectile vomiting? It's just the flu.

He bent her fingers back and lifted one of her palms closer. Her pale hand had a fine sheen of sweat that made it sparkle. She smelled like Easter lilies.

"I'm fine," she said.

There. A tiny brown speck, on the base of her thumb near her wrist. Archie steadied himself. He touched it with his finger. "What's this?" he said, looking up.

Susan slid her hands out of his and squeezed them under her armpits. "A freckle," she said. "I was not attacked. I think I would have noticed."

Archie turned back to the table. Ngyun, Heil, and Flannigan hadn't moved. They were all looking at Susan. The fridge was grinding up a storm. "Bag it," Archie said to Heil. Heil blinked at him, and then snapped to, produced an evidence bag from his pocket, and used a pen to guide the key off the table and into the bag.

Archie turned back to Susan. "Where did you get the key?" he asked.

"It was in my purse, like I told you," Susan said. "I found it when I was at the assisted living facility. But I don't know how long it's been there."

"Okay," Archie said. He had to think, make sense of this, sort out the timeline. "When was the last time you cleaned out your purse?"

Susan frowned. "I don't clean out my purse. I just buy a new one and put what I need in that."

Archie pulled out one of the two empty chairs for her and motioned for her to sit. "I want you to tell me everywhere you've been the past few days," he said.

She tossed her purse on the table next to the tampons and slumped down in the chair. "Oaks Park," she said. "The newspaper. The morgue. Waterfront Park. The hospital. Home. The Mississippi Magnolia

212

Assisted Living Facility." She shot Archie a wry look. "Which, by the way, does not have a magnolia anywhere near it." She threw up her hands. "And here."

"Have you been away from your purse?" Archie asked. "Maybe set it down somewhere?"

"No."

"You didn't put it aside at the hospital. Leave it on the back of a chair? Set it down at the park while you were tending to Henry?"

"I wear it," she said. "I don't put it down." She gave the purse a little shove. But it was stuffed so full it didn't move. "It has my cigarettes and phone in it."

The purse sat between them all on the table, like an odd centerpiece. It had a woven leather body, double handles, and a leather chest strap that clipped on to either side with a gold buckle. There was no zipper or flap and the top gaped open. Archie could see the corner of a wallet, the cap of a water bottle, and a pair of sunglasses that Susan wouldn't need until July.

"It's open," Archie said.

"It's a Bottega Veneta tote," Heil said. "It's supposed to be open. That's the style. Reese Witherspoon has one just like it."

"Exactly," Susan said.

Archie and the other two detectives looked at Heil.

"My wife leaves *InStyle* out in the bathroom," Heil said.

"How do you wear it?" Archie asked Susan.

She looked at him like he was crazy. "You've seen me with this purse a hundred times."

He didn't remember ever having seen her with that purse, but that didn't mean anything. Some detective.

"Put it on," he said. "Please."

She put her palms on the table, pushed out her chair, and stood up with an exaggerated sigh. Then she grabbed the purse and slung it over her shoulder, so the body of the purse rested behind her left hip. "There," she said. "Happy?"

"Turn around," Archie said.

Susan turned, and then looked over her shoulder, at the purse, at the detectives at the table, at Archie.

Archie took a step toward her, so that there was barely a foot between them, and moved his hand over the open top of the purse. Susan's eyes followed his hand.

"He just came up behind her," Ngyun said.

"That motherfucker," Susan said.

The killer had been close enough to touch her, and her reaction was to be pissed. Archie liked that about Susan.

Archie heard a knock and looked over at the door, which Susan had left ajar, to see a female patrol cop peering in at them. He didn't know her — she was one of the officers that the chief had sent to help. But she was holding a sheet of paper in each hand, and fluttering them like drying Polaroids.

"Yeah?" he said.

"I think I found something," she said, coming into the room. "I was going through missing persons reports, like you asked. It's out-of-state, so it didn't turn up right away." She moved to the table and slapped down the grainy surveillance photo of the boy leaving the hospital. Then she put down another picture — unmistakably a school photo — from a missing persons report.

Archie looked from one image to the next. The shape of the head, the symmetry of the features, the hair color — it looked like the same kid.

"His name is Patrick Lifton," the patrol cop continued. "Nine years old. He left his house in Aberdeen, Washington, to walk to a friend's house three blocks away and never made it." She pointed to the date across the top of the page, the date when the boy had left his house that last time and the missing persons report was filed.

It was a year and a half ago.

The kid had been missing a year and a half, and Archie had had him in his arms.

And let him go.

"Get out," he said to Susan.

"What?" she said.

Archie recovered himself. "Please," he said. "We need to have a meeting. You can wait for me in my office."

She crossed her arms. "Why do I have to wait?"

"Your purse," Archie said, searching for a reason. "We need to print it. I'll call a tech."

Her eyes fell on the bag and he thought she was going to protest.

"Can I get my phone and cigarettes?" she said.

"Go ahead," he said.

She picked up one of the tampons off the table. "And I'm going to need this," she said.

CHAPTER 28

Archie's office was a square room with one window, a desk, three chairs, and a bookcase. It was bare-bones. Susan thought it looked like one of those porn sets from the eighties in which the intern gets bent over a desk by an executive wearing nothing but a blue-and-red-striped tie. She'd never told Archie that. Obviously.

His desk chair didn't even have arms.

She spun around slowly on it.

He'd blame himself. For losing the kid.

There was a computer on Archie's desk. The monitor was flat and black, but the CPU was older than the ones at the *Herald.* It was probably password-protected. But it didn't matter. Susan plucked her phone off the desk and Googled "missing 'Patrick Lifton' Washington."

A page of results popped up.

Smartphones. You had to love them.

She clicked on the first result. It was a

Web site run by the family. The home page had a snapshot of Patrick Lifton, age eight, grinning and holding a soccer ball under his arm. He was missing one of his top front teeth. HAVE YOU SEEN ME? cried the bold letters above his head.

The information was all there. Patrick Lifton had been born and spent his first eight years in Aberdeen. Susan knew the place — a small town at the gateway of Washington's Olympic Peninsula that had been gritty even before the mills had closed down and the local salmon runs had dried up.

His father worked at one of the remaining paper mills, and his mother was described as "self-employed." Their son left home on a Saturday afternoon to walk three blocks to his friend's house. It was the third time he'd been allowed to walk there alone. The mother of the friend called a half hour after Patrick left. He'd never arrived.

The rest was too familiar. Patrick's parents searched for him. The police were called. Soon a massive search was under way. An Amber Alert was issued. No one saw anything. It was a rental neighborhood. There were a lot of apartment buildings. People didn't really know each other.

There were no witnesses. And no suspects.

Susan hoped the police report had more

information. If the man who'd poisoned Henry and killed three other people had taken the kid, then the kid had probably been through hell.

And it had been at the hands of a man who had been close enough to her to drop a key in her purse. She ran through it again and again in her mind. Had she been alone, in a crowd? All the others had happened near the river. That's where it must have happened. She and Archie and Claire had moved through so many people, looking for Henry. All those faceless raincoats. She shivered. Had he planned on poisoning her and then changed his mind? Or had she turned away at the last minute?

"I'm sorry if I was short," Archie said from the doorway.

Susan held up her phone. "I've been catching up on a Scrabble game," she said.

"Sure you have," he said. He stalked in and took a seat in one of the chairs across from her. Then he folded his hands in his lap and looked at her with a level gaze. She knew a lecture coming when she saw it. "This thing about the kid, we need to keep that quiet," he said. "We don't want the parents to know until we're sure."

Susan had already thought this all through. "You could check for his finger-

219

prints on the key he left under the bed. I'm sure they got his prints after he disappeared, right?"

He didn't move. "I know how to do my job, Susan."

"Right," she said. He'd thought of that, too.

They were both quiet for what seemed like too long.

"Do you want your chair?" she asked finally.

"It's a blue-ringed octopus," he said.

She wasn't sure she'd heard him. "What?"

"The toxicology report came back early this morning," he said. "It's a small cephalopod. Very deadly. Its bite causes respiratory paralysis. There's no antivenom. They think if Henry makes it twenty-four hours, he'll be okay. You can look it up on your phone."

All Susan could say was, "You lied to me at the hospital?"

He sighed and looked away. "We didn't want it public."

She remembered the spots on the palms, his concern with inspecting hers. "The marks on the hands," Susan said.

"Yes."

"So someone is . . . is . . ." She faltered, searching for the words.

"Using an octopus to kill people," Archie said.

"A blue-ringed octopus," Susan said.

"Yes."

She examined his face for some glimmer of humor. "Is this a joke?"

"No."

"Why are you telling me?"

He spread his fingers. "You can have the story."

"You said you didn't want it public."

"I didn't," he said. "Now I do."

It was the kid. Archie's bosses didn't want the octopus story out there. People were going to freak out. The city was flooding. They had enough to deal with. But Archie had decided that it was worth upping their chances of catching the guy, and saving the kid.

"I'm not a journalist," Susan said. "I was fired."

"You're a freelance journalist."

Henry. Archie had said there was no anti-venom.

"Twenty-four hours?" Susan looked around the office for a clock. "What time is it?" she asked.

He didn't even have to glance at his watch. "It's almost noon. Six hours to go, give or take."

Susan spun around again slowly in the chair. "This guy takes a kid and keeps him for a year and a half. Then uses a poisonous octopus to kill three people, put a fourth in the hospital, and he leaves keys on all of them."

"The keys are his signature. The octopus is his weapon. I don't know how the kid figures in."

"Why did he give me a key? Was I almost a victim?"

"I have no idea."

"It's kind of like a Peter Benchley novel."

"Okay," Archie said.

"How much time do I have? For an exclusive?"

"Two hours and I send out a press release."

Her phone rang. She knew that ringtone. "Number of the Beast." Iron Maiden.

"It's Ian," she said.

"You can take it."

She let it go to voice mail. "I'll call him back," she said. A serial killer with an octopus? She could get that story run anywhere. But she knew that once she did, any hope that Ian would hire her back was over. She'd have to make a living as a freelancer, or move to a city with more media outlets.

There was a second option.

She could use the exclusive to get back in with the *Herald.* Ian would have to take her back. She'd make him sign something. Everything could go back to the way it was.

"Can I smoke a cigarette and have five minutes to think about it?" she said.

"Sure," Archie said.

Susan stood up. She looked at Archie. He waited.

"Are you giving this to me because you're worried I was almost murdered and want to keep me around so you can keep an eye on me?" she said.

He held his thumb and forefinger out an inch apart. "A little," he said.

CHAPTER 29

Susan hunched under an overhang next to a garbage bin outside the task force building and lit a cigarette with a lighter from her raincoat pocket. The drizzle was relentless. The noon sky was flat and dark. She could hear the gutters running all around her, a constant gush of water spilling onto concrete. The streetlights from the nearby intersection swung back and forth in the gentle wind, flashing red.

The cigarette tasted really good.

She didn't bother to check Ian's message on her voice mail. She hardly ever listened to voice mails — if people had something important to say, well, that's what texts were for. He probably needed her to fill out some paperwork or do an exit interview or something.

"Number of the Beast" started up again.

He was like herpes.

She let Iron Maiden sing a verse before

she picked up.

"What?" she said flatly. She was going to make him work for this. If she was going back there with the story, she was going to get a better task chair, maybe even a view of the river.

"I'm sorry," Ian said.

She would not have been more surprised if he'd said, *Aliens have landed and they want to give you an interview.* Maybe he had the wrong number.

"It's Susan," she said.

"I know," he said. "I'm calling to say I'm sorry."

"What?"

"I behaved badly. You can have your job back."

Susan let that sink in. She took a drag off her cigarette. Examined it. Flicked some ashes into the trash can. There was something hinky going on. She had been driving Ian crazy for almost a year. She was always late to meetings, was hardly ever at the office, tried to expense everything, insisted on her own story ideas, and had twice broken the third-floor candy machine trying to get M&Ms out by reaching up through the flap. But she'd managed to land incredible stories — to be right in the middle of them — so she'd always figured her job was safe, despite his occasional threats. Also, there was the fact that she had slept with him, and he knew that if she ever told (which she wouldn't) he would be ruined. It had been during her older-married-men-with-authority phase. Thinking of it now gave her the willies.

"Did you hear me?" Ian said. "I'm offering you your job back."

"Why?" Susan asked.

"We need you," Ian said.

"No, you don't," Susan said. She took a drag of her cigarette. "I mean, you do. But you don't know that."

"Don't be difficult," Ian said with a little of the old edge back in his voice. "You think you're going to find another job out there?" He paused. "Sorry. I'm sorry. I'm in a jam here. Just come back. I'll make it up to you."

"Okay," Susan said.

"Okay? Really? You'll take your job back?"

"Sure," Susan said. "You bet."

"That's great," Ian said, with a relieved sounding sigh. "Thanks, babe."

"Oh, Ian?"

"Yeah?"

Susan smiled and stretched the moment as long as she could, grinding the cigarette out on the brick wall. There was no way she was giving him this story. She didn't work for the *Herald.* She was a freelancer. She said, "I quit." She waited for the gasp on the other end of the phone before she hung up and tossed the butt in the trash.

She wasn't done.

She got another cigarette out of her purse and lit it. She hadn't had two cigarettes in a row since grad school. The second one made her feel light-headed and warm. She had no regrets. She just had to get another job with insurance before she got lung cancer.

An orange peel went by, swept along by the gutter rapids.

Susan called Derek.

"Hey, there," he said.

She wasn't in the mood for small talk. "Did you call Leo Reynolds and tell him I got fired?"

Derek was in his car. Susan could hear NPR in the background. He turned it down and the host's voice dropped to a low burble. But he didn't answer the question. He didn't have to.

"I'm going to kill you," Susan said.

"Ian is a moron," Derek protested. "You didn't deserve to get fired. You do good work. When you get around to it."

When she got around to it? "What do you mean by that?"

"Just that you spend a lot of time hanging out with your police friends."

The cigarette bent in Susan's hand. "That's me working. How do you think I get stories?"

"You don't ever wonder if you're too close to them?" Derek said. There was a characteristic in his voice that Susan didn't like — air quotes around "close," an implication of something sordid.

Susan was irritated by air quotes in general. But there was something about these particular air quotes that really got under her skin.

She took an angry drag off the bent cigarette. "Sure, yeah," she said. "Which is why I didn't want to write the story about Henry. It would have been inappropriate. I know the line."

"Where are you right now?"

Susan turned so she was facing away from the task force offices. She felt ridiculous. It's not like he could see her through the phone. "Shut up," she said. "I'm mad at you."

"So I called Leo Reynolds," Derek said. "You got me. His family knows the Overtons. You may have noticed the Overton-Reynolds Wing at the museum." Susan hadn't. "And he obviously likes you. So I called him and I told him you'd been unfairly fired, and that if he really liked you, getting you your job back might be a grander gesture than slowly burying you in floral arrangements."

"How did you get his number?" Susan asked. She happened to know that Leo was unlisted.

"You wrote it in Sharpie on your desk," Derek said.

"Oh." She remembered that now. She hadn't been able to find a Post-it.

"I still think he's bad news," Derek said. He paused. "But he sure got through to Ian." Susan could hear the smile in his voice. "You should have seen him get the call."

Susan couldn't help but smirk at the thought of that conversation.

The radio noise stopped, and she heard Derek open his car door. Wherever he was going, he'd arrived.

"So Ian unfired you?" Derek asked.

"He did."

"Great," Derek said. He sounded happy. He was out of the car. She could hear city sounds on his end, traffic, the slap of footsteps in water.

"Then I quit," Susan said.

"Susan," Derek said. He stretched the

word out, turning it into a disappointed sigh.

She heard a siren then, someone on a loudspeaker, police radios yelping, the buzzing commotion of a hundred urgent conversations.

She felt suddenly very fond of Derek. "Where are you calling from?"

"Waterfront Park. Ian's got me down here covering the sandbagging effort. Gotta go. On deadline."

If she told Derek, he'd run with it. It would be a headline on the paper's Web site in ten minutes. *You don't ever wonder if you're too close to them?* She couldn't say anything. Besides, what was she supposed to say, *Keep an eye out for an octopus-wielding madman?*

She threw the rest of her cigarette in the trash.

"Derek?" she said.

"Yeah?" he shouted. She could see him, phone against one ear, fingers pressed against the other, wearing some stupid sport coat and a tie, *Herald* ID on a lanyard around his neck. He'd wear that thing in the shower if he could.

She was being mean. He'd make a good

boyfriend. For someone normal. Someone not her.

"Be careful," she said to the dead air.

Chapter 30

Susan had left a tampon on his desk. Archie had noticed it while he was on the phone with Claire.

No change.

That's what Claire had said.

Archie wasn't sure if that was good or bad. If Henry's body was processing the toxin, shouldn't his vital signs be getting better?

He opened his desk drawer, slid out the flash drive, and turned it over in his hand. It had been six months since Gretchen had given it to him. Her last move in their demented psychological chess game.

Archie had yet to plug it into his computer and look at the files. He had promised Henry he wouldn't.

He put it back in the drawer and checked his watch. It was after noon.

An e-mail bounced up — the electronic file of Patrick Lifton's missing persons report. The FBI had come through.

He was scanning it when Susan came back in.

"I'll do it," she said. "The story. I called the national editor at *The New York Times* while I was outside. Can I have a desk to work at?"

"You leave the boy out of it for now," Archie said.

"Yep," Susan said. "Now give me back my purse. I need my notebook."

Archie's phone rang. He saw Heil's number and snapped the cell to his cheek.

"Where are you?" Archie asked.

"In the front," Heil said.

"You're calling me from the office?"

"It was faster. There's someone here. Says he's the one who moved Stephanie Towner's body."

"Here, now?"

"I'm looking at him. Says he's the caretaker at Oaks Park."

"I'll be right out," Archie said. He looked at Susan. "You can work in my office," he said. He immediately regretted the offer.

August Hughes had broad cheekbones and a wide nose, and white hair that receded halfway back his scalp. Deep folds were stacked on his dark forehead, and dimples had long ago deepened into shallow trenches on either side of his mouth. White whiskers spotted his chin. His collared shirt was ironed. He was wearing red suspenders.

His son, Philip, had brought him in. He'd taken care of the congenital receding hairline by shaving his head and growing a beard.

Archie had decided against interviewing them in the interrogation room, and instead suggested the conference room where they now sat.

The list of possible key purposes was still on the dry-erase board.

Heil sat next to Archie; August and Philip Hughes, side by side across the table.

August Hughes swallowed hard. "I'll accept full responsibility," he said.

His son looked away.

They hadn't asked for a lawyer.

"You moved the body to the carousel?" Archie asked.

"I did."

"Why?" Archie asked.

"I'll accept full responsibility," he said again. His irises looked almost black, the whites of his eyes more cream than white, and threaded with red blood vessels.

"Why did you do it?" Archie repeated.

Philip Hughes placed a hand on his father's back. "Tell them, Pop," he said.

August's shoulders slumped. "At first I pulled her off the bank because I was afraid the river would wash her back out," he explained. "I laid her in the grass." He shrugged a little and frowned. "But it didn't seem right. She just looked so cold. So scared. I didn't want her found like that."

Archie raised an eyebrow. "So you put her on the carousel?"

"Carousel's been there since 1923," August said. "It's on the National Register of Historic Places, and recognized by the National Carousel Association. All wood. Hand-carved. It's the prettiest thing in the park." He shook his head, eyes closed. "I knew it was wrong. Knew it when I did it. But sometimes right is wrong, know what I mean?"

"You might have destroyed valuable evidence," Archie said. She had been in the water two days; any trace evidence had certainly been long gone. But August Hughes didn't know that. "Something that could have helped us catch her killer."

August's eyes opened. "She was murdered? I thought she drowned."

Philip Hughes took a breath, removed his hand from his father's back, and laid it on his father's hand. "It's okay, Pop."

"Why didn't you report it?" Archie asked August.

"How could I explain what I'd done?" the old man said. "Besides, I knew the work crew would find her. They take their smoke breaks over there. But it ate at me. I finally told my son this morning. Asked him to bring me down to you all."

People did a lot of strange things, for strange reasons. Archie had seen some of those things up close. But this? It was up there.

"Why the ostrich?" Archie asked.

August Hughes looked at his hands. "No reason. Thought she'd like it. You can tell a lot about someone by the carousel animal they get on. Rooster. Stork. Frog. Zebra. Most people, they get on the jumping horses, the dragon, the lion, the tiger — you know, the classics. We got two ostriches on that carousel. Some kids, they cry when their moms try to set them on one. They want to ride on the dragon. Some kids, they go right to the ostriches. They have secret names for them. You see them whisper in their ears. Those are the kids with heart. I thought she was one of them."

"My dad's a drinker," Philip said.

"I drink beer," August said, looking up. "Just enough. Not more."

236

Archie was forty-one and his whole body hurt most of the time. He couldn't carry his kids more than a few blocks. This old man, he'd managed to move a body in the dark, after a few beers? Dead bodies were a lot harder to move than most people thought. There was a reason people talked about "deadweight." Dead people weren't any heavier than they were when they were alive. But it felt like it. "You picked up that girl, got her over the fence, carried her a hundred feet, and got her up on the carousel?" Archie asked. "By yourself?"

"I didn't say I did it quick," the old man said.

"Dad's strong," Philip said. "He still goes to the gym every day. He boxed in the army. Then worked at the shipyards." He patted his father's hand. "The roller rink was destroyed back in '48, and after that they put the floor up on pontoons. My dad, he was working at the park during the Christmas flood of '64. Saw the brown water coming in, and he cut the floor loose from supports with a chainsaw. Saved the roller rink."

"Nineteen-forty-eight," Archie said. "That was the Vanport flood, right?"

The elder Hughes nodded. "Water had to go somewhere, once it washed away the town. The Willamette rose fifteen feet. The park was underwater for thirty days, trees dead, rides warped. Course, I didn't work there then."

"You weren't supposed to be there on Sunday night, either," Archie said. He had seen the schedule for that week. "So what were you doing at the park?" he asked.

"I go there a lot at night in the winter," August said. "Place is closed. Don't want anyone getting into things, getting into trouble. Kids jump the fence and fool around. I know them all. I know all their parents."

It was a hunch. Nothing more. Archie had the case file in front of him. He opened it and took out the hospital surveillance image of the boy and pushed it over to August Hughes.

"Have you seen this kid?" Archie asked him.

Philip Hughes leaned forward. "Is that the boy on the news?"

August frowned. "He's not any trouble."

Archie's heart quickened. "You've seen him? Are you sure?"

"He comes around for the goldfish," August Hughes said. "The older kids, they come to the park and spend a fortune throwing darts at balloons to get those fish. Jump all around when they win one. You'd think they'd gotten themselves a trip to Paris, the way they bounce around. Ten minutes later, they couldn't care less. I find those bags on the Ferris wheel, in the bathroom, on benches. The kid asked if he could have them. I don't care. They don't belong to anyone. They only live a few weeks."

"When was the last time you saw him?" Archie asked.

"He came by the park every couple of days last summer. Haven't seen him since the park closed for the season back in October."

Patrick Lifton had been in Portland at least sixth months.

"Did he ever tell you his name, where he lived? Anything?"

"Said his name was Sam. Other than that, nothing. He was quiet."

"Did you ever see him with anyone?"

"No. He was always alone. But most of the kids I see are. They find their way. Parents want them out of their hair. He okay?"

"Is it the kid from the news?" Philip Hughes asked again.

"We're going to need your clothes from that night. And your fingerprints, and a DNA sample."

"Anything," the son said.

"You committed a Class C felony. There's prison time. Up to five years."

Philip gave his father's hand a squeeze.

"I'm ready for what I've got coming," the old man said.

"He's eighty-five," Philip said.

"We haven't made an arrest yet."

Philip glanced at his father and then back at Archie. "What are you saying?"

"Thanks for coming in," Archie said.

The old man hesitated. "We can go?"

"I'll have a detective escort you home," Archie said. "To pick up those clothes, and do a DNA swab." Archie turned back to Philip. "He stays in town. Available if we need him." Archie took out a card and handed it to August Hughes. "You see this kid, you call me."

August Hughes took the card and put it in his pocket. Then he glanced over at the moaning fridge. "You need a new bearing on your condenser fan," he said.

CHAPTER 31

Susan put together a bare-bones outline of the facts of the case for *The New York Times* on Archie's computer — he'd made her leave the room while he typed in his password. Someone else would get quotes. And a third person would make it all sound good. The three of them would share a byline.

It was not the way Susan had imagined her first story for the *Times* going, but the national editor wanted it up on the Web site ASAP, and this, apparently, was the fastest way to do it. She hoped they didn't list the byline names alphabetically. She was always getting screwed by that.

The expanded story — the one that would run in tomorrow's print edition — that was all Susan's. And she had the rest of the day to get it in.

She hit send, and waited for the editor to e-mail her back.

Susan, then, found herself with a moment of idle time alone in Archie Sheridan's office. She did not decide to snoop. It just happened. She looked down and she'd opened Archie's desk drawer. She was that kind of person. The kind of person you didn't want house-sitting.

There, inside the desk drawer, along with all the paper clips and pens and notes on official-looking stationery, under a flash drive, was a photograph of Gretchen Lowell. It was not such a strange thing, for a detective who'd spent most of his career hunting a killer, to have an image of that killer in his office. It was a famous case. A lot of detectives probably had a photo of Gretchen Lowell in their offices — hung on the wall, with darts sticking out of it. But Susan also knew that part of Archie's recovery process was that he was supposed to move on. It's not like anyone could totally avoid Gretchen's image. But he didn't have to see her every time he needed a paper clip.

Susan heard a voice from the doorway say, "Find anything interesting?"

She shut the drawer, nearly snapping off her fingertip in the process. "Ouch," she said.

Anne Boyd had arrived from Washington,

D.C., and now stood in the doorway to Archie's office. Susan gave Anne a sheepish smile, embarrassed to be caught snooping by anyone, but especially a criminal psychologist.

Anne was the only black female profiler in the FBI and, as she had once told Susan, she was also "the most stylish." She cinched the belt of her patent leather trench coat the color of grape jelly and grinned. "He still keep a picture of her in there?" she asked.

Anne had worked on the Beauty Killer case. She knew what it had done to Archie. Perhaps better than most. But Susan still sidestepped the question. "I was just looking for a pen," she said.

Anne looked at her for a second, and then smiled. "Good answer," she said finally. Her attention was drawn down the hall. "Here comes our fearless leader now."

Susan pulled her hand down from her mouth just as Archie appeared next to Anne.

"You're late," Archie said. There was no pleasure in his expression. No hey-how's-it-going-welcome-back.

Susan knew that face.

She could tell by Anne's shift in posture that Anne knew it, too. "What happened?" Anne asked.

"National Guard called in another body," Archie said.

An e-mail popped up on the computer screen — a response from the *Times* editor.

"Let's go take a look," Anne said.

Susan glanced at the e-mail's subject line. "Need more detail," it read.

Susan stood up, knocking her knees on Archie's desk. "Can I come?" she said.

Archie hesitated.

"I'd like to stick with you," Susan said. She tried to look vulnerable and a little scared. It wasn't hard.

Archie's shoulders dropped. "Fine," he said.

Susan set about gathering up all her personal items — phone, cigarettes, notebook — and then hurried around the desk after them.

"How are you doing?" Anne asked Archie.

"How do I look?" Archie said.

Anne took a step back and looked him up and down. "Better," she said. "Bad for most people. But good for you."

CHAPTER 32

The river was a monster. The break in the rain had done nothing to calm it. If anything, it seemed even fiercer. The water churned with eddies and whirl pools, and ribbons of debris bumped along on the surface.

"So tell me," Anne said. "What is it you people have done to piss off the good Lord?"

Archie parked next to the patrol car on the east side of the Burnside Bridge. He had filled Anne in on the case en route. Susan had been weirdly quiet, scribbling notes in the backseat.

Heil, who'd followed them from headquarters, pulled up beside them in a green Nissan Cube. It wasn't police-issue. But it was new, and Heil insisted on driving it.

The bridge was up, always a strange sight, four lanes of road and sidewalk, all at nearly a ninety-degree angle, streetlights almost parallel to the earth. It was closed to traffic, but the caution sawhorses had been blown over and were easy to drive around.

The rain had slowed to a light drizzle — the kind of rain you couldn't see fall if you looked out a window from inside.

Archie was silent. He didn't know what to say. Both Anne and Susan occasionally looked at him a little too closely for comfort.

They took the staircase that jackknifed down from the bridge's pedestrian walkway to the esplanade below, where Officer Chuck Whatley was unspooling yellow plastic crime scene tape with the help of a National Guard soldier.

The sky was the texture and color of freshly poured concrete. This part of the esplanade was high enough that the river lapped at it, but didn't overflow. The body was under a blanket on the dry side of the pavement. The blanket was the same gray as the sky.

Whatley tied the tape to a stake as he talked. "Just got here about fifteen minutes ago," he said. He was wearing a bright yellow plastic rain bonnet snapped over his hat, and it was beaded with rain. "A National Guardsman found the body in a logjam about thirty minutes ago." He caught himself. "Guards*woman*," he corrected. He lifted his hand in the direction of the person who'd been helping him with the tape. "Anyway, this is her."

The soldier was a young black woman, and clearly pregnant. She snapped her heels together and stood at attention. She was wearing an orange reflective vest over her maternity fatigues and holding one of the ten-foot steel poles Archie had seen them using to break up the floating debris.

"Private Jen Auster, sir," she said.

"What were you doing over here?" Archie asked gently.

"Clearing flotsam, sir. They sent us over here to push the larger logs out. Helps break up the smaller stuff. Keep it all moving."

A massive logjam clotted the area under the bridge, held in place by the massive concrete pilings. The fifty-foot mass of rolling logs and snapping branches was a death trap. Getting a body disentangled from that would have been no easy job. Not with these currents.

"Who got him up on land?" Archie asked.

"Him, sir," Private Auster said.

A lanky man in National Guard fatigues trotted their way. Archie recognized him immediately.

"Carter," Susan said.

Carter loped toward them, grinning. "They sent me over here to get me away from the reporters," he said. "Something easy, they said. Easier than hauling sandbags, I guess." His eyes brightened. "I lassoed him."

"Let me guess," Susan said. "You did rodeo, in addition to lifeguarding."

"Got a gold belt buckle for calf roping. Grew up in Pendleton, ma'am. Not a lot else going on."

Archie didn't have the heart to tell him that he should have left the body to the cops. It would have been nice to at least have a photograph before it had been moved. The retrieval and the blanket may have contaminated evidence. What was it with people moving bodies in this town? They needed to run some public service announcements about that. "You've had a busy twenty-four hours," Archie said.

"You, too, sir. Sorry to hear the kid went missing."

"You covered him up?" Susan asked Carter.

"Right after we called you all," Carter said. He gave her an awe-shucks grin. "It seemed like the respectful thing to do."

"That's so nice," Susan said.

Archie turned to Heil. The two soldiers needed to be interviewed before they got to talking and merged details. Even the most well-meaning witnesses, given the chance to exchange versions, would adapt aspects of the others' memories as their own. It was subconscious. Two people see a bank robber. They talk about it. One saw a man in an orange shirt with a mustache. The other saw a man in an orange shirt, but didn't see his face. Pretty soon they'll both swear on their mother's lives that the guy had a mustache, and they'll tell you all about it — shape, color, whether it was neatly trimmed. The guy never had a mustache. But the first person gets it wrong, and it goes viral.

Heil seemed to know exactly what Archie was thinking. "I'm on it," he said, and he pulled out his notebook and led Carter away.

Archie turned to Anne. Having worked the Beauty Killer case, he'd seen more bodies than most detectives saw in their entire careers. He'd never gotten used to it, but he'd learned to mind it less. "Let's take a look," he said.

"Thought you'd never ask," Anne said.

"What about me?" Susan said.

Archie hesitated. He had no reason to let Susan see the body. She wasn't even a reporter anymore. He'd already exposed her to enough death.

"I found Henry," Susan said. "I might be

able to help. To recognize a clue or something."

"Fine," Archie said. He wasn't in the mood to argue. "Try not to step on any evidence."

They walked to the body, and Archie pulled the blanket back. The smell of decomposing flesh blew forward, a faint whiff of old meat.

He had smelled much, much worse. This was dank and sour, but not very far along. The body was relatively fresh. The young man still looked human. Archie didn't see any misshapen flesh where gases had built up. No bluish stains where blood had settled. Rigor hadn't set in. Cold water could slow that process some. He'd been beaten up a little. There was an open wound on his forehead, deep enough that Archie could see a flash of white skull. But there was little blood, and Archie guessed the wound was postmortem, a result of getting knocked around in the logjam.

"What do you think?" Archie asked Anne. "A few hours?"

"Seems right to me," she said.

"Me, too," said Susan. Archie slid her a look. "What?" she said. "I know a little about forensics."

The blanket was still in Archie's hand and

he pulled it all the way off and dropped it to the side of the body.

A rope was still knotted around the dead man's ankles from where Carter had lassoed him. Lifeguards tied ropes around their waists during rescues. It would have come in handy the night before. Carter had made sure he'd be ready for the next time.

Corpses lose something they had in life. When the muscles slacken, the face gets soft, wider, dimples and laugh lines vanish. It's one of the reasons people sometimes misidentify remains, and it's why Archie didn't recognize the street kid at first. It was the tribal earring that gave him away. Then the braided beard, the army surplus jacket, the skateboarder shoes. "I know him," Archie said.

"Freeze," Archie heard Robbins bellow. "You know I hate it when you peek." Archie took a small step back from the body, and Susan and Anne did the same. Robbins jogged up from under the freeway, followed by two forensic investigators, all three dressed in identical white Tyvek suits, hoods up. Robbins knelt next to the body, opened up a plastic toolbox, and snapped on latex gloves. He gave Carter's blanket a disdainful snort. "Tell me some jackass didn't throw a nasty old blanket on my corpse."

Susan glanced in the direction where Heil was interviewing Carter. "Not so loud," she said. "You'll hurt his feelings."

"Bag it," Robbins said to one of his investigators.

Archie, Susan, and Anne took another few steps back. One of the forensic investigators started taking digital photographs of the scene. The other snapped on gloves and carefully folded the blanket into a large evidence bag.

All Archie cared about at that moment was getting a look at the body's hands. But he knew better than to rush Robbins.

Archie heard a siren approaching, and then saw an ambulance slam to a stop on the bridge above them. Two EMTs hopped out and started down the stairs. "I think it's a little late for lifesaving measures," Archie said to Robbins.

"I'm taking him to Emanuel for autopsy. My office, as you'll recall, is submerged."

"So you called an ambulance?" Susan said.

Robbins didn't even look up. "You want to help me get him into my car?" He turned his head back toward the EMTs. "We're okay here," he yelled. "Give us a minute." The two EMTs stopped in their tracks and looked at one another, clearly unsure how to proceed.

Archie sighed and lifted his badge. "Just hang out for a few minutes," he yelled. "We're fine. He's dead. Thanks."

"Who's that doofus?" Susan asked. Archie followed her gaze farther up the stairs, where a man was gazing out over the river with his hands on his hips. Archie was excellent at noticing small details about people. He could recall the curve of a person's earlobe, the angle of a stance, the pattern of the freckles on an exposed clavicle. He knew body language. Facial expressions. The sentence structure people turned to when they lied. He could read people. But social categorization escaped him.

Still, Archie could see what Susan meant with this guy.

"I called him," Robbins said before Archie could comment.

Their visitor looked to be in his midthirties. He was wearing a red scarf knotted nattily around his neck, and the type of plaid newsboy hats that enough young men in Portland had started wearing so that even Archie had noticed.

He saw Archie looking up at him, waved heartily, and started trotting down the stairs.

"Is he a haberdasher?" Archie asked.

Robbins was busy directing his minions.

"You wanted an expert," Robbins said. "This is the part of the case where you call them in, right?" He tilted his hooded head at Anne. "Criminal Psychologist, meet Octopus Guy."

Octopus Guy realized he was being talked about and hurried down the remaining stairs.

"This is Any Mingo," Robbins said as Octopus Guy approached. "He teaches marine biology at Portland State."

Archie was hoping for someone from the Oregon Coast Aquarium in Newport. Professionals told you what you needed to know. Academics told you what they wanted you to know they knew.

Mingo wiped his hand on his pant leg and offered it. "I teach freshwater invertebrate zoology," he said. He was wearing glasses with lenses the size of coasters, which, based on the lack of refraction, he didn't seem to need. He had a broad, fleshy face with delicate features and a pronounced chin highlighted by sideburns that stretched to his jawbones. He wore a woven leather cuff snapped around each wrist.

Archie shook his hand. Mingo's fingertips were callused — the fronts, not the tips. Stand-up bass, Archie guessed. "Thanks for helping us out."

"I'm Susan," Susan said. "I like your hat."

"Agent Boyd," Anne said. "FBI."

Mingo sniffed the air. "That smell," he said, "reminds me of a giant octopus I discovered in Tasmania. Twenty-one feet. Washed up dead on a beach." He leaned in near Susan. "The sperm packet that a giant male octopus deposits in a female is nearly one meter long."

Susan looked over at Archie and raised an eyebrow.

Robbins lifted one of the corpse's hands and leaned in close to examine it. "Professor Mingo likes himself some cephalopods," he said. "I've informed him about our octopus problem."

Mingo was standing between Archie and Susan, within two yards of the body, but he seemed to make a point of not looking at it. "These aren't aggressive animals," he said. "They basically spend their lives alone, in hiding. The only reports of attacks are when they're stepped on or handled."

"He's got a mark on his hand, just like the others," Robbins said.

Archie's throat tightened. That made four. Five if you included Henry. And they still knew next to nothing about the killer.

The forensic investigator beside Robbins slipped a plastic bag over the corpse's hand

and used a twist-tie to secure it around his wrist.

"You said you know him?" Anne asked Archie.

Archie unzipped his coat. He was hot. The humidity was getting to him. "He was at the camp last night," Archie said. "He knew we were looking for someone, knew about the octopus attacks. I warned them. Specifically." If they couldn't protect people who knew to be careful, knew what to look for, how would they protect a city full of people who didn't even know to be afraid?

"So he wouldn't have picked it up," Anne said. "He knew not to. But he might take it in his hands before he knew what it was. If it came from someone who didn't appear to be a threat. Someone he knew. Or someone he had reason to trust. With the exception of Henry, they've all been found in the water?"

She didn't wait for the answer. She knew it. She was just talking it through now. "The killer waits for them to die, then pushes the bodies into the river," she concluded.

Archie nodded. "He likes to watch."

"Or she. Women are more likely to use poison." She wheeled around to Mingo. "What happens to the victims? After the poison hits?"

But Mingo was looking at the body now, his eyes wide behind the fake glasses. Archie had seen it before. Once you looked, you couldn't look away. The professor's pallor went from Northwest pale to ash. "The toxin causes respiratory paralysis," he mumbled.

This was why Archie didn't like bringing amateurs to crime scenes. Pretty soon Mingo would be in the bushes vomiting, and then they'd have that smell to deal with on top of the decomp.

"No, I mean step by step," Anne said. She took Mingo's pointy chin in her leather-gloved hands and gently turned his head. "Look at me. Not him." She smiled at him. He blinked. Took a breath. Adjusted his cap. His Adam's apple rose and fell. "There, now," she said. "You're okay. Now tell me, this toxin, what does it feel like?"

He frowned and thought for a moment. "It happens fast," he said. "A lot of people, they don't even know they've been bit. It doesn't hurt. They suddenly feel nauseated. Their vision blurs. They'd be blind within a few seconds. They lose motor skills, their senses of touch, smell, their ability to speak. They find themselves unable to swallow. Within ten minutes they experience total body paralysis. They might be aware of what's going on around them. But they can't move, their lungs stop working." He looked around at the group. "Basically, they suffocate."

The logjam groaned, straining against the force of the river, and Archie heard the crack of timber as it broke free.

That's why Henry had dropped his phone. He'd pulled it out to call for help, but had lost motor function and dropped it. Then stumbled and collapsed. He was probably just feet away when Otter had found it, but had been unable to cry out.

"How is Henry still alive?" Susan said. "If he was bitten at least an hour before we found him."

"He must not have gotten a full dose of venom," Mingo said. "The venom is in the saliva. It's not injected by the beak. The beak pierces the skin. But it's not like a snakebite. If the detective was able to react quickly, disrupt the attack and apply pressure to the wound, he might have bought himself some time. Is he a big guy?"

Archie nodded.

"That would help, too."

Henry had been on the ground, unable to move or speak, barely able to breathe, yet completely aware. Archie knew what that was; he had experienced it in Gretchen's basement. It was one of the reasons he left the lights on when he went out.

"Do you know how the octopus is being transported?" Mingo asked.

"We found a Ziploc freezer bag near where Henry was found," Archie said. "Smelled like salt water. We're having it tested."

"It was empty?" Mingo said.

They all looked at each other, the question so obvious no one bothered to say it. *Where was the octopus?* If the bag had been used to transport the octopus, and Henry *had* disrupted the attack, and the killer hadn't stayed to watch, had instead fled, leaving behind the bag —

He'd left the octopus behind.

They all turned and looked across the river, in the direction of the Japanese American Plaza. The seawall was high enough that Archie couldn't make out the people closest to the river, only their heads and arms as they stacked the last layer of sandbags. But he could see the tops of the emergency vehicles that still crowded the park, the white festival tents set up as volunteer stations, the hundreds of people that still milled around farther into the park. "How long can one of these things live outside the water?" he said.

"A half hour, tops," Mingo said.

They'd searched every inch of that plaza.

"These octopuses can get around pretty well," Mingo continued. "They can crawl from tide pool to tide pool, fit through a hole the size of a pea."

"Heil," Archie called. Heil looked over from where he was interviewing Jen Auster. "We need to search the plaza again. Make sure that octopus didn't crawl into a pea-sized hole and die." Archie's gaze fell on the surging Willamette. "It can't survive in there, right?" he asked.

"Not a chance," Mingo said.

Susan was still staring across the river. "So the killer has more than one octopus? I mean, if he left the bag. Maybe he put the thing in a bucket or his pocket. Carried it away. He has to get it out of the bag, right? Or does he just open the bag up and get people to pull it out?"

"Maybe he uses tongs," Archie said.

No one laughed.

"Does it know him?" Susan asked Mingo.

"Oh, come on," Archie said.

"If you put a crab in a bottle," Mingo said, "and drop it next to one of these things, they can figure out how to uncork it to get at the crab. They can learn. It's possible this thing has learned that its owner isn't a threat. But if that's true, it would be spectacular. I'd want to write a paper on it. Can I write about this? For a professional journal?" He looked off into the middle distance. "CONSULTING WITH THE POLICE TO CATCH THE OCTOPUS KILLER." Then he chuckled nervously and fumbled with his glasses. "You know what they say, publish or perish."

Anne was focused on the body, not having any of it. "So let's assume he's got more than one."

"We're talking about exotic animals here," Mingo said. "He'd need a species tank. Fifty gallons of salt water, at least. A filtration system, a protein skimmer. Constant temperature monitoring. Ideally you'd want to run the tank for three months before you even put an octopus in it. And you'd need a tank for each octopus. They don't like roommates."

"Any luck with aquarium supply stores or pet shops?" Archie asked Heil.

"Everything's closed," Heil said. "I'm trying to track down the owners. Ngyun's looked online and contacted some of the sites that sell them. Nothing yet."

Susan hugged her arms. "Why do people want to own these things?"

Mingo huffed, sounding a little offended.

"They're beautiful," he said, as if it were obvious. "Most of the time they're the color of sand, but when they're agitated they produce blue rings the size of eraser heads all over their bodies. The rings circle black spots, and the blue is this amazing luminous neon color. These rings, they pulsate with color. Children love them." He paused. "Those are the casualties you usually see — some kid on vacation in Australia sees a blue-ringed octopus in a tide pool and picks it up." His mouth turned down with exaggerated disdain. "Tourists," he explained. "The locals know better. Most cephalopod enthusiasts resist the urge to own one, though. They're hard to take care of, don't live long, and there's always the chance that your grandkid is going to reach in the tank and go home in a box." He gave Archie a jab with his elbow and winked. "You know what they say about mushrooms and women. The more beautiful they are, the more dangerous."

Archie felt something hit his cheek and looked up at the concrete sky. The rain was getting worse. It quickened from a drizzle to a constant patter. The others turned their heads up to the sky, too.

"It was too good to last," Heil said, turning up his hood.

Robbins and the EMTs hurried to load the body onto a gurney and get him in the ambulance.

Mingo adjusted his cap against the drizzle and Susan took shelter under the bridge a few steps away.

"You think they went to the Mission?" Archie asked Heil.

"I called last night. They all made it."

"You're kind of a softie," Archie said.

"I know," Heil said. His phone rang, and he stepped away to take the call.

At least they knew where to find the street kids, Archie thought. Maybe their friends had seen something. Maybe they hadn't. But either way, the task force needed to know.

Robbins came jogging back down from the ambulance with something in his hand. He held it out to Archie. In an evidence bag.

"What's that?" Archie said.

"You know what it is," Robbins said. "It was in his pocket."

Archie took the bag. Inside it, lying on its side, was a *Star Wars* Darth Vader action figure.

Heil returned. "That was the crime lab," he said. "Fingerprints on the key you found under the boy's hospital bed are a match to Patrick Lifton."

Archie closed his eyes for a moment. When he did, the sound of the river blotted out everything.

"There's a detective on the Aberdeen PD who worked closely with the family," he said finally. "His name's in the case file. Call him and let him tell them the news. But let's keep it out of the media for now. Our guy's kept him alive this long. We don't want him panicking." He held out the evidence bag Robbins had given him.

"What's this?" Heil asked, taking it.

"Get it to the crime lab," Archie said. "My guess is they'll find Patrick Lifton's prints on it, too."

However the boy was wrapped up in all this, it was only getting more complicated.

"Hey," Susan said from under the bridge. Something had attracted her attention in the river. "Look at that whitewater," she said, pointing to a thick beige froth that snaked along the riverbank, lapping at the water's edge.

Mingo was closest to her. "It's pollution," Archie heard him say. "A stew of sewage, chemical runoff, and bacteria. Terrible for marine life. I wouldn't go in that river if my life depended on it."

Archie coughed, trying not to think of the

water that had ended up in his lungs the
night before.

CHAPTER 33

Archie pulled as close as he could to the task force offices to let Susan and Anne out. The rain was really coming down now. The sky looked lower and darker. He had the windshield wipers on their highest setting and their insistent back-and-forth swoop seemed frantic.

Heil had stayed behind to supervise the crime scene investigation around where the corpse had been found. Archie didn't envy him. Nothing like tiptoeing around a flooding riverbank in the rain looking for tiny clues among the floating trash and muck.

Mingo had gone back to wherever he'd come from.

Susan slid across the backseat, opened the car door, and sprinted for the building with her notebook under her arm.

Anne didn't move.

The windshield wipers went back and forth.

The engine wheezed.

"Are you going to get out of the car?" Archie asked.

Anne lowered her chin and turned to look at him. "How long have you had that cough?" she asked.

"Not long."

"Since you went in the river?"

"I don't know."

"Talked to your doctor?" Anne asked.

"Not yet."

Anne made a clucking sound. "Your immune system isn't what it used to be," she said.

"I've been filled in about that," Archie said, staring straight ahead.

It turned out that you could live without a spleen just fine. But the fist-sized organs weren't exactly useless. Spleens cleaned old red blood cells from the blood supply and produced and stored white blood cells. Those white blood cells produced antibodies when your body needed to fight an infection. If you happened to lose your spleen to a beautiful psychopath, the liver was expected to help take over some of this duty. Unless, of course, your liver happened to be damaged from a two-year-plus addiction to painkillers.

He could feel her still looking at him.

He needed to go, to get to the Mission, he needed her out of the car.

He broke, and turned back to her. "I'm a little busy, Anne."

Anne picked up her purse and put it on her lap, and reached for the door handle. "You're a stubborn martyr with a white knight complex," she said, opening the door. "You know that, right?"

"I want a profile by two," Archie said as she closed the door.

"You call your doctor if you get any worse," he heard Anne call as he pulled away.

CHAPTER 34

There were two Portland Mission buildings on Burnside, three blocks apart. The old mission, founded in 1949, was in a nineteenth-century brick structure with a neon sign in the shape of a light house out front. The new building, the result of a fund-raising campaign, was steel and glass. Mary Riley's office was in the old building, which was usually used as an emergency shelter for men, but had been opened to all comers during the flood watch.

It was where they had put up Nick and his friends. Mary Riley had them waiting in her office. "Don't touch anything," she told Archie before she left him, and he wasn't sure why, since the office was a tornado of files and books and chipped mugs ringed with coffee sludge.

Nick and his friends — minus the kid who was by now rolling into the hospital morgue — sat on an old couch that looked like it belonged on a porch. Archie took a seat in Mary Riley's desk chair. One of the plastic armrests was split jaggedly down the middle as though the chair had been heaved against the wall at some point.

Archie was the only one in the room who hadn't showered and changed in the last twenty-four hours. He almost didn't recognize the women without their soaked shrouds. He could see now that, in fact, they didn't look anything alike. One had dark hair and bright, even features, the other had bleached-out hair and was clearly older and more street-weary.

Archie took down all their names this time, writing them in a notebook open on his thigh.

The younger woman was named Kristen Marshall. The older woman was named Liz McDaniel, but she went by Sister. The man with the bushy beard was named Devin Longman. Nick's last name was Campbell.

He'd already gotten their full names from Mary Riley, who required full names from everyone who spent the night at the facility, but he'd wanted to start a conversation, and asking people their names was always an easy start. Everyone knew the answer. He went down the line, and they each said their names and spelled them for him.

"Got it," Archie said. They were all kids, no one over twenty-five.

"What happened to you?" Nick asked. Even in his donated homeless shelter sweats and Colorado Rockies T-shirt, he held himself with easy confidence. The man in charge.

Archie ran a hand through his wet hair and coughed. "It's raining."

Did he look that bad?

"Thanks for helping us out with the dogs," Nick said.

Archie had done this next part more times than he cared to remember. In the Beauty Killer days, when the body count challenged the imagination, Archie had always felt that he needed to be the one. The family deserved that — to get the news from the head of the task force himself. Besides, Archie wouldn't wish causing that kind of pain on anyone else.

"We found a body today, in the river," Archie said. He paused to let that sink in, but as he glanced from face to face he saw that they instantly knew; they always did. And as much as they knew, they hoped they were wrong. "I saw him with you last night. The kid with the braided goatee."

The younger woman, Kristen, lifted her hands over her mouth. "D.K.," she said through her fingers.

Archie wrote down *D.K.* in his notebook. Then asked, "Do you know his full name?"

"Dennis something," Nick said. He turned to the others. "Keating? Keller?"

"Keller," Kristen said behind her hands.

Archie wrote that down. "You know where he was from?" he asked.

"K-Falls," Bushy Beard said. Klamath Falls was a high desert town near the Oregon-California border. Archie checked his notes. Devin Longman.

Kristen let her hands fall from her mouth onto her lap, in tight fists. "His mom lives there," she said. "And a stepdad. They didn't get along." She squinted at Archie skeptically. "He's dead?"

"I'm sorry," Archie said.

"I left him," Nick said. His gaze was fixed on the floor, but his eyes shone with fierce intensity. "Last night, I left him behind."

"What happened?" Archie asked.

"There's this spot under the train trestle along the Steel Bridge. It's like a crawl space right under the tracks. You have to crawl over some of the timber trestles and get over one set of tracks — it's between the two lines. It's not big enough to get all the way into, but we used to store beer up there sometimes, when we had it. But it wasn't worth the hassle. D.K. thought someone might be living under there."

"Why?"

"He found this toy. A *Star Wars* figure. It was outside the opening. He tried to crawl in, but you can't see into the space more than a few feet, and it's so loud up there under the bridge that you can't hear anything. This crawl space? It's small. Like only big enough for a kid."

Archie's mind went to the toy they'd found in D.K.'s pocket. "Darth Vader," he said.

"Yeah."

"He thought it might belong to the kid you were looking for," Devin said.

"He didn't tell us until after you'd left," Nick said.

Kristen chewed on a nail. "D.K. left K-Falls when he was twelve. His stepdad used to beat him up really bad. He thought maybe this kid had run away, too. He didn't want to narc on him."

"D.K. went to look for him," Archie said.

"He was going to ask him to come with us," Devin said. "He was worried the kid was up in there. That he'd drown or whatever."

"We waited," Nick said. "But the van from the Mission came, and the people for the dogs. D.K. didn't always do what he said. He'd get distracted."

"He'd get high," Sister, the older woman, said, wiping her nose with her fist. It was the first thing she'd said since she'd spelled her name for Archie.

Nick was shaking his head, eyes fixed to that spot on the floor again. "We shouldn't have left him."

They could have waited all night. D.K. wasn't coming back.

Archie put the tip of his pen to his notebook. "Where exactly is this crawl space?" he asked.

Nick described how to get to it, and Archie wrote it down.

"Don't blame yourself," Archie said when he left them. But he knew Nick would. Archie and Nick were alike that way.

Archie called the task force as soon as he was out of the building. The sooner someone got to the boy's hiding place, the better.

CHAPTER 35

Something was happening. Susan heard a raised voice coming from the task force office's main room. Not yelling; more the sound of someone relaying urgent information. She got up from Archie's desk and hurried out there.

Heil was doing something with his gun. He had the magazine out in his hand and he looked at it and then snapped it into the chamber. Ngyun and Flannigan were putting on dark blue windbreakers that said POLICE in all-caps white letters across the back.

The uniformed patrol cops they had tracking down tips were sitting at their desks talking on the phone or clicking through Web sites, but Susan could see their eyes following the detectives.

Susan looked around for Anne and saw her sitting at an empty desk, with a laptop open and stacks of files and notes around her.

"What's going on?" Susan said.

Heil was reholstering his gun. "We're going to check something out," he said. "You're staying here."

"But —" Susan said.

"Not open for discussion," Heil said.

Susan stalked over to Anne. "Do you know what's happening?"

Anne kept her gaze firmly on her notes. "They have a lead on where the boy might be," she said. "That's all I know."

"Ask if we can come," Susan said.

"Nope," Anne said.

"You're not going to fight it?"

She looked up at Susan and sighed. "I have two kids," she said. "When they say it's not safe, I listen."

Susan's phone rang. It wasn't the *Times* editor calling her back; she had already programmed in a ringtone for his number — "Big Apple Dreamin' " by Alice Cooper. This was just the default ring. She didn't recognize the number.

Ngyun tossed a windbreaker at Heil. He tried to catch it but missed, and the windbreaker fluttered to the floor. Heil leaned over and picked it up.

"Hello?" Susan said into her phone.

There was a pause. "Susan Ward?"

"Yes," Susan said slowly.

"This is Frances Larson. I'm Gloria Larson's daughter. You wanted me to call?" Susan had nearly forgotten that she'd called Brad at the Mississippi Magnolia Assisted Living Facility and asked him to get a message to Gloria's family.

Ngyun, Flannigan, and Heil were putting on baseball caps now. The same blue, the same white letters that spelled POLICE.

"Are you there?" Frances Larson said.

Susan returned her attention to the call. "Yes," she said. "Yes, thank you." She tried to figure out a simple way of explaining everything. "I wrote a story yesterday for the *Herald* about a skeleton that was found a few days ago in the Columbia Slough. The skeleton's old, dating back to the forties or fifties. Your mother read my story and called me. She said she thought she knew the identity of the man." Susan mentally crossed her fingers. "Someone named McBee?"

"I'm sorry my mother bothered you," Frances Larson said. "But she gets confused. She likes to read the news, and it agitates her sometimes."

Susan gave it another try. Just to be sure. "You never heard her mention someone named McBee?"

277

"I'm sorry, but no."

"Did she ever live in Vanport?"

"No," Frances Larson said. "She grew up in the Kenton neighborhood. Lived there until she moved in with me. She was a secretary at Portland Union Stockyards. After she and Dad got married, she stayed home."

Susan looked around for a pen and paper. Her eyes settled on a ballpoint on Anne's desk, and she snapped it up.

"Hey," Anne said.

Kenton, Susan wrote on her hand. *Portland Union Stockyards. Secretary.* She was grasping at straws. "Do you mind me asking when they got married?"

"Nineteen-fifty-four."

Susan wrote that down on the base of her thumb. Gloria Larson would have still been single in 1948. "What was her maiden name?" Susan asked.

"Green. Gloria Green."

Susan wrote the word *Green* across her palm. "And she never mentioned someone named McBee, or the Vanport flood?"

"The Vanport flood?" Frances Larson paused. "She talked about it. When I was growing up we knew a lot of people who'd lost their homes and moved to North Portland. A lot of them had conspiracy theories

278

about how the Housing Authority let the city flood. Get rid of all the black folks." She paused again and chuckled. "But my mother never believed it."

"Okay, then," Susan said, trying to hide her disappointment. "Thanks anyway."

"Sorry I couldn't help."

Susan hung up. The detectives were gone. Anne was holding out her hand, palm up. Susan put the pen in it.

"I couldn't go with them anyway," Susan said. "I have too much to do."

She went back into Archie's office and slumped into the chair facing his computer.

It was true. She did have too much to do. She had sent the *Times* the info about the killer's most recent victim, but she had a lot of work yet to do on the actual story. The Word document she was working on was open on the screen. The cursor blinked at her insistently.

Susan minimized the window, opened Archie's Internet browser, and Googled "Gloria Larson." Over twenty-six thousand hits came up. So she tried " 'Gloria Larson' Vanport." Nothing. " 'Gloria Larson' 'Portland Union Stockyards.' " Nothing. " 'Portland Union Stockyards' Vanport."

Bingo.

The first hit was a PDF from the Oregon

Historical Society documenting the flood. Susan scanned it for highlights. W. E. Williams, the president of the Portland Union Stockyards, had been the first one to call and report the levy break. One of his employees, Floyd Wright, had been patrolling the railroad fill and had seen the roadbed give way. He'd raced back to his stockyard and alerted Williams, who immediately called the Housing Authority.

Williams and Wright waited, but didn't hear an evacuation siren, so Williams had called back. "For God's sake, alert those people!" he was reported to have shouted into the phone. And the siren sounded not long after. Thirty-five minutes later, Vanport was under fifteen feet of water.

Gloria Larson had worked for the Portland Union Stockyards.

It was a stretch, but it was a connection.

Susan clicked print.

She'd told the national editor that she'd cover the press conference. That gave her two hours. She Googled " 'Vanport Flood.' " It was worth a shot. Sometimes the best research happened when you didn't even know what you were looking for.

CHAPTER 36

Archie's watch was a Timex. It had a titanium band with a black face, numbers that glowed in the dark, and Swiss movement — whatever that was. He had paid $14.99 for it. Archie was looking at it while he was walking down the ICU hall, which was why he didn't see his ex-wife until he was standing right in front of her.

She was growing out her hair. She had always worn it very short, and now it fell in curls below her earlobes. Archie was still getting used to it. Her freckles glowed brown in the hospital light. She had only looked happier and younger since they'd finally broken up.

"It's you," he said dumbly.

"You should have called me," she said. "I had to see it on the news."

She was right. Debbie had known Henry as long as he had. Henry had been there for her every day when Archie was missing, and then for the long month in the hospital after. He'd been to their kids' birthday parties. She'd deserved to hear it from him. "I'm sorry," Archie said. How many times had he said that to her? "I was trying to protect you."

"Well, stop," Debbie said with a gentle smile.

Archie craned to look around her, into the room where Henry lay like a sarcophagus in a tomb. Claire was still in the chair she'd claimed, reading a book. "How is he?"

Debbie looked away. "The same."

"Where are the kids?" Why did it seem like a personal question?

"With Doug, at home," Debbie said. "I can help Claire. I've done this before, you know."

Before. When Archie had been in a medically induced coma. When she had sat in a chair by his hospital bed. Before Archie had confessed everything.

"Her sister's here," Archie said.

"Her sister is an idiot," Debbie said.

"Claire's handling it pretty well."

"You're an idiot, too."

"Only emotionally," Archie said.

"Yes," Debbie said. "There's that."

She waited, and they were quiet. He could

tell she was working out how to say something.

"One of the doctors came and talked to Claire," she said finally. "They told her that Henry might have suffered cerebral hypoxia." She paused. "It's caused by lack of oxygen to the brain."

Archie had to look away for a moment, to keep it together. "What are we talking about?"

"Oh, it's an eclectic menu," Debbie said. "Shortened attention span, loss of short-term memory, poor judgment, uncoordinated movements. People can recover. To varying degrees. Then there's the severe cerebral hypoxia. The patient enters a prolonged vegetative state. They can breathe on their own. They can open their eyes. They sleep. But they don't respond to their surroundings; they don't know you're there." She looked him in the eye. "They usually die within a year."

"Not Henry," Archie said.

She squeezed his arm. Her mouth formed the word *No,* but no sound came out.

Archie coughed. The effort of it hurt. Sputum filled his throat and rattled around in his lungs. He sounded like he belonged in the ICU himself. He wiped his forehead with his sleeve.

283

Debbie's brows furrowed. "Are you sick?"

Archie looked away. "It's just a cold."

She appraised him for a long moment. "O-kay," she said slowly. "I'm going to get some food. Do you want anything?"

He hadn't eaten since morning. "Yeah."

"What?"

Archie's phone rang. "You know what I like," he said. He got out his phone and glanced down at the caller ID. "I have to take this," he said, looking up. But Debbie had already turned and started down the hallway.

He brought the phone to his ear. "Go ahead," he said.

"We found it," Heil said excitedly. "They were right. The opening is small. But we snaked a camera in and it widens up a little once you get in there. Looks like a kid was definitely up there. We found more *Star Wars* figures, bags of dried fruit, a flashlight. No sleeping bag or blankets, though. So maybe he cleared out."

"Take the sleeping bag and leave the *Star Wars* figures," Archie said. "You don't have kids, do you, Heil?"

"No, sir."

So the kid was staying under the bridge during the day. Which begged the question, where did he go at night? Archie knew the answer. Patrick Lifton went back to his captor — just as he had returned to him from the hospital. The boy had been under the kidnapper's control for a year and a half. Children were especially vulnerable to Stockholm syndrome. Giving Patrick room to roam, and always having him come back, was probably part of the killer's whole power trip.

Wherever the kidnapper was staying, it was close enough to the river for the boy to come and go by himself.

"Oh," Heil added, "and we found some more of those keys. Like the one under the hospital bed. Six more so far. All the same size. Look old. All look like they fit different locks."

CHAPTER 37

Archie woke up coughing, stiff and sore in a chair in the ICU waiting room. His feet were on the coffee table next to a half-eaten burrito. He felt clammy and cold. His muscles ached. He remembered Debbie leading him in there to eat and take a nap, but he had no idea how long it had been since then. He checked his watch.

"You've only been asleep an hour," he heard a voice say.

He glanced up and found Anne was sitting in the chair across from him. He didn't know how long she'd been there.

"Henry?" he asked.

"No change," Anne said. "I picked you up some things from the pharmacy downstairs," she added. She lifted a white paper bag off the floor by her purse, set it on the coffee table, and started emptying it, setting each item on the table. "Cough syrup. Cherry lozenges. Decongestant. Tylenol.

Vitamin C."

"Can you write me a prescription for Vicodin?" Archie asked.

She ignored him, her lips pursed with
concern. "You have a fever. Still low-grade.
For now."

"You can tell that by looking?"

"I'm a mother."

"How did you know I'd be here?"

She raised an eyebrow at him, as if it were
obvious.

Archie opened the bottle of Tylenol and
washed down two pills with a swig of cough
syrup.

"Nice," Anne said.

"I have a lot of experience taking pills."

She lifted a hand and gestured vaguely to
the hospital. "How does it feel to be here?"

"In the ICU? It's a walk down memory
lane."

"What room were you in?"

"Ask Debbie. I was unconscious for most
of it. You have a profile for me?"

"I didn't just come to bring you cough
syrup." She waved a notebook. "I have some
idle thoughts and observations."

Archie had learned a long time ago that
Anne's idle thoughts and observations were
more reliable than most people's academic
dissertations.

He sat up.

She didn't open her notebook. She didn't have to. "The killer watches them die," she said matter-of-factly. "Immobilized, powerless. No threat. The killer has all the power. This is a person who wants the victim to know what's happened to them, wants them to know what he's done. Wants them to experience death."

"Why an octopus?" Archie asked.

"Why not?" said Anne. "It's worked pretty well so far."

"What kind of people keep aquariums?" Archie asked.

"You mean besides psychopaths and sushi restaurants?" Anne said. She rolled her eyes. "All sorts of people have aquariums, Archie. Many of us find them very soothing." She raised a finger. "Saltwater aquariums, though, take a special enthusiasm. They're high-maintenance. Keeping a cephalopod tank is a whole other level. They've got a life span of two, three years, if you're lucky. You're not going to experience a huge level of emotional attachment. They're not dogs."

"So how does he feel about the kid? Is he another specimen? Something to keep and observe?"

"I think he finds the kid useful." She crossed her boots at the ankles, leaned forward. "I'm interested in the killer's ability to get so close to victims. Even Henry. Even after suspected poisonings. You had warned that street kid specifically about an octopus. This killer blends in, appears trustworthy. In cases like this, we'd consider someone disguised as law enforcement, except that the street kid wouldn't have trusted a cop or someone in a National Guard uniform. A woman. Someone feigning jeopardy. She needs help. The victim goes to her aid, and she pushes the octopus into the victim's hands. It's dark, the person takes the thing reflexively, before they even know what they've got. They're bitten instantly. The poison enters their system. They're disoriented. The killer retrieves the octopus. Watches as the victim dies. Then pushes the victim into the water."

"He's using the kid as bait," Archie said.

Anne nodded. "If so, the child has watched at least four people die. It explains why he left the hospital, why he'd try to find his way back to this person. He'd be entirely dependent. And terrified." She thought for a second. "This person has been in chat rooms, exchanged information with other cephalopod fans online," she said. "And talked the ear off aquarium store clerks. There's a trail. If you can find it."

Chief Eaton poked his head in the room. "The parents are here," he said to Archie. "They want to meet you."

Archie cleared his throat. "Of course," he said. He stood, thinking the parents were downstairs, that he would be following Eaton to find them, but when Eaton opened the door wider Archie saw that Patrick Lifton's parents were right there.

They stood in the doorway, Eaton behind them. They didn't come in. They seemed almost physically wary of Archie. He'd seen that before. Crime victims sometimes associated cops with grief and anxiety. Everything had been fine before the cops had showed up.

"I'm Detective Sheridan," Archie said. He held out a hand and Daniel Lifton took it. He had a firm handshake and he looked Archie in the eye from under the bill of his baseball cap. "We appreciate all you're doing," he said.

"I wish I could do more," Archie said. He extended his hand to Diana Lifton. She wrapped her hand around his, but she didn't shake it. She just held it for a moment. Her palm was smooth and warm.

"How did he seem?" she asked. "When you saw him?"

Archie didn't know how to answer that. It

was dark. And Patrick Lifton had been drowning. How had he seemed? He'd seemed scared and wet and lost.

"He's a fighter," Archie said.

Diana nodded.

"Thank you," Daniel Lifton said.

Why weren't they livid? Why hadn't they gotten in Archie's face and demanded how he'd had their lost child only to let him walk off alone into the night?

"Okay," Chief Eaton said to the parents. "Let's go." He looked at Archie. "I'll give you a few minutes to prepare yourself," he said.

The door closed, and Archie and Anne were alone.

"I'm not okay," he said before she could ask.

"I didn't think you were," she said.

They were waiting for him. It was time to parade the parents in front of the TV cameras. Archie's eyes settled on Anne's purse. "Press conference," he said. "Do you have enough tools in there to make me look human?"

"Honey," she said, "I've been waiting to brush your hair since we met."

CHAPTER 38

This is how you kill someone, he thought.

You let them experience it slowly. By natural means. You let them move through terror to understanding. He liked to step back and watch their eyes as they felt the poison's first effects. They all panicked. Stumbled. Fell. Struggled. It was the human condition to fight. To rage against the dying of the light. Just as it was in our nature to let go. The body knew when to give up the ghost. The brain released endorphins. Pain vanished.

He watched their chests rise and fall, slower, slower.

Peaceful at the end.

Their eyes smiling.

And through it all, they were silent as mice.

It was a lot like drowning.

The Willamette had been killing people, one way or another, for a long time. Toxic pollution, heavy metals, PCBs, dioxin, poly-cyclic aromatic hydrocarbons. Industrial and urban waste; agricultural runoff. A six-mile stretch of the river through Portland was considered a Superfund site. The river violated temperature, bacteria, and mercury standards. You couldn't eat most of the fish.

It was a lovely sight, to see her rise up. He had waited a long time for it.

He was patient. They had been standing there for almost an hour, his steel-and-nylon-mesh-gloved hand on the boy's shoulder, both their backs up against the brick wall of the empty fire station.

The boy was entirely cloaked in rain gear — rain pants, hooded slicker, rain boots. All dark colors. The coat was too big and the cuffs hung over his hands. The hood fell over his forehead and obliterated his profile.

The man wore green waist-high rubber waders under a light jacket, and a black baseball cap.

They were dressed for the weather.

He had let two National Guard soldiers pass by. They had trotted down the espla-nade. One carried a long pole, one looked to be on patrol. They couldn't see him or the boy. People didn't see things they weren't looking for.

Water sloshed at the man's boots. The

world had never been louder. The throb of helicopter blades in the sky above the city; the thunder of the brimming, surging river; the static of rain hitting standing water. The noise seemed to be building to a fever pitch.

The man looked down at the boy to see if he could hear it, but the boy didn't look up. The boy was very quiet. Some days he didn't say a word.

Movement caught the man's eye and he glanced up at the esplanade and saw another National Guard soldier loping in their direction. The soldier's hat was pulled low. He was on his way somewhere, head down.

The man pushed the boy forward with his heavy-gloved hand.

"Can you help my son?" the man called.

The boy stumbled, the weight of the bucket throwing him off balance.

The soldier stopped and looked up. He was still a good thirty feet away.

The man waved.

The soldier grinned and waved back.

He came over to them in a slow jog. When he got within a few feet he stopped, put his hands on his thighs, and bent down so that he was eye-level with the boy. "What's the problem, kiddo?" he asked.

The boy didn't answer.

The man nodded at the bucket. "He

found this on the sidewalk," he said. "We think it's hurt."

"What is it, buddy?" the soldier said.

"Show him," the man said.

The boy made a sound. Somehow it bubbled up above the roar of rotors and river. One word. Clear as day.

"Run."

The man grabbed the bucket from the boy, lifted it, and heaved its contents at the soldier.

The water slopped against the soldier's face and chest. He cried out in surprise. Then looked at the ground, his face knitted with confusion.

The man was breathing hard, his heart pounding in his chest. The blue-ring lay at the boy's feet, a soft yellow ball of flesh, its neon rings a bright pulsing blue. He scooped it up in his glove and lowered it gently into the bucket. If they got it back in its tank soon, it might live.

The soldier hadn't moved.

That was a good sign.

The man looked over at him. The soldier lifted his hand to his cheek, brought it back down, and looked at it. The man could see a small red mark forming. But the injection point was tiny. There wasn't any blood.

The soldier fell to his knees, facing the

boy. He looked surprised.

"You," he said.

The word hung in the air for a moment before the soldier fumbled for his radio, dropped it, and collapsed.

This time, there wasn't time to watch.

The man picked up the bucket and put a gloved hand back on the boy's shoulder. "That's how you kill someone," he said.

CHAPTER 39

The press conference was at the hospital. It was a compromise. The press had descended on Emanuel after they'd learned that Henry had been poisoned. The hospital had responded by bringing in extra security to keep them out. This way, the press would get their hospital shots.

The public information officer was at the mike giving flood updates, with Robbins, the mayor, the chief, and Archie standing behind him. Patrick Lifton's parents sat holding hands in the front row.

Apparently the media had gotten the press release. There were a hundred chairs in there, and it was still standing room only.

Archie had been met with a barrage of questions when he'd entered the room.

"Have you seen Gretchen lately?"

"How are you feeling?"

"Should she get the death penalty this time?"

They were always the same.

The PIO continued. The number of sandbags that had been filled. The number of volunteers who'd participated. The press dutifully took notes.

Then it was the mayor's turn. He gave the no-need-to-worry-everything-is-under-control speech. The seawall was holding. The city had a crack task force headed up by Archie Sheridan on the trail of the killer. They had some good suspects. (*Now, that would be news,* thought Archie.) It would all be resolved shortly.

He didn't take questions.

Chief Eaton stepped up. He had to adjust the mike down a foot. The lights in the room dimmed, the chief clicked a remote in his hand, and a projected image appeared on a screen behind him, above Archie's head.

"This is a blue-ringed octopus," Eaton said matter-of-factly. "They are currently recognized as one of the world's most venomous animals. They can be recognized by their characteristic blue and black rings and yellowish skin. They hunt small crabs, hermit crabs, and shrimp, and may bite attackers, including humans if provoked." Archie knew the material — it was the exact wording from the Wikipedia page. "Our medical examiner has discovered a toxin from this animal in the bodies of four people recently believed to have drowned in the Willamette. Dennis Keller. Stephanie Towner. Zak Korber. And Megan Parr. It was also the toxin that was used to poison Detective Henry Sobol, who remains in critical condition upstairs."

The hands were already up. Twenty, thirty. Everyone straining to be highest.

"We believe that someone is using the octopus as a weapon," Eaton continued. "These are saltwater creatures which require a very specific habitat to survive. They cannot live in our waters." A few of the hands went down. "The person we are looking for is someone with an interest in aquariums. He or she has at least one saltwater tank."

Eaton took a breath and glanced back at Archie. Archie gave him a nod.

The chief turned back to the microphone. "The suspect is also a person of interest in a missing persons case." He hit a button on the remote and the image above Archie's head changed. Archie saw the boy's parents flinch and their grip on each other tighten. The room got louder. "Patrick Lifton," the chief said, quieting the press with a hand. "Age nine. He went missing from Aberdeen, Washington, a year and a half ago. We believe that this is the boy that Detective Sheridan rescued from the river last night." He paused. "As you know, the boy went missing from Emanuel Hospital several hours after that."

Archie wondered how that was going to play in the media.

Eaton must have wondered, too. Because this was when he decided to turn things over to Archie.

Archie stepped forward, adjusted the microphone, and looked out at the crowd. Fifty flashbulbs went off. Archie cleared his throat. He had prepared remarks. They were on index cards in his pockets. But he was having second thoughts. This guy wanted control. It's what fed him.

Someone needed to challenge that. Archie needed to fight him for the boy.

"Patrick Lifton is alive," Archie said into the mike. "He is either wandering the streets or he is in the custody of the serial killer who stole him from his parents. Either way, I will find him." Archie looked directly at the boy's parents sitting in the front row. "I. Will. Find. Him." He looked back up at the crowd, and this time addressed the row of TV cameras. "Patrick Lifton is going home."

Archie sighed. His head hurt.

"Any questions?"

CHAPTER 40

Susan had to stand at the back of the hospital conference room during the press conference. Archie had taken questions for twenty minutes. She had kept the Patrick Lifton angle off the record, and now Archie and the chief had announced it to the world without so much as a heads-up. She was a little bitter about that before she remembered that her problems were petty compared to Patrick Lifton's. The mood in the room was grim, but once the press conference ended, it was Armageddon as everyone scrambled to get stories in. Susan managed to get a chair in the chaos. She was sitting cross-legged on it, with her laptop on her knees, typing up a stringer piece on the press conference for the *Times,* when she smelled Stetson.

"Oh," she said, as Derek took a seat on one of the plastic folding chairs next to her. "That's good. You're alive."

"You finally noticed," he said. He worked his jaw a little. "Saw the online piece for the *Times.*"

"Yeah," Susan said. She gestured to the press badge on the lanyard around her neck. "I'm covering the press conference," she said.

Derek examined the badge. "You totally printed that out on your computer," he said.

She pulled it away from him. "They haven't sent me a stringer badge yet."

"Ian's pissed," Derek said. "You should have come to us."

"Ian fired me," Susan said. She finished typing the sentence she was writing and clicked send.

"I have to go," she said, snapping her laptop shut. She lifted her chin at Archie and Robbins, who were in conversation near the podium. "I have to talk to my vast array of insider sources."

She left Derek and made a beeline for the front of the room, which required a lot of dodging and weaving. She tripped on one laptop cord, stepped on three feet, and beaned a kneeling KGW cameraman with her elbow. Archie and Robbins were leaning up against the wall. They stopped talking when they saw her. People did that a lot.

"Any news on Ralph?" she asked Robbins.

He squinted at her. "I really only understand about twenty percent of what you say."

"The Vanport skeleton," Archie said.

Robbins blinked. "Since when have we
decided he had anything to do with Vanport?"

"Timing's right," Susan said. "Location's
right."

"Give or take ten years and five miles,"
Robbins said. "The age of the bones is an
educated guess. I've been busy with the
fresher bodies. There's a nine-year-old boy
missing, you know. Not sixty years ago.
Right now."

Susan's face burned.

"I got a tip," she said. "From a reader."

Robbins crossed his arms. Archie was silent.

"She gave me a name," Susan said. "Mc-
Bee. Fifteen bodies were recovered after the
Vanport flood. Fourteen more were reported
missing and never found. Elroy McBee. He
was a firefighter with the Vanport Fire
Department. Last seen two hours before the
dike broke. His body was never recovered."

"Is this supposed to matter to me because
I'm black?" Robbins asked.

Susan sputtered for a second. "No." She
dug around in her bag. "Look at this," she
said, holding out the page she'd printed in

Archie's office. "A lot of people wonder why it took so long to sound the alarm when the dike broke? I found this story." She told them the story of W. E. Williams and the stockyards, and searched for a moral that would serve her purpose. "He didn't have to call back. He'd done his part. But he went the extra mile."

"Her source suffers from dementia," Archie said.

Susan slid him a look. "It comes and goes," she said.

"We have more important business right now," Archie said. "This can wait."

They still didn't get it.

"Find out anything about those keys?" Susan asked.

"Flannigan is on it," Archie said. "He showed some pictures to a locksmith, but didn't turn up anything."

"You know how everyone has a tiny talent?" Susan said. "Like parallel parking? Or catching serial killers? Mine is Googling. I am a really excellent Googler." She opened her laptop, hopped on the hospital wi-fi, and opened an eBay page. It was a listing for a key. She flipped it around so they could see.

Archie's mouth opened.

"It's a mailbox key," Susan said. She

glanced around at the screen — and the photograph of a small black key that had three bidders for a total of $4.50. "From Vanport. They salvaged hundreds of them from the mudflats after the flood. People collect them."

Archie looked off, his eyes darting back and forth. He rubbed his face. "When did your column run, on the skeleton?"

"Thursday," she said.

He sighed and turned to Robbins. "The day before the first murder."

"I sent the bones up to Lewis and Clark," Robbins said.

"Get them back," Archie said.

"I was going to go talk to Gloria Larson," Susan said. She widened her eyes innocently at Archie. "Did you want to come?"

CHAPTER 41

"Wipe your feet," Gloria Larson said. She looked regal. Not what Archie had expected at all. For one, she was white.

"This is my friend Archie," Susan said. "He's a police detective. Do you remember me?"

Gloria turned and padded back into her apartment, gesturing for them to follow her. "I'm making tea," she said.

Archie wiped his feet, and Susan took off her rainbow rain boots and left them by the front door.

"Sit," she said from the kitchen, and Archie and Susan took seats on a striped sofa in the apartment's main room. "Chamomile or peppermint?" she asked.

He didn't even like tea. "Chamomile," he said.

"It will help clear your lungs," she said. "I'll add some honey."

He wasn't sure how she knew he was sick.

He hadn't even coughed.

"Peppermint, please," Susan said. "Can I help you?"

"I'm fine, dear," Gloria said.

The TV was on. They were running the clip of Archie at the press conference. "I will find him." Then the screen showed a photograph of Patrick Lifton.

Gloria came around the kitchen bar with two pretty teacups on saucers. She set one in front of Archie and one in front of Susan. "Let it steep," she said.

She went back into the kitchen and prepared her own cup.

Archie looked down at the coffee table. There was a half-eaten Jolly Rancher next to his teacup.

Susan saw it, too. She pried it off the table and put it in her mouth. "That's mine," she said.

Gloria returned, set her tea on an end table, and took a seat in a striped chair across from Archie.

"McBee's first name, what is it, Elroy?" Susan asked.

"Elroy McBee," Gloria said, but Archie couldn't tell if she was confirming it or merely repeating it.

He sat forward a little. "What makes you think the skeleton in the slough is this

307

person McBee?"

"There were three," she said, peering into her teacup. "Only three men who went missing. It was children mostly."

"The other two were black, weren't they?" Susan said. "McBee was white."

Gloria turned and looked at the TV. It was a different photograph of Patrick Lifton now. A snapshot of him with his arms wrapped around a black Labrador retriever.

Gloria looked concerned. "That poor boy. Did he drown?"

"No," Archie said.

"Is he your son?" she asked.

The question startled Archie. "No," he said. "He's missing. We're looking for him."

She was twisting the bottom of her cardigan around her fingers. She stopped and folded her hands in her lap and looked off toward the door, like she was expecting someone.

"Are you all right, Mrs. Larson?" Susan asked.

Gloria looked at Susan and smiled. "I went to watch them float the Fremont Bridge in yesterday," she said. "We packed a lunch and took the children. They floated the whole center piece down the river on a barge and lifted it into place. It was marvelous."

"That was in 1973," Archie said to Susan.

His phone rang. It was Flannigan. This exercise appeared to be about over anyway. "Excuse me," he said, picking up the call.

"Hey," Archie said to Flannigan. "What's up?"

"It's Carter," Flannigan said. "That National Guard soldier. He's dead."

"Are you married?" Gloria asked him.

Archie plugged his free ear and turned away from her. Carter? Dead? They had just seen him, hadn't they? "What happened?" he asked Flannigan.

Flannigan sighed. "He wasn't responding to his radio, so they went looking for him. Found him facedown near the fire station on the east bank. There's a mark. But not on his hands. It's on his face."

Archie should have closed down the waterfront. Screw the seawall. He should have gotten everyone out of there. Let the whole city flood. It was just property. "I'll be right down," Archie said.

He hung up.

Susan had paled. "What's going on?"

"I will find him," Archie said on the TV. *"I. Will. Find. Him."*

They had taken separate cars.

"Carter's dead," Archie said. "You should go home."

Susan's brow knitted. She swallowed hard. "I have work to do," she said. "I need more quotes. I have to fact-check."

Archie caught her gaze. "Stay away from the river, okay?"

She nodded.

He stood. "I have to go," he said to Gloria. "Thanks for the tea." He had yet to take a sip.

"Are you?" Gloria asked again. "Married?"

"I'm divorced," Archie said.

"Have you ever had an affair?"

"Only one," Archie said.

Gloria lowered her chin girlishly, her white hair falling around her face. "I've had more than that," she said.

CHAPTER 42

Carter had died trying to radio for help. He was facedown on the concrete, one arm outstretched, his walkie-talkie a few feet away where it had landed as he fell. He had probably watched it for a while as his body shut down. Heard the radio calls. Watched the red light blink steadily.

The river lapped over the bank, sending a current washing over the fire station driveway where Carter lay, and leaving a sticky froth of residual pollution on the pavement. The water had shorted out the walkie-talkie's batteries. It had still been working when they found him. It was what led the Guard soldiers who went looking for him to the body — they had heard the static of the radio. But it was dead, too, now.

Rain tickled the back of Archie's neck. The sky was settling into dusk.

Carter's eyes were open. Just slits. His eyelashes were beaded with water.

Flannigan glanced nervously at the river. "We need to move him out of here," he said. He was the third person to say it since Archie had arrived. The fire station driveway was twenty feet above the river, protected by a steep foliage-covered bank that dropped to the river below. Today there was no bank. The spindly trees that grew at its top swayed and shimmered, one already snapped in half by the current.

The river sounded like thunder. Chopper blades beat overhead. And louder than all of that was the squawk of gulls. They danced at the driveway's edge, taking flight a few feet in the air, but always returning, their eyes on Carter's body.

They were hungry.

"In a minute," Archie said.

He squatted next to Carter and examined the pea-sized red lesion that marked his right cheekbone. The lesion was bigger than the others, but it was also on a more sensitive area. The killer had gotten the others to handle the blue-ring somehow. But not Carter. Carter had the thing thrown at him.

A film of water and foam washed over the pavement, causing the fingers of Carter's outstretched hand to move slightly.

Carter had been found within the same time frame of being poisoned that Henry had been. But Henry was still alive, for now, and Carter wasn't.

Archie glanced around the wet pavement. There was nothing there. Any potential evidence had been lifted and taken by the river. The kid's face was all over the news. Something would turn up. He'd been out in public. At Oaks Park. People had seen him. Someone would spot him now.

"Hey." Robbins stepped up beside Archie, the Tyvek suit he'd put on over the one he'd worn to the press conference already streaked with rain. "We need to move him out of here."

"Okay," Archie said.

Archie's phone rang. He let it ring a few times before he checked the caller ID, but he snapped it to his cheek the second he saw who it was.

"It's me," Claire said. "You need to get to the hospital."

CHAPTER 43

Susan stared at her laptop screen. Now that she had her laptop, she didn't need Archie's computer, so she'd decided to work in the conference room. She could spread out in there, and the chairs were more comfortable. Also, she'd managed to find a leftover burrito in the fridge, which didn't seem to be working anyway.

She'd updated the editor at the *Times* about Carter. They were sending the paper's Northwest Bureau chief down from Seattle. The story was now too big for a stringer, he said.

The cursor in front of her blinked. Crap. She couldn't even figure out how to finish the story she'd pitched. She'd never sweated over thirty column inches so hard in her life.

Heil came in, saw Susan, and stopped.

"You're still here?" he asked.

"You're still here, too," she pointed out.

His forehead creased. "I work here," he said.

Good point. "I'm almost done," she said. He was wearing a jacket. Not the police windbreaker this time — a black jacket that zipped up the front. "Are you going home?" she asked.

"I finally got in touch with some local aquarium supply shop employees." He held up a list. "Aquarium nerds. I've got interviews with five of them."

She saw the bottom address. Division and Twentieth. "That's on my way home," she said. "Want me to do it?"

Heil glanced at the list in his hand. "You can read that from there?"

"You write big, like a girl."

He smirked and pocketed the list. "Go to the Academy," he said. "Work patrol. Make detective. And then call me." He walked to the fridge and opened it. After a few seconds he said, "Did you eat my burrito?"

Susan cringed. The foil was still in front of her. "I didn't know that belonged to anyone," she said.

"It was in a bag with my name on it," Heil said. "Written big. Like a girl."

"Sorry," she said.

"I'll get something while I'm out," Heil said with a sigh. "Something's got to be open." He turned and walked to the door, and then turned back.

"You okay?" he said. "About Carter?"

"Sure," Susan said, turning away so he couldn't see her face. "It's not like I knew him."

Heil left, and she tried to get back to her story, but her mind kept returning to Carter. The *Times* wanted news. A National Guard soldier murdered. But it didn't do him justice.

She opened Safari and went to eBay to check on the key. She wasn't looking for anything in particular. It was just something to do. But as soon as the key appeared on her screen, she unplugged her laptop and went searching for Ngyun.

She found him at his desk typing a message on an octopus fan chat board.

"That key on eBay?" she said, turning her laptop so he could see the screen. "Someone just bid ten dollars for it."

He took her laptop and set it on his desk, and she came around behind his chair and looked over his shoulder.

"Doesn't really mean anything," Ngyun said. "Except he really wants the key."

"Check out the user name," Susan said, pointing at the screen.

Vanport48.

"He's willing to spend ten bucks on an old key," Ngyun said. "I think it's clear he's interested in Vanport."

"Can you find out who it is?" she asked.

"Like contact eBay and have them tell me the guy's real name and contact info?" Ngyun said.

"Exactly," Susan said.

"Nope."

"Really?" Susan said.

"Not without a warrant," Ngyun said. "And reckless financial decisions aren't probable cause."

"I thought the government had access to all our online accounts."

"Homeland Security, maybe," Ngyun said. "Not us. And you're not supposed to know about that."

She saw his eyes flick back to his own monitor.

"Come on," Susan said. "There's something you can do."

Ngyun hesitated. "Okay," he said. "A lot of people have a user name and stick with it for all their accounts. I, for instance, am huggybearxp for almost everything not work-related. This guy probably uses Vanport48 for other things. I can keep an eye out for it. If I see him in any of the cephalopod-related chat rooms, we might have probable cause." He started typing on his keyboard. The noise his fingers made tapping the keys sounded a lot like rain. "I rock at this," he said.

Susan was satisfied.

She took her laptop back to the conference room, plugged it back in, and resumed staring. Carter was dead. And now he just lay there on the page. She had written that he'd been instrumental in the river rescue, that he'd recovered the body of Dennis Keller. But his personality was missing. Then something occurred to her.

After a few minutes of browsing, she had what she needed. "Alex Paul Carter grew up in Pendleton, Oregon, where he was a lifeguard, varsity swimmer, and Boy Scout. He won a gold belt buckle for calf roping at the State 4-H rodeo competition."

She stared at the screen some more.

Then she clicked send, packed up, and headed home.

CHAPTER 44

"There," Claire said. "See?"

Archie had seen it. Henry's eyelids had fluttered. Claire reached for Archie's hand and gave it a squeeze.

Henry had been breathing on his own for almost thirty minutes.

The oxygen mask was gone, and Archie could see Henry's face again. His chin and scalp were prickly where salt-and-pepper hair the color of his mustache had grown out to stubble, but his color was better. His blood pressure was up. He looked like he was alive.

Claire let go of Archie's hand, picked a scab of dried saliva from the corner of Henry's mouth, and flicked it on the floor.

The room seemed weirdly quiet without the sound of the artificial respirator.

The doctors and nurses were in and out at a regular clip. Everyone was smiley.

Henry's eyes fluttered again.

"There," Claire said.

Her face lit up every time it happened.

Henry's neurologist swept into the room for the fourth time in ten minutes. She was Indian and wore her thick black hair in a braid that hung against the back of her white lab coat. She glanced at the monitor.

"He fluttered again," Claire said.

The neurologist smiled. "That's a good sign," she said, and she typed something into Henry's chart and left.

"She doesn't think he'll wake up," Claire said.

"He'll wake up."

Claire rocked her head back and gazed at the ceiling. "I shouldn't have called you," she said. "You shouldn't be here."

"This is important."

She blinked at the ceiling for a long moment and then looked at Archie. "Go," she said. "Try to find that kid."

Archie hesitated.

"Go," Claire said.

Archie stood up. "Call me if anything changes?"

"Yep."

He reached his hand out and laid it on Henry's chest. The cloth of the hospital shirt felt insubstantial. Archie coughed and lifted his hand to his mouth. "Okay," he said.

He turned and made it a few steps.

"Archie?" Claire said.

"Another flutter?"

"No," she said.

He turned. Claire was standing now, both hands over her mouth, eyes shiny with tears.

Henry's eyes were open.

Archie hurried back to the bedside beside Claire.

Henry's lids were heavy, his eyes slits. But they were open.

The neurologist appeared, briskly ushering Claire and Archie toward the foot of the bed.

She whipped an ophthalmoscope out of her lab coat pocket and shone it back and forth between Henry's eyes.

"Henry?" she said in a loud clear voice. "Can you hear me?"

Claire gripped Archie's arm.

Henry squinted at the light. "Yeah," he croaked.

"Oh my God oh my God oh my God," said Claire. She let go of Archie, squeezed around the doctor, and took one of Henry's hands in hers.

Henry gazed up at her and smiled. "Hey, baby," he whispered.

Claire laid her head gently on Henry's chest. Tears streamed from her eyes and her shoulders shook, but the grin on her face was luminous.

"Do you know your last name?" the doctor asked.

"Sobol," Henry rasped.

"Do you know who the president is?"

Henry touched the back of Claire's neck with his hand.

"Gary Hart."

The doctor stiffened.

He coughed. "Kidding."

"I need to talk to him," Archie said.

The doctor raised a hand. "Not now," she said.

"Archie?" Henry said, lifting his head to look around the room.

"Do you remember what happened?" Archie asked.

"He's not going to remember anything," the doctor said. "His brain has been through a terrific trauma."

Henry lifted his hand from Claire's neck and made a beckoning motion at Archie.

Archie inched forward, past the neurologist, and leaned in as close as he could.

Claire didn't move.

A stain from her tears spread on the thin cotton of Henry's hospital gown.

Henry's voice was barely more than a rasp. "White male. Early forties. Rubber waders. He had a kid with him."

CHAPTER 45

The defroster in Susan's Saab didn't work, so she had the windows rolled down to keep the windshield from fogging up. Rain slapped her in the face. She hunched forward over the steering wheel and squinted in an attempt to make out shapes in the darkness ahead.

The traffic lights on Division Street were all out. Some of the streetlights had blown. Even with the porch lights and house lights, it was hard to see the street. Susan slowed as she crossed the railroad tracks. She didn't see any other cars on the road. Apparently everyone was taking this curfew thing pretty seriously.

Her radio was blasting. A DJ broke in with a news update. The serial killer had claimed another victim. Sauvie Island was flooding. The port was flooding. Swan Island was flooding. The Willamette was expected to crest later that night. Susan changed the station.

She didn't realize how deep the water was until she was in it.

It had pooled in the intersection, creating a vast black swamp. The water surged around her tires and she could feel the pressure of it pressing against the car. "Fuck," she said. She put the car in reverse and turned around to back up. But the engine stalled.

Her heart skipped a beat as she turned the ignition key once, twice, three times.

"No," she said. "No, no, no, no."

Not even a sputter.

She sat up a little in her seat and peered over the hood of her car. The headlights were still on, skimming the surface of the water, illuminating the rain. Then they went out.

The radio stopped.

It was dark and still and quiet. And the car started to slide. It happened slowly at first, an almost imperceptible shift, something more like vertigo than actual motion. Then it fishtailed.

Susan didn't have time to react. Not that there was anything she could do. She just held on and braced for impact.

It didn't come.

She unclenched her eyes and looked around.

She was still in the intersection, only now she was facing up Twelfth Avenue. The car had stopped moving. *The car had stopped moving?*

Yes.

She looked out the window. She was still in the water. It was all around her. She tried the handle, half expecting the pressure of the water to pin it closed, but it opened, skimming over the top of the water. She grabbed her purse off the passenger seat and stepped out of the car. The water was maybe five inches deep, above her ankle. She could feel its chill through the rubber of her boots.

She already had her phone out when she turned and saw her car moving again. It floated peacefully for a moment, before scraping along a parked pickup truck and coming to rest nuzzled against it.

Susan dialed 911.

All the operators were busy.

"You're kidding me," Susan said.

They were probably up to their eyeballs with calls. Flooding. Mudslides. Traffic accidents. Citizens concerned about their neighbor's aquarium.

She called Archie. He didn't pick up.

326

She looked up and down Division Street, and then up and down Twelfth Avenue. She didn't see any headlights coming.

At least her car was out of the path of traffic.

She wrote a note on a page from her notebook and tore it out. *My car hit your pickup truck,* read the note. *Sorry.* She added her name and cell number. She waded over to the pickup and tucked it under the windshield wiper. The paper was already wet enough that the ink was bleeding.

She was across the intersection when she realized that her laptop was in the backseat of the car. She decided to leave it. She was twenty-three blocks from home, and she didn't want it getting rained on.

She put her hood up and started walking.

It wasn't that far. They were short blocks. And she remembered that Heil was going to an address around here. She decided to take Division most of the way, and keep an eye out for his car. She had to walk through deep puddles on the sidewalk in places, but she had her rainbow boots on. And it was relatively warm out. That was the bright side — if all this was coming down as snow, Portland might be even more screwed. After a few blocks she'd worked up enough body heat that she had to unzip her raincoat.

A few more blocks after that, she'd had enough.

Her feet hurt. She was getting blisters between her toes. She needed Band-Aids. Her jeans were soaked.

She lit a cigarette and called Archie again. Once again, his voice mail picked up after one ring. It was making her a little mad. "It's me," she said. "Susan. Again." She didn't know what he could do, just that he could do something. Call a tow truck or something. Get her a ride. Then she saw the mint-green Nissan Cube.

She searched out a street address off a nearby house. The two thousand block of Division.

"Never mind," she said to Archie's voice mail. "I see Heil." And she hung up.

It had to be Heil's car. How many mint-green Nissan Cubes had been sold nation-wide? Five? Six, maybe?

He was parked in front of a weird little boxy house with a steeply pitched roof. The houses on either side looked pretty similar. The house number was 2051. It seemed familiar. She thought she remembered that being the first address from his list.

Curb space was plentiful, so Heil probably would have parked right out front.

It had to be the house.

Susan stood in the rain, suddenly filled with uncertainty. Rain pelted her coat. She'd call him. She'd call and tell him she was outside, explain what had happened, and ask for a ride.

She looked up his number in her contact list and clicked on it. It rang. He didn't pick up.

He was probably interviewing the aquarium nerd and didn't want to be interrupted.

She stood there some more. She could feel strips of wet hair sealing to the sides of her face.

She took a drag off the cigarette.

It was just a ride. She'd talk to him, and then she'd wait on the porch.

She hurried up the walk, took the four steps up the stoop in one leap, and rang the doorbell before she lost her nerve. At the last moment she remembered to put out the cigarette.

A man answered the door. He had dark hair. Maybe in his forties. Archie's age. He didn't look like him, though. He was round in all the places Archie was angular. Not fat, just a little soft. But he was taller than Archie. He loomed.

Susan looked up and smiled. "Is Detective Heil here?" she asked.

"Come on in," he said. "He's right here."

She only blanched for a second. Heil was inside. Plus the guy had a kid. She could see *Star Wars* toys on the living room carpet behind him.

He held the door open for her.

She thanked him as she stepped inside.

CHAPTER 46

Susan didn't notice the man's army-green chest-high rubber waders until she got inside. They were held up by black suspenders over a golf shirt. The boots were beaded with water up to the knees. A trail of wet footprints led down the carpeted hall behind him.

"Basement's flooded," he explained.

Susan didn't move from just inside the door. "That sucks," she said.

Rain smacked against the front window. It sounded like water boiling.

The living room was small but organized. Paperbacks were lined up perfectly on the bookshelf. The CDs were housed in wicker CD towers. He had a gray leather couch, and one of those rattan half-shell chairs a lot of people bought in the seventies and which had been populating thrift stores ever since. There was a deck of Uno cards on the glass coffee table. Besides the *Star Wars* figures, it was the only other sign of a kid in the room.

She didn't see Heil.

The man stooped and started gathering up the action figures. "I think the storm runoff put pressure on the water main," he said. "Your friend's downstairs. He was helping me move a few things."

Susan's shoulders relaxed a little.

He dropped the action figures in a shoe box and put the shoe box on the coffee table next to the Uno deck. "You can come in," he said. "Take a seat. I'll give him a shout."

She started to take off her boots.

"Don't worry about it," he said. "I've already tracked muck all over the rug. I have to get a steam cleaner in here anyway. Can I take your coat?"

"Um, sure," Susan said. She could feel rivulets of water running down her neck and between her breasts. She peeled off the wet vinyl slicker and held it out, and he hung it on a hanger in a closet by the door. Susan caught a glimpse of the black jacket Heil had been wearing on the hanger next to it.

"You're drenched," he said. "Hold on, I'll get you a towel."

She stood dripping on the mat while he disappeared down the hall, presumably to the bathroom.

She was chilled now that she was inside. Her black jeans stuck to her skin, gathering too tightly in all the crevices. When she got home, she was taking a bubble bath.

A door creaked open. There followed the sound of shuffling downstairs, and then a muffled voice. Good. He was telling Heil she was here. He'd be up in a minute, and they could go. If he wanted to be a Good Samaritan he could come back after he took her home.

She looked around the room some more. He had a framed Wyland poster above the couch — a glowing moon rising over a pod of orcas. There was a shooting star in the purple and pink sky. White cursive script ran across the poster below the image.

Susan inched forward to read it. It was a quote from the artist.

THE SEA IS FILLED WITH LIGHT AND CONSCIOUSNESS.

Gag me, she thought.

"Here you go," the man said, tossing her a thick magenta towel.

She caught it and dried her face, and then squeezed a tablespoon of water from her hair. "Thanks," she said. She looked behind him, but he was alone. "Did you tell Heil I was here?"

"He'll be right up," the man said. "Have a seat."

Susan rubbed the towel along her legs, patted down her neck, wrung her hair out again, and then lifted her sweater up, slipped the towel underneath, and, as delicately as she could, blotted her chest and underarms. "Excuse me," she said. Then she folded the damp towel, set it on the couch, and perched carefully on it. The couch wasn't real leather anyway.

He sat in the rattan chair. His waders squeaked. "Shouldn't be long," he said.

She looked around some more. The whale print was the only marine-related thing in the room. He didn't seem like much of an aquarium nerd to her.

"So you're into fish?" she said.

"I have a few aquariums. They're all in the basement. That's what your friend was helping me with. They're running on emergency power now, but the generators won't last, and once the systems shut down I'm going to have a lot of dead fish on my hands."

It was suddenly making sense. Heil was the kind of guy who'd get suckered into some sort of massive goldfish airlift. The man probably had Heil doing all the heavy lifting.

The man. She still didn't know his name.

She held a hand out and smiled. "I'm Susan Ward," she said.

He leaned forward and shook her hand. "Nice to meet you," he said.

Then he glanced toward the basement. "I should get back down there," he said. "There's a lot to do."

"I'll come with you and say hello to Heil," she said.

He looked at her boots. "It's deep," he said.

She ran her hand over her hair — it felt like seaweed. "I don't think I can get any wetter."

She followed him to the basement door. There was a big industrial flashlight on the carpet and he picked it up, turned it on, and pointed it down the steep, skinny wooden stairs. "I had to throw the breaker," he said. "Most flood-related deaths are due to electrocution."

But it wasn't dark, exactly. She could see light reflecting on the water.

"I've got those IKEA push lights," he said. "Battery-operated. You just stick them right on the wall."

"Heil?" Susan called.

"He's in the aquarium room," the man said.

"The what?"

"It's the old root cellar. I'll show you."

She could already taste the sourness of old concrete and laundry detergent in her mouth.

She should have just walked home.

"You go first," Susan said.

"Sure," he said. They both had to turn sideways for him to get by her and for a moment they were face-to-face, or rather face-to-bottom-of-chin. Then he pressed against the wall and slipped past her.

When he got to the bottom of the stairs, he shone the flashlight back for her to follow. The water came up to just below his knees.

Susan took each stair carefully, one hand on the rough concrete wall, one hand on the splintered wooden railing. "Have you called someone?" she asked.

"Half the basements in town are flooded," he said. "They say it might be four days."

She got to the bottom, to the water's edge. The stairs led to a large unfinished room with a washer and dryer in the corner next to a stained utility sink. Two round lights the size of salad plates were affixed to two of the walls, providing about as much light as you'd find in a bar bathroom. Just enough to do your business, but not enough to see anything that might trouble you.

The man turned off the flashlight, but didn't put it down. There was nowhere to put it. The water was opaque and bobbed with basement flotsam — a box of dryer sheets, a Christmas ornament, a soccer ball.

Susan dipped the toe of her boot in the water and felt for the edge of the step. Then another, and another. Until she was standing on the basement floor. When she took the last step she heard a sucking sound, and cold water rushed into the tops of her boots, filling them.

"I want to see Heil," Susan said. Her feet felt heavy and cold. She had to drag them to take a step.

"He's in here," the man said, wading to a far door. The door was the newest thing in the room.

"I told him I could handle it," the man continued. "But he said he wouldn't leave until he'd saved the queen angel. They're expensive. Five, six hundred."

"Dollars?" Susan said, trudging after him.

"Sure. Your friend recognized her right away. Apparently he's a bit of an aquarium enthusiast himself."

He opened the door and Susan was engulfed in tranquil blue light.

She heard Heil shout her name from

somewhere inside the room. But she didn't have time to respond. All at once she was stumbling, her center of gravity gone, her feet out from under her. She didn't know why at first. Then she realized that she'd been pushed from behind. She couldn't recover from it — she fell forward, belly-flopping into the water with a splash. It was disgusting. She got water in her mouth. In her eyes. In her hair. She flipped over and sat up, the water to her armpits, and looked accusingly at the door. It was closed. He'd pushed her in and closed the door behind her.

"Asshole," she said struggling to get up.

"Susan," she heard Heil say again. She looked over and saw him now, standing in the water in front of a wall of ghostly blue tanks. He glanced at the water, his face tense. He was perfectly still. "Don't move," he said.

CHAPTER 47

So this was the aquarium room. There were tanks on all four walls, lined up side by side on floor-to-ceiling shelves. There were at least fifty of them. They were the room's sole illumination, a Caribbean blue filtered through gels. Some of the tanks were lit with black lights, creating a dizzying array of incandescent fish and coral. Pink. Blue. Purple. Susan's hair had been all those shades.

Heil's voice was smooth and firm, each word carefully enunciated. The black light made his eyes and teeth a dazzling unnatural white. "Now stand up, very, very slowly."

"What. The. Fuck?" Susan said.

She followed his gaze to a wall of aquariums. All four of the room's walls were lined with shelves of aquariums. But the aquariums on this wall were empty.

"There are seven of those tanks," Heil

said. "Each one had a blue-ring in it."

It took her a second to understand.

They were in the water. She was sitting in it up to her chest.

She made a strangled cat sound and started to get up.

"Stop," Heil said quickly.

His urgency froze her in her tracks.

"Listen to me," he said. "They're not aggressive. They'll only bite if you brush up against them. You just need to stand up slowly. Don't slosh."

Susan's mouth felt dry. How did you stand up from a seated position without sloshing? She was on her butt. Her hands were on the floor behind her. Her legs were out in front, bent at the knee. If she stood up, she'd have to move through the water. She'd touch one of those things and it would bite her and she'd suffocate and her heart would stop. She was just going to stay where she was. She would sit there in the water and wait for someone to come get them out of there.

"Stand up, Susan," Heil said.

She didn't move. "Why can't I stay like this?"

"Because they're swimming around in here, and your odds of getting in one's way are directly related to the surface area you

340

have in the water."

An excellent observation.

"I thought they couldn't survive in this kind of water," Susan said.

"They can live briefly in it," Heil said. He rubbed his forehead. "I don't know."

"Okay," Susan said.

But she still couldn't move.

"Are you going to stand up?" he asked.

"Yes."

"Okay."

She wondered if her teeth looked like that.

"Give me a minute," she said.

She looked down toward her right hand and began to incrementally lift it to the surface of the water. Every cell in her arm hummed with electrical current, ready to react at the slightest contact with solid matter. When her hand broke the surface and eased out of the water, it was like Susan had never seen her hand before. It looked incredible and marvelous. A hand!

"What are you doing here?" Heil asked.

"My engine stalled," Susan said.

She moved on to the other hand now. "I was walking home and I saw your car." Measured, steady breaths. "I wanted a ride." Finally, she had both hands up above the waterline. Now all she had to do was get to her feet. She inhaled deeply, mentally anchored her feet to the floor, and lunged slowly forward.

It didn't work.

She couldn't get the leverage without her hands.

"Use your stomach muscles," Heil said.

She was going to die because she didn't have rock-hard abs.

Then she saw a dimple in the water, just a few feet away from her knees. Heil saw it, too. She heard his intake of breath. The adrenaline was enough to power her forward and up on her feet. She didn't do it slowly. Water streamed down her body and rippled outward all around her. She hugged her arms and waited for something to bump against her leg. The water settled.

Susan's panting slowed.

She looked over at Heil. "So I guess he's the guy you've been looking for?"

He swallowed hard. "Yeah."

"Is help on the way?"

He didn't answer.

Surely he'd called for backup. "Is it?" she said.

He looked her in the eye. She'd never seen his face so serious. "My phone doesn't work down here."

She let that sink in. Okay. That was bad. But they still had options. She had a phone.

A smartphone. If she couldn't get anyone on the horn at 911, at least she should update her Facebook status. *Susan Ward is: being menaced by octopuses and wants her friends to save her.* "I'll try mine," she said. The realization hit her as soon as the words left her mouth. "Oh, no."

"What?"

She could see it sitting at the foot of the fake leather sofa. "I left my purse upstairs."

"I thought you never put your purse down," Heil said.

"Shut up."

She looked up at the ceiling and cupped her hands around her mouth. "Hey!" she shouted at the top of her lungs. "Someone help us! We're down here! Hey!"

"I think it's soundproof," Heil said softly.

She squinted. He was right. There was some sort of thick padding on the walls and ceiling, held in place by a metal grid. She felt the prickly sensation of panic under her skin.

"I've tried," he said.

Why would someone soundproof a room full of aquariums?

Then she realized: "He kept the kid down here," she said.

"There's a folded-up cot over there," Heil said, lifting his chin toward a wall of electric-

343

blue tanks.

The toys upstairs. The deck of cards. She was shaking. She couldn't stop herself. "So where's the boy now?" Susan said.

"I don't know," Heil said.

"I called Archie," Susan said. "I left him a message. I told him that my car broke down and I saw you." She looked down at the cold water. The light from the aquariums reflected off the surface, giving it a turquoise sheen. *Don't move,* she told herself. *Just don't move.* "He'll come for us," she said.

CHAPTER 48

It was hard not to move. Susan's leg was cramping up. She couldn't stop shivering. How long had it been? Fifteen minutes, twenty? Her feet ached from the cold, from standing in flat rubber boots on concrete.

She should have stayed with the car. You were supposed to stay with the car. Everyone knew that.

Where was Archie?

"My leg hurts," Susan said.

The blue glow all around them was not tranquil anymore. It made her head hurt. The black lights made everything look radioactive.

Heil was scanning the water. She noticed that he had a pattern, like he was tracing the spokes of a wheel. She hardly knew anything about him. Now she felt bad about that. She should have shown an interest.

He took his gun out of his shoulder holster and leveled it at the water in front of him.

"What are you doing?" Susan asked.

"I'm going to try to get to the door," Heil said. "And if I see one of those things, I'm going to shoot it."

Susan looked around at all the glass and concrete. Wouldn't a bullet ricochet in there?

"Why don't we wait?" she said.

"I'm going to try to get to the door," he said again. He swallowed hard and slid one foot forward an inch, eyes trained on the water along with his gun.

He was going to get himself killed. They should wait for Archie. He was on his way.

Heil inched his other foot closer to her, to the door.

"Keep talking to me," he said.

She couldn't think of anything to say. "Do you like fish?"

"I used to."

"What kind?"

He tilted his head at the north wall of aquariums. "See those weird silver fish that are shaped like little axes?" he said.

Susan scanned the tanks until she saw a dozen shiny silver fish with flat tops and large beer bellies. "The ones zipping around the top of their tank?" she said.

"They're hatchetfish," Heil said. "Good, dependable aquarium fish. They're social.

They like to hang out. Jump around. They'll jump right out of the tank if you don't keep a lid on it. They live longer if they have friends. So you want to keep a school of at least six."

He was only a few feet away from her now, halfway to the door.

The water rippled between them. "Did you see that?" Susan said.

He leveled his gun at it. "Yes."

"I think you should stand still." She felt something move past her leg and she yelped.

"What?" Heil said, alarmed.

Susan lip started to quiver. "I think something bumped me."

"Where?"

"On the knee," she whimpered. Had she been bitten? She couldn't tell. "Does it hurt, when they bite?" she asked.

"I don't think so," Heil said.

She was breathing too fast. Hyperventilating. "I can't catch my breath," she said. She bent over, gripped her thighs with her palms, and tried to think of something besides dying. Song lyrics. Think of song lyrics. *Load up on guns / bring your friends / it's fun to lose and to pretend.*

She could feel her breathing slowing back down to normal. She was okay. "I'm okay," she said. "I'm okay."

Heil didn't answer.

She stood up. "Heil?"

He was studying his hand.

"What is it?" she said.

He looked over at her with a perplexed expression on his face. "My hand feels numb."

Then he turned his head, leaned over, and vomited into the water. The vomit swirled and then sank, leaving an acidic tang in the air.

"I think I need to go to the bathroom," Heil said. "I . . ." He took a couple of sharp, short breaths. "I can't feel my hands."

"It's okay," Susan said. She worked to keep her expression calm. It took every ounce of her willpower not to burst into tears. "You need to come to me. Before you fall."

He looked up at her. The gun fell from his hand with a plunk into the water.

Susan held her arms out to him as if he were a child. "Come to me," she said.

Heil was looking at the spot in the water where the gun had dropped.

"Leave it," Susan said. "You don't need it."

He turned his neon-white eyes up toward her and stumbled forward.

She caught him under the armpits as he

fell, so that his face was pressed into the front of her shoulder.

"We'll be okay," she said. "We'll be okay."

He was too heavy. She couldn't hold him like this; he was already slipping from her grasp. She lowered him into the water on his knees and cradled his head against her hip with both hands.

"I know you can hear me," she said.

CHAPTER 49

The hatchetfish swam happily in their tank, their silver bodies shimmering like coins.

Heil had not taken a breath in a long time.

Susan still hung on to him.

"You're okay," she kept saying. "You're okay."

She hadn't seen any more ripples in the water. But she'd stopped looking. She didn't want to know. If she didn't see them, then they weren't there.

The hatchetfish seemed so content, not a care in the world. She hated them.

Heil sank an inch lower and she repositioned him. Her whole body was stiff. Her feet ached. She was standing in knee-high water, wet and cold and shivering. But she was not going to let him go.

She heard someone at the other side of the door. She didn't know if it was the killer or a rescuer, and she didn't care. "Hello?" she cried. "I need help! Please! Let us out of here!"

The door swung open.

Susan's heart sank. The man was back. He still wore the waders, but now he had added a coat, like he was going somewhere. He stood in the doorway for a moment, the aquariums bathing him in blue light.

"I need you to help me," he said to Susan.

Susan turned away from the door and hugged Heil tighter. "I'm not leaving him."

The man tromped through the water over to her and put a hand on the back of Heil's neck. Then he checked under his jaw for a pulse.

"He's dead," the man said.

Susan could feel tears slipping down her cheeks.

The man looked at the water. "They're still alive," he said. "If they were dead they'd be floating."

That's why he was here, Susan realized. The blue-rings were going to die soon. With them gone, she might have gotten out of there. She would have had a chance.

The man pulled Heil out of her arms and pushed him into the water. Susan could barely breathe.

He yanked Susan's arms behind her back and tied her wrists together with some sort of twine while she watched Heil sink below the water's surface.

"I'm going to pick you up," the man said.

One of the hatchetfish flung itself against the lid of its tank.

Susan's whole body was trembling.

He scooped her up, carrying her as if she were an infant. She sobbed, relieved to be out of the water, terrified to be in his arms. He hauled her out of the aquarium room and through the laundry room to the bottom of the stairs, where Patrick Lifton sat just above the waterline gripping a *Star Wars* figure between his hands.

"Patrick?" Susan said.

The boy scurried up a few steps to make room, and the man set her down on her feet a few steps below.

Susan wiped the tears and snot from her face. "Everyone's looking for you, Patrick. Your parents miss you."

The boy's eyes darted to the man and then back at Susan.

"Let's go," the man said, and he gave Susan a push. The boy sprang up and took the steps two at a time. Susan trudged behind him. When they got to the kitchen the man told the boy to get his coat and the boy left the room.

The man was going to kill her. Susan knew it. He was going to take her somewhere and kill her and they would never find the body.

"What's your name?" she asked him.

His eyes were small and he blinked at her for a moment. "Roy," he said.

She nodded. Now she was certain. She was going to die. He wouldn't have told her his name if he'd planned on letting her live.

The boy returned, wearing an oversized black raincoat.

"Can I have a glass of water?" he asked the man.

It was the first sentence Susan had heard him speak.

"Hurry," Roy said.

The boy went to the sink and got a glass from a dish drying rack on the counter, filled it with tap water, and drank a few sips. Then he poured the rest down the drain and set the glass on the counter in front of him.

"Come on," Roy said. He opened the back door, cursed at the rain, and put up his hood. Then he put his hand on the back of Susan's neck and led her outside, behind the house, into the night. There was an unattached garage back there, and a car parked in the driveway in front of it. A sedan. Dark-colored. Nondescript. Even looking right at it, Susan couldn't have described it.

The rain hissed all around them.

"Where are we going?" Susan asked. Raindrops pelted her bare head and stung her hands.

"To get supplies."

Roy opened the back door and shoved her, shivering, in the backseat. The boy got in after her, and she slid over to the other side to make room, leaving a damp stain in her wake. She noticed he didn't have the *Star Wars* figure anymore.

Roy got in the front seat and fingered a switch, and the chrome lock on Susan's door snapped down with a deadening finality.

As they pulled out onto Division, Susan saw the blue and red glow of police lights straight ahead at a distant intersection.

They had found her car.

CHAPTER 50

Archie hunched against the weather. The patrol cop who'd found Susan's car was closing off the intersection, setting up reflective saw horses so other drivers wouldn't make the same mistake that Susan had. The pool of standing water was a vast glassy black and deeper than it looked. The raindrops exploded as they hit it, making the water look almost like it was simmering.

Archie had checked the abandoned vehicle report after he'd gotten Susan's messages. Her Saab, which had drifted into the middle of Twelfth Avenue, had just been called in.

So much for the nap that he'd been planning.

The Saab had clearly been knocked around. The driver's-side mirror was missing, and the paint job had been scratched bumper to bumper. Archie looked around for what she'd hit, and spotted a pickup truck with a crumpled fender. He made his way over to it and saw a folded piece of paper under its windshield wiper. She'd left a note.

He leaned over the hood, lifted the wiper blade up, and peeled the sopping paper from the wet glass. He recognized the size of the lined paper as a page from Susan's notebook. The ink had bled, but he could still make out the gist of what she'd written.

He folded the note in half, put it back under the wiper where she'd left it, and returned to the Cutlass.

"Anything?" he asked Flannigan when he got in the car.

"Heil's still not picking up. Ngyun hasn't heard from him since he left the office."

"She said she was going to walk," Archie said.

Flannigan held up his notebook, showing a page covered in a hurried scribble.

"What's that?" Archie asked.

"It's the list of addresses Heil was tracking down. Ngyun found them in the MapQuest history on Heil's computer."

Archie took the notebook and tried to make out the words. It looked like it was in another language.

"There are two in this neighborhood," Flannigan said. "One in Ladd's Addition, and one at Twentieth and Division."

Archie looked out the rain-streaked window. The world was a dark and blurry place.

Division would have been on Susan's way home.

He could tell that Flannigan was thinking the same thing.

"Let's go," Archie said.

He backed down Twelfth and took side streets around to Division, avoiding the flooded intersection.

Division was a two-lane street, but it was an arterial and usually busy. Not tonight. Archie only saw one other set of headlights as they made their way east, passing under dark traffic lights and past closed bars. The commercial buildings quickly gave way to the residential ones, with small bungalows on one side and older, larger houses on the other.

Water gushed along the curbside.

"There," Flannigan said.

Archie saw it, too. Heil's car.

Flannigan glanced down at his notes and then squinted at the house numbers. "He's parked right in front of the house," he said.

Archie turned the wheel and pulled into the driveway, sending a spray of water up from the gutter.

The house was simple and compact. One-story. No frills. The living room light was on, but the curtains were drawn.

It had been over an hour since Susan had left her second voice mail. If she had stumbled upon Heil and everything was fine, they wouldn't still be here.

Archie and Flannigan got out of the car and walked up to the front door. Archie bent down and picked up a mushy cigarette butt from the concrete stoop. It had berry lipstick around the filter.

He rang the doorbell.

They waited.

No one answered.

The rain flowing through the house's gutters sounded like a waterfall.

Flannigan banged on the door with the side of his fist.

"Look around back," Archie said.

Flannigan jogged off across the muddy yard and disappeared around the side of the house.

Archie tried the doorknob. It was unlocked. No one in Portland locked their doors. It was one of the reasons the city had such a high burglary rate.

He opened the door. "Police," he said. "Anyone home?"

Archie listened. All he could hear was the sound of the overwhelmed gutters and the rain sweeping against the windows.

A trail of wet footprints led away from the door and across the carpet. "Hello?" he said. He took a small step inside, just onto the mat, and looked around.

He unsnapped his holster and put his hand on his gun. His eyes immediately fell on Susan's purse sitting by the sofa.

His shoulders tensed. "Susan?" he called. "Heil?"

Archie drew his gun. "This is the police," he said again. "I'm coming in." He moved slowly into the house and made his way to the kitchen, following the footprints.

Flannigan met him at the back door. "Car's gone," he said. "There's a garage out back."

"Susan's purse is in the living room," Archie said. The footprints ended at the basement door. "Call for backup. I'm going down there." He swung the basement door open and saw the brown water below. "Shit," he said.

"This is the police," Archie yelled. "I'm coming down the stairs."

He drew his weapon and took the stairs sideways with his gun held at a forty-degree angle. The flooded room at the bottom of the stairs was empty, but there was another door. It had been left ajar and Archie could see the distinctive blue glow of aquarium lights.

He moved into the thigh-deep water, bracing against the cold, and made his way to the door. A round glass Christmas ornament floated past him. "Susan?" he called again.

The door was steel — a fire door — the owner of the house wanted to protect whatever was in there. Archie raised his gun and pushed it open.

The room was full of fish.

The tanks lit the room with an aqua gleam.

There was no one in there. They were gone.

Archie lowered his gun.

Then he saw something in the water.

It bobbed at the surface, a knot of flesh — the size of a golf ball. Archie took a step back. The water in the room was full of blue-ringed octopuses.

He counted a half dozen, at least.

They were all at the surface, limp, not moving.

Dead. Nothing could live in that water for long.

"What's going on down there?" Flannigan called. "You okay?"

"Yeah. Stay up there," Archie hollered.

"I've got dead octopuses down here." He looked down at the water. He hoped they were all dead.

Archie had backed out of the room and was closing the door when he saw the shadow. It was nothing he could really discern, just a sense of something, a shape, under the water.

Still, he felt a sickening tug at his gut.

There was a person under there.

He holstered his gun and stumbled forward into the room, feeling under the water until his hands found clothing, solid cold flesh, hair. Archie lifted the person's head and shoulders out of the water.

It was Heil.

The dead blue-rings floated all around them.

"Call for EMTs," Archie called up the stairs. "It's Heil."

Heil's skin was chilled meat. Archie felt for a pulse and got nothing.

Bodies didn't sink until the lungs had filled with water.

He needed to get him to a flat surface so he could start CPR.

Archie pulled Heil through the water, out the door, and into the main room of the basement.

Flannigan was at the bottom of the stairs.

"Jesus Christ," he said.

"Help me get him to the kitchen," Archie said.

Flannigan took Heil under the arms, Archie grabbed under his knees and they half carried, half dragged him up the stairs. When they got to the kitchen they laid him flat on his back on the linoleum, a puddle of brown water already seeping from his clothes.

Flannigan knelt next to Heil's head, so he could turn it to the side if Heil started coughing up water, and Archie started chest compressions. It was like pushing on rubber.

"He's dead," Flannigan said.

Archie kept working. "They can save him."

"He's dead, Archie. He's been dead for a while."

But Archie didn't stop. CPR had worked on Henry.

Sirens wailed in the distance.

Archie kept up the compressions. He focused on the count. One. Two. Three. Four. Push.

Flannigan reached out with a shaky hand and closed Heil's eyes.

The sirens got louder.

Archie heard the emergency vehicles pulling up, then the front door opening.

"In here," he yelled.

The EMTs trotted in and slid into squats next to him. One took over compressions, while the other checked Heil's vitals, then peeled back his eyelids and checked his pupillary response with an ophthalmoscope. "He's dead."

The first EMT lifted her latex-gloved hands from Heil's chest. They both looked at Archie and Flannigan.

Archie pulled himself to his feet.

He could hear more sirens now.

A *Star Wars* figure was sitting on the kitchen counter. Archie took a step toward it. He didn't know which character it was, but could tell that it was supposed to be female.

The kid had been in the house. Maybe even earlier that night.

Archie looked closer. The action figure had a Jolly Rancher on its lap.

Flannigan was still sitting on the floor, back against the wall. "What is it?" he said.

"I don't know," Archie said. There was something under the figure — a slip of paper. Archie slid it out and unfolded it. It was a credit card receipt from Aquarium World.

"I know where they are," Archie said.

CHAPTER 51

Roy could tell the reporter was afraid.

He liked it.

The boy hadn't been afraid like that for a long time.

"Do what I want and I won't hurt you," he said to her, and he pushed her ahead of him toward the store's aquarium display. Floodwater had seeped in from outside, and her boots smacked against the wet linoleum as she floundered forward.

"Is that what you told Patrick?" she asked.

The store's power was off, and the moan of the generator running the tanks echoed through the room. The halide fixtures glazed everything with blue.

He turned to the boy. "I need a trickle filter," he said. "An overflow box. A protein skimmer, and a couple of power heads." The boy nodded and went in search of them.

The reporter turned and looked around.

"So this is where you get your fish?" she asked.

He had been a faithful customer. Until the detective told him the store had given out his name. It was poor customer service. They deserved to be robbed.

"I need you to help me carry the tank," he said. He took a step closer to her, but she backed away from him.

"You'll have to untie me," she said.

He took another step and she attempted to do the same, but he pinned her against a wall of freshwater tanks.

He put his face next to hers, nuzzling her neck, twisting his tongue around her wet hair, tasting it. "If you try to leave, I'll punish him," Roy whispered. He put his open mouth against her ear and licked his lips. "He cries when I punish him."

He placed a hand flat against her chest and felt her heart fluttering under her breast, her nipple hard under his palm. Good. She was scared again.

If you wanted a loyal dog, the first thing you did was beat the hell out of it.

He pressed against her and reached around her hips with both his hands. He could feel the pant of her breaths against his neck, the wet knit of her sweater against his arms. He slid his hands down her arms to her wrists, and then untied her. She whimpered as he pulled the twine loose. He made sure she saw him drop it to the floor. He didn't need it anymore.

"Good girl," he said. He could smell the sweat between them. He bent his head down again and rested his face on the crown of her head.

"I have the stuff," the boy said.

Roy stepped away from the reporter and she let loose a gasping sob. The boy was looking at them, his arms full of supplies. "Put it over there and get an air pump," Roy said.

It wasn't like the boy to interrupt him, and it crossed Roy's mind that the boy had done it on purpose.

No, Roy decided.

The kid didn't have the nerve.

CHAPTER 52

Aquarium World was on Naito Parkway, crammed into the first floor of one of the elegant old buildings facing the river. It had a small sign out front, no parking, and a front window painted to look like a tank full of fish.

Archie and Flannigan had made it to First Avenue, one block west of Naito, with two squad cars behind them.

"SWAT's having trouble getting through," Flannigan said. "Half the roads downtown are impassable."

What had Heil said? Two feet of water was enough to sweep away a car?

"We need to continue on foot," Archie said.

Downtown was dark and the falling mist was so fine it looked like fog. Water dribbled from awnings and fire escapes and gushed down the curbsides. The three-story buildings that lined First were ornate, their windows and roofs frosted like wedding cakes. But the first-floor storefronts and the offices upstairs had been evacuated, the electricty shut off, and their black windows were now illuminated only by the reflection of streetlights and the emergency beacons of the patrol cars.

The city seemed utterly abandoned. There were no people. No parked cars. Traffic lights were out. Water ran down the pavement like a wild brook. The thin wisps of trees lining the sidewalk shuddered, bare-leaved, in the wind. The whole world glistened wet and black, like the Pacific Ocean at night.

Archie didn't bother to park. He just stopped the Cutlass in the middle of the road, got out, and walked around to the trunk.

The two patrol cars following them stopped. Their red and blue lights were strangely comforting. They were something familiar in an environment suddenly defined by everything it was lacking — shoppers, office workers, bicyclists, buses, homeless teenagers with their dreadlocks and cardboard signs.

Archie opened the trunk and took off his jacket.

"Suit up," he called to the uniformed

cops, who were already stepping out of their cars. They were both young and skinny, clean-shaven, one light-haired, the other dark. "We're walking," Archie said.

He pulled a flak jacket out of the trunk and strapped it on, then handed one to Flannigan.

Flannigan put it on.

No one spoke.

Choppers droned invisibly overhead. They had become such a part of the downtown experience that they barely registered. It was just another sound, like the drum of rain on the hoods of cars.

Archie put his jacket back on over the bulletproof vest and faced Flannigan and the two patrol cops.

Up close, in the light from the headlights, Archie could see the silhouette of fuzz on the blond officer's upper lip. He was trying to grow a mustache.

"This is a hostage situation," Archie said. "Protect the victims first. We can always catch the bad guy. We can't bring someone back from the dead."

The two officers nodded, their hair already wet.

"Okay," Archie said. "Follow my lead."

He leapt, attempting to clear the wide swath of water running along the curbside, but landed ankle-deep and had to take another stride to get to the sidewalk.

Flannigan was next to him, the patrol cops a few steps behind. The trees spit rain at them from their wet, windblown branches.

Archie didn't draw his gun. He didn't want the others to. This was a public place, and anyone could appear at any moment. Downtown had been evacuated, but that didn't mean that people weren't dense enough to ignore the warnings.

The wet sidewalk sucked at his suede shoes as Archie walked and the cold water squished into his socks.

The name on the Aquarium World receipt was Elroy Carey.

It had been easy to bring up his driver's license photo once they had a name and address. He was forty-three years old, with a soft, unlined face, rounded shoulders, and eyebrows lifted in surprise. His brown hair was parted on the side. He looked like an overgrown kid.

Carey had gotten his Oregon driver's license three years ago, and registered a Dodge sedan at the same time. Before that, he'd lived in Everett, Washington, just a couple of hours by car from where Patrick Lifton had disappeared.

Were Archie's feet somehow getting even wetter?

They had turned onto a side street and were headed down to the parkway. The water on the sidewalk was definitely deeper here. It splashed up Archie's pant leg as he walked. Standing water. Not wet pavement. Not a puddle. Not storm drain backup. This was a cold inky blanket of water that lapped against the concrete. Archie could see the edge of it slowly creeping up the length of the street.

This water had a current.

Under the noise of the helicopters, under the splatter of the rain, Archie could make out a faint new sound — like a waterfall or a filling bathtub.

Flannigan heard it, too. "What's that?" he asked.

"The water," Archie said.

Flannigan squinted up at the starless sky.

"It's not the rain," Archie said.

It had started.

Downtown was flooding.

On cue, Flannigan's walkie-talkie crackled to life. "We've got a report of a breach in the seawall," dispatch reported.

Flannigan pressed the talk button. "This is Flannigan," he said. "We're on Ash between First and Naito. There's two inches of water here, and rising. What's going on?"

"There's a hole in sector eight near the Burnside Bridge. You need to get out of there, sir."

"Are they sending a team to fix it?"

"Roger. But you need to evacuate. We've been told that whole wall could give."

"What happens then?" Archie said.

"What happens then?" Flannigan repeated into the walkie-talkie.

There was nothing but static for a moment. "You ever see a bug hit a windshield?" came the eventual reply. "It'll be like that. Only you'll be the bug, and the windshield will be a ten-foot wall of water."

The two patrolmen glanced at each other.

Archie wasn't sure if Carey and the others were even downtown. Maybe they hadn't made it. Maybe the receipt was misdirection. Maybe Archie had misinterpreted it. Maybe Carey didn't even have Susan or the kid. Maybe they were already dead.

Archie had cost Heil his life. He couldn't risk any others but his own.

"You better get out of here," he said.

Flannigan hesitated. "What about SWAT?" he said into the walkie-talkie.

"I'm sorry, sirs. But they've been ordered to stand down until we get the all-clear."

A streetlight popped across the street and

began to smoke and send sparks arcing into the night air.

"Don't go back to the cars," Archie told them. "Stay on foot. Head west."

The patrol cops didn't need their arms twisted. They backed away a few feet, turned, and started to run.

Flannigan didn't move.

"I know how to swim," he said.

CHAPTER 53

By the time Archie and Flannigan got to Naito Parkway the black glass of the water was above their ankles.

The parkway was flooded, and beyond it Waterfront Park had all but vanished into darkness. It was all underwater, Archie realized. The vast expanse of grass. The promenade. The park benches. The monuments and fountains. Two helicopters hovered over a section of the seawall, shining their spotlights down, and Archie could see the cascade of black water spilling over a fifty-foot section where the emergency levee had given way. The churn they'd heard earlier was ten times louder here.

He could see the aquarium store four doorways up the street, a faint, now-familiar blue glow radiating from within — the tanks must have been powered by a backup generator. A row of sandbags was stacked along the seam where the sidewalk met the buildings, and Archie had to drag a hand along the top of them to keep his feet from going out from under him. Flannigan was close behind. Somewhere a car alarm started blaring.

The glass front door was broken.

"They're here," Flannigan whispered.

Archie peered into the store and listened. But if there was something to be heard above the sound of the choppers and the car alarm and the roaring water, Archie couldn't make it out.

"Elroy?" Archie yelled. "This is the police. The river has breached the seawall. This area is flooding right now. I need you to give me the woman and the boy, so we can get you out of there."

He directed his flashlight's beam into the store. The water was bleeding in, finding every means of entry. It covered the store's floor, reflecting the blue gleam of the aquariums.

Archie drew his gun and stepped over the knives of glass that still held in the doorframe.

The car alarm swelled in volume as Archie turned and looked past Flannigan to see the car in question float by, honking madly, parking lights flashing, half submerged in the water. Then the alarm stopped, the lights extinguished, and the car was gone in the darkness.

He took a step and raised his weapon.

"Susan?" he called.

Aquariums lined every wall, marine worlds encased in blocks of glass. They were fitted with black lights to highlight the neon of the colorful fish and exotic coral. Bright pink rocks. Fish of every size and color, feathery, plump, tiny, long. The tanks bubbled and gurgled. If Archie never saw an aquarium again, it would be too soon.

He took another few steps inside.

"You like fish, Elroy?" he called. "I like fish." He tried to think of names of fish, and could only come up with the ones he liked to eat. "Salmon. Halibut. Black cod. Filet o'."

"I like Leopard Wrasse African Blue Stars," a small voice said.

Archie swung his flashlight in the direction of the voice, and saw Patrick Lifton sitting cross-legged on an orange molded plastic chair in front of a large tank of small red fish. He was wearing dark rain pants and a dark raincoat, but the hood was down. He had something in his lap.

A plastic bucket.

The hairs on the back of Archie's neck bristled.

The kid appeared to be alone. Out of the corner of his eye, Archie saw Flannigan duck down an aisle to get at the kid from the other side.

"What do you have there, kiddo?" Archie said in as calm a voice as he could manage.

Patrick's eyes flicked past Archie to a point somewhere behind him. "He wanted another one," Patrick said.

Archie snapped his flashlight around, tracking the gun after it. But he saw only more fish. They jerked around in their tanks like anxious spectators. "Where is he?" Archie asked Patrick.

"I know you," Patrick said.

"I'm Archie," Archie said. "We met in the river."

The kid blinked in the light, but his eyes didn't waver. He looked directly at Archie. His eyes were a startling dark green, with a brown rim around the irises.

"I need you to hand me the bucket," Archie said slowly.

"I can't," Patrick whispered.

They didn't have time for this. Archie needed to find Susan and get her and the kid out of there. What did the parenting books say? Never negotiate? "I have something that belongs to you," Archie said quickly. "Your Darth Vader figure. You lost him near the river. I found him. I'll trade you."

Patrick looked down at the bucket and seemed to hesitate.

Archie put his flashlight under his arm, and extended his hand, and took a step toward the boy.

"Archie," he heard Susan say from behind him.

If it had been anyone else, he might have reacted differently. He might have secured the boy first before turning around. But it wasn't anyone else, it was Susan, and Archie acted on instinct, swinging his gun around to his left, following her voice, away from the boy. The flashlight was still pinned under his arm and its beam careened sideways. He dropped it, caught it in his hand, and lifted the light to find Elroy Carey holding Susan in front of him, one arm around her waist, the other hand securing her by a fistful of her hair. The top of her head came to the top of his shoulder. Archie aimed his weapon at Carey's head.

"He'll put his hand in the bucket," Carey said. "If I say so."

Archie couldn't see Patrick. The boy was behind him. If Archie turned, it would mean taking his gun off of Carey. "It's okay, Patrick," Archie said. "You don't have to do what he says anymore."

Susan was limp in Carey's arms, her head twisted back like a rag doll. "Heil's dead," she said. It sounded like an accusation.

Archie couldn't see if Carey had a weapon. If Archie shot him, he'd have to kill him, or risk him hurting Susan, and he'd have to kill him instantly. SWAT called it "aiming for the apricot." The apricot was the medulla oblongata — the lower half of the brainstem. It controlled involuntary movement. Done right, Carey wouldn't even flinch. But Archie wasn't a marksman. And Carey kept moving, rocking back and forth, shifting his feet. And Susan was so close.

"Did you hear me?" Susan said. "He killed Heil."

"I know," Archie said. He kept his gun trained on Carey, along with the flashlight, hoping the light might limit his vision. He needed to buy time for Flannigan to work his way around to the boy.

"You need to help me get everyone out of here, Elroy," Archie said. "It's flooding."

Susan's body stiffened. Archie thought it was the threat of the flood.

Carey adjusted his grip on her, still rocking, moving in and out of Archie's sights. "My name's Roy," he said. He was hunched over Susan, his chin on her shoulder, their heads pressed close, like a couple posing for a photograph.

Archie's feet ached from the cold water. Carey and Susan had been there longer. Their feet had probably moved through pain to numbness. It could make Carey clumsy.

"Okay, Roy. My name's Archie."

Carey's attention shifted to a spot behind Archie. "Come here, Sam," he said.

Archie couldn't let Carey get the boy. If Archie had ever had an ounce of parental authority, he needed it now. "Stay there, Patrick," he said.

Archie listened. He could barely make out the sound of the generator powering the tanks. Aquariums gurgled. The water was a few inches deeper now. The whole room flickered with aqua light. It reflected off the water, the metal fixtures, the empty tanks. Archie steadied his weapon and lined the sight right at the center of Carey's chin. Recoil would push the shot upward, and if Archie had to fire, he wanted to be sure to kill the bastard.

Carey's lip curled.

"I like the name Elroy," Susan said. She was talking to Carey, but her gaze was leveled right at Archie. "It's a good name. Why did your parents choose it?"

What was she talking about?

Carey's lips peeled back in a strange smile. "My mom named me after my granddad," he said.

"That column tacked up above your sink," Susan said. "I wrote that."

"I know who you are," Carey said.

"What column?" Archie said.

"About Ralph," Susan said.

Carey yanked her head back by the hair and examined her face. "You look different than your picture."

"I dyed my hair."

Archie's stomach knotted. "What was your grandfather's name?" he asked, anticipating the answer.

"Elroy McBee," Carey said.

"Vanport," Archie said softly.

Carey's face clouded. "My grandmother carried my mother and a suitcase for five miles. She lost everything. Her husband. Her house. Strangers took them in. No one remembers." He looked past Archie at the boy. "Get your ass over here, Sam."

Archie heard the boy get up off the chair, the soft splash of his rubber rain boots slipping into the water.

"Your name is Patrick Lifton," Archie called to the kid. "Your dad works at a lumber mill. Your mom works from home building Web sites. You've got a black Lab named Fly. They've never stopped looking for you, Patrick. They want you to come home."

"Bring it to me, you little fucker," Carey snarled. "Or I will hurt you."

Archie needed to distract Carey, give him something else to focus on other than the boy. "The skeleton from the slough hasn't been identified," Archie said. "You don't know it's your grandfather."

"The flood got a lot of kids," Carey said. "Women. A few couples, that worked the nightshift, died in their beds. There were only three men on the missing list. Two black. The paper said the skeleton was a white man. It's him."

"Are they dead?" Patrick asked.

"Who?" Archie said to Patrick, his gun still trained on Carey's chin. "Your parents? No. They're fine."

Patrick's voice wavered. "The blue-rings."

Who knew how many murders the kid had witnessed, but he was worried about the octopuses. "No," Archie said. "No. We saved them."

Carey's eyes narrowed. "He's a liar, Sam. He'll put you in jail."

There was the briefest of commotions

behind Archie. "Give that back!" the boy called.

"I've got the bucket," Flannigan hollered to Archie. "It's okay, Patrick," Archie heard him say to the boy. "I'm a policeman. I'm here to help you."

Patrick Lifton apparently didn't buy it. Archie heard a flat splash — the sound of the chair getting knocked over. Then the frantic, spastic splash of small rain boots.

"What's going on?" Archie called.

"He's headed for the back door," Flannigan cried.

Archie had to go after the kid. He had to leave Susan.

Carey's forehead twitched. His baby face gleamed with sweat. He smiled. He knew where the kid was going, Archie realized. They'd find each other. Just like before.

"For fuck's sake," Susan said. "Go get him."

Archie took a step back and then turned and ran toward the back of the store, the back door, the boy. He glanced back once, just in time to see Susan elbow Carey hard in the stomach.

Chapter 54

Susan had seen Patrick flee.

She was not going to lose him.

She hit Carey again, her elbow slamming into the soft flesh just under his rib cage. He gasped. She had pointy elbows. People had always told her that. His grip on her hair loosened a bit and she pulled away, squirming out from the deadweight of his meaty arm as he doubled over in pain. She winced at the sting of hair ripping from her scalp as she did.

She scrambled toward the back of the store, pulling empty aquariums from the shelves behind her as she ran. They splashed and some shattered, littering the path behind her with glass.

Carey was lumbering after her, a yarn-sized lock of her raspberry hair still in his fist.

The door at the back of the store was still closing from when Archie had gone through it. Susan threw herself against the door's metal push bar. It was called a panic bar. Now she knew why.

The door opened onto a back hall leading to another door, this one with a green exit sign and a flashing emergency strobe mounted above it. Susan kept running, her heart pounding. The water wasn't as deep back here. The strobe light bounced and flickered through the corridor. She waited for the sound of Carey coming through the door behind her, but it didn't come.

When she got to the emergency exit door and pushed it open, she could hear Archie and Flannigan calling Patrick's name.

The door opened onto a side street.

She had stumbled drunk down this street before, leaving clubs at two-thirty in the morning, looking for her car when she should have been calling for a cab.

The voices were coming from the east, toward the river, so Susan took a right and headed in that direction. It was pitch-black. If she hadn't spent her early twenties throwing up on that street, she would have snapped an ankle for sure.

She clomped through the floodwater, trying to ignore the cold biting through her rubber boots.

Carey still hadn't come through the door.

She considered calling out to Archie, but she didn't want to scare Patrick if he was still around.

Her clothes were still damp and gooseflesh rose on her arms from the wind.

If she were a kid, where would she go?

Not far. That was for sure. Not in the dark. Not in this weather. Heil had told Susan about the kid's fort under the bridge. He liked to hide. It was dark enough on that street that you could hide in plain sight. But there was another spot, a big green Dumpster parked next to the kitchen entrance of a bar, where Susan had been surprised more than once by some drunken frat boy with his dick out, peeing against the bricks.

Susan squinted in the darkness, barely making out the hulking shadow of the Dumpster, and headed for it.

"Patrick?" she whispered when she got close. "It's me."

She heard Archie yell Patrick's name again. He was close, where the street met the parkway. Susan could see his flashlight beam cutting through the darkness.

The Dumpster stank, ripe from two days without garbage pickup. Susan put one hand on the slimy, cold metal and thrust the other into the dark emptiness where the back of the Dumpster abutted the building.

"Take my hand," she whispered.

She waited, her hand outstretched, feeling like an idiot.

Archie's flashlight beam was getting closer.

She was about to call to Archie, to let him know that she was all right.

Then she felt small cold fingers fold around hers.

She squeezed them. "We need to get out of here," she said.

Patrick's form materialized from the darkness. He stepped forward, and she pulled him into her arms.

Archie's flashlight beam streaked past them, then doubled back and landed on Susan.

She peered into the light.

"I've got him," she said. She scooped up the boy and carried him forward, following the light to Archie. "We're okay. I don't know where Carey is."

At the intersection with Naito, the water was mid-thigh-high and moving fast. Susan had to fight against it to stay upright. Archie took her face in his hands and held it, not saying anything.

He put an arm around her shoulder. "Come with me," he said. They started wading north. He was leading them toward the

Burnside Bridge, she realized. There were rescue crews up there. She could see their emergency lights.

Archie waved his flashlight skyward, signaling them, then toward Flannigan fifty feet ahead, his own halogen glow bobbing in the dark.

They only had a block to go, but the strength of the current made it hard.

Archie tried to take Patrick, but the boy clung to Susan, refusing to let go, and she was secretly pleased not to give him up.

The two helicopters buzzing in circles over the river sent out rings of concentric ripples.

She turned back to look for Carey, half expecting to see him come splashing up behind her.

There was no differentiation between park or street or sidewalk. It was all underwater now. It would take months for the city to recover from this. Maybe years.

"Listen," Archie said.

She didn't hear anything but sirens and helicopters. And then, somehow, she did. Low, almost subsonic at first, like a stomach growling, and then, all at once, a vast white noise that seemed to bleed into all five senses. Every hair on Susan's body stood up.

She couldn't hear the helicopters or sirens

anymore. Only the oncoming water. But she didn't turn to look. She didn't want to see it.

There wasn't any point.

There was no time to run.

Archie wrapped his arms around her in a bear hug, and she put her forehead against the crook of his neck, the boy sandwiched firmly between them. Susan could feel the boy tense.

"Take a breath," Archie said.

Susan braced herself.

CHAPTER 55

He lost them immediately when the water hit. It was like being swallowed, forced down a tube by peristalsis. There was no staying on the surface. Archie was sucked under, tumbling, the water thundering in his ears. He had no sense of direction, no clue which way was up. He managed to get his flak jacket off, and when he slammed against something hard he somehow had the instinct to grab hold of it and grapple his way to the surface.

It was a streetlight.

The water seemed to draw back, like the undertow of a great wave breaking shore, and Archie had to hug the streetlight with all his strength to keep from being sucked off toward the river.

And then it was over.

Suddenly everything was incredibly still, the water waist-high, cold, and black, without a ripple on its surface.

"Susan," Archie called, his voice hoarse, looking around in the darkness. "Patrick?"

The damage was obvious all around him. Half the cherry trees from the Japanese American Plaza were gone, a car was on its side, half submerged, all the windows of the storefronts were broken. The chair from inside the aquarium store floated by.

He heard splashing nearby, and turned to see a man's clawing hand emerge from the water. Archie reached for it instinctively. It grabbed hold, and Archie pulled the person to the surface, expecting to see Flannigan.

But it was Elroy Carey who came up bellowing.

He exploded from the water and got his hands around Archie's neck. Archie was knocked off balance and fell back into waist-deep water. Carey fell on top of him, and Archie flailed at Carey's wrists, trying to pry them off, but the water stole all his leverage.

It also stole Carey's.

Archie held his breath, put his feet together, bent his knees, and kicked Carey in the shins. The force pushed Carey's feet out from under him and he belly-flopped forward, losing his grip. Archie got out from under him and came to the surface for air.

But Carey got his footing back and turned

and came back at him.

Carey's head was matted and bleeding. He'd been knocked against something when the flood surge hit. His skull had been cracked open. Archie could see the pink shimmer of brain tissue where Carey's wet brown hair parted around the wound. Rage and adrenaline were the only things keeping him on his feet.

Archie reached for his gun, but the flood had ripped the holster right off his belt.

Carey lunged for him.

But Archie was ready. Carey had killed Heil. He'd taken Patrick Lifton from his family. He'd tried to kill Henry. He deserved to die.

Archie clenched his fist and swung hard for Carey's head wound. His fist slammed against bone and hair and something slippery. It knocked Carey over on his side, back into the water.

Carey pulled himself to his feet, doubled over, heaving, soaked in filthy water.

He lifted his head and looked sideways at Archie.

Blood gushed from his scalp, over his face, into his eyes, and down his chest. He adjusted the suspenders of his waders. His eyes rolled back. And he sank to his knees, disappearing almost completely beneath the water. He managed to stay there for a moment, only his forehead visible, the gaping wound pulsing blood. Then it sank below the surface. Archie watched until the bubbles stopped. It only took a few minutes. He waited a few minutes more, just to be sure. Then he felt for the body, and lifted it by the shirt collar.

Carey's scalp was clean. Archie could see the full extent of his injuries now — a two-inch section of his brain exposed. The wound had stopped bleeding. He was dead. Archie looked around. He was alone. He released Carey's body and watched it sink and vanish in the river.

CHAPTER 56

Susan surfaced and took in a great gasp of air. She was alive. She'd been tossed and tumbled and rolled underwater until she thought her lungs were going to burst, and she was still alive. Air — humid, fetid, flooded-city air — had never tasted so good. She was still in the water, but she was swimming, above the surface. She could breathe.

Then the absence struck her.

Where was Patrick?

She'd lost him when the water hit.

"Patrick?" she yelled. She paddled in frantic circles in the water, searching for him in the darkness, calling his name again and again.

But he didn't answer.

"Archie?" she called.

He wasn't there.

They were both gone.

Or maybe she was the one who was gone.

She looked around for landmarks, but

couldn't orient herself. She didn't see any buildings. Rain pattered against the surface of the water. Compared to the water she was in, it felt warm.

The floodsurge was still moving, and taking her along with it. She could feel it all around her — a billion pounds of pressure all rushing in the same direction. She realized then that she wasn't swimming. She was treading water, paddling against the current.

The muscles in her arms already burned. She was getting more exhausted by the second.

She strained again to get a bead on where she was. And then she saw the shadow of something overhead. A bridge.

She was in the middle of the river.

Frantic now, she swam for the shore, wide strokes, straight kicks, employing every ounce of energy in her possession. She swam like an Olympian. Like Esther Williams. But every force she exerted was met with twice the resistance. The current was too strong. She couldn't fight it.

CHAPTER 57

Archie stumbled through the waist-deep water, calling out for Susan, for the boy, for Flannigan. He coughed after each name, as if even the effort of producing sound were too much for his lungs. He didn't know if it was from his cold or all the water he'd inhaled.

The flashlight was gone, along with his shoes, torn away in the flood. His phone was dead. Some of the buildings had exterior emergency lights, and the flashing white and yellow beacons illuminated the scene in splinters of light.

He kept walking. Kept calling for them.

His knee jammed into something immovable underwater. He put his hands in the cold river and ran them over the obstacle. A concrete public trash can. He could see its former contents now, a trail of paper cups and red plastic straws, crumpled take-out bags and water bottles, stretching out in a vague trail across the water. Archie found his way around the trash can, and then nearly lost his balance going over a curb. A branch swept past and Archie grabbed it, using it to trace the ground ahead like a blind man.

He could wade out. Make his way up to the rescue crews on Burnside. Get help. But it would take valuable, maybe crucial minutes.

The Willamette had pulled them in opposite directions, Archie guessed. If he was right, if Susan wasn't nearby, then she was in the river.

The helicopters still hovered overhead, only now their spotlights scanned along the edge of the waterfront. They were looking for survivors.

Archie could hear sirens. And see some kind of light gliding on the surface of the water, getting closer.

He saw other lights then. Skating along the water, appearing from behind buildings and dispersing.

Rescue boats.

The first light he saw was headed toward him, moving north down what had been the parkway.

"Here!" Archie yelled, waving his arms. "Here!"

A spotlight beam hit him in the face and stayed fixed on him until the boat was right at his side.

An arm reached under each of Archie's armpits and pulled him, belly first, onto the black Zodiac. Someone put a blanket around him.

When Archie looked up he saw two National Guard soldiers wearing black life jackets.

"You find anyone else?" Archie asked.

They shook their heads no.

Archie coughed, and when he caught his breath he looked out toward the river. He knew what the current was like out there. If Susan and Patrick had been swept into the Willamette, they'd be a half mile away by now.

"How fast can this thing go?" he asked.

CHAPTER 58

Susan stopped swimming and let the river take her. She tried to inhale deeply and float on the surface like she'd done a thousand times in a hundred hotel pools, but the water was too rough, and pulled her under, and rolled over her face, leaving her even more exhausted and disoriented and sputtering. So she stayed vertical, her socked feet kicking, the boots long gone, arms shoveling water, her head like a human buoy on the surface. There was so much junk and wreckage in the river that she had to stay vigilant just to keep from getting beaned by a log or loose street sign. She kept her paddling arms near the surface and her strokes wide, so that she might brush with her hand anything headed her way. So far she'd swatted away split wood and branches and what felt like the rearview mirror of a car. Her hair was matted with twigs. Her hands felt like they were bleeding. Her skin shuddered.

A frigid chill had settled deep inside her bones.

She turned her face up at the midnight sky, the rain hitting her lashes.

It was as black as the water, except for one bright star.

Not a star. A planet.

Venus.

No, Jupiter.

She could never get those two straight.

It was too big to be a planet. It was close. Susan felt the water flatten around her just before the wind from the chopper blades hit her face.

"Hey!" she yelled, swallowing some water. She choked and lifted her hands to wave, but that only made her sink up to her hairline. She kicked hard, as hard as she could, and managed to lift one arm up and beat it against the sky. "Down here!" she yelled. "I'm here!"

But it streaked overhead without pausing, and she was left alone again and without light.

They couldn't see her. It was too dark. There was too much debris.

She was going to die.

She started to breathe hard, sharp little pants, and her eyes burned with hot tears. Her head felt light. She bit her tongue and tasted blood.

They might never find her body. She'd sink. Get stuck under all that crap and be carried off and end up decaying under a dock somewhere. If she was lucky the bacteria in her stomach would create enough gas for her bloated body to disentangle itself and bob to the surface.

Susan didn't want to die.

Her legs were cramping up, her lungs throbbed. She needed to calm down, to slow her breathing.

The first stage of drowning was fear.

She thought of Patrick, out there alone, scared, if he was still alive.

Talk to yourself, Susan thought. *Talk yourself through this.* That's what reporters did, didn't they?

They took notes.

They did research.

And they hoped that one day all of that useless knowledge they'd stored up would come in handy.

The water was cold, and Susan clawed at it, trying to keep her chin above the surface. It was dark and she couldn't see anything. She didn't even know which way the current was taking her. The river water tasted like mud and metal. All her life she had been told not to drink water from the Willamette, that it was polluted with mercury and sewage and radioactive runoff from Hanford. Now she'd probably swallowed a keg of it. If she didn't drown, she'd die of cancer.

Most people who were drowning didn't cry out for help. They were too busy trying to breathe.

It's not like you see on TV.

It's silent.

People just slip under the surface, and are gone.

Sticks and debris snapped against her legs, focusing her mind like a slap in the face. The river groaned and roared. It was the only sound.

Her body burned with exhaustion.

It took everything she had to take that last breath. She could have held it. Bought herself another few minutes. But she'd never been the type of person to go quietly. So she yelled. That whole lungful of sweet oxygen — she let it go in one word. "Archie." It rang in her head as loud and clear as a bell, but she wasn't even sure she'd said it out loud. His name echoed in her brain, fading into a mantra as she sank below the waterline.

Archie.

It took her a split second to realize she

was underwater. It was quiet, the roar of the river a distant hum.

She stretched a hand up and managed to find the cold night air with the tips of her fingers, but she had no leverage, no way to push herself above the water. She could feel her body panic, like a spark bursting into flame, and she inhaled water, a great cold gulp of it. She choked, and it hurt. But she couldn't stop. She inhaled more of it.

Her brain wasn't working. She searched sloppily for some sentence to hang on to.

The second stage. The epiglottis sealed the airway. The body's way of protecting the lungs from filling up with water.

She was calm now, and so tired. The water carrying her. It was a relief to stop fighting it, to let her body rest.

She wasn't cold anymore.

She thought of her dad, dying in his hospital bed, and how in the end, after all those months of fighting, dying had seemed peaceful.

She thought of her mom, and how pissed off she would be by this.

What was the third stage? *Unconsciousness.* It would happen soon, and then she would go into cardiac arrest. Her heart would stop. She would be clinically dead. It wouldn't hurt. She'd be asleep.

Four minutes.

That's how long you had between clinical death and biological death. CPR. Defibrillation. You could restart the heart, if you got there in time.

Four minutes. About the length of an average pop song.

That's how long Archie had to save her.

CHAPTER 59

He'd heard her voice.

No one else in the boat had. But Archie was certain that he'd heard Susan calling his name.

"Quiet," he said.

The soldier piloting the Zodiac shut off the outboard motor, and Archie called back to her. But there was nothing. Only the choppers. The endless staccato of the rain. The crescendo of the current.

Archie searched the blackness and tried to pinpoint the location.

"That way," he yelled, and the outboard kicked once again to life and headed twenty feet up and west until Archie said, "Here."

One of the soldiers was on his radio calling in a dive team and directing a helicopter to their position. Someone threw a life preserver into the water. It made a dead splash. Someone else swung the boat's spotlight around, scanning the surface of the water. But they didn't have time for all that.

Archie jumped off the boat and went under.

It wasn't the first time he'd plunged into this kind of darkness.

In Gretchen's basement, when she'd cut into him, the blackness had been an enveloping comfort; and later, after she'd let him go, all those nights when he'd fallen asleep with seven Vicodin in his system, he had longed to let his mind go again to the abyss.

The floodwater was that place, given physical form and weight.

He reached clumsily, feeling around underwater, fingers splayed. His ears pounded and ached from the cold. He dove deeper.

A martyr with a white knight complex, Anne had said.

Except that the people he tried to save died.

Even underwater he could hear the roar of the river. The current twisted around him, nearly turning him over. His inner ears ached from the cold water. He opened his eyes under there and saw only blackness. He propelled himself deeper, struggling against the current. He could feel it moving him. His lungs pulsed with pain.

He dug through the water, stretching his

arms and legs, hoping to make contact with her.

But he needed air.

He swam up, breaking the water with a sputtering cough.

He looked around. The boat was a hundred feet away. The current had washed him downriver fifty yards in just a few minutes.

And then, all at once — light.

He was bathed in it. He had to squint against it for a moment before he could see. The light was filled with a trillion tiny glittering raindrops. The beam encircled him and went straight up into the sky.

He was in the spotlight of a Coast Guard helicopter.

The chugging rotors that had become such white noise over the past several days sounded like the trumpet of a cavalry charge.

Then, from above, he saw something in the light. They were lowering a rescue basket. They were trying to rescue him.

No.

Archie couldn't even get a full breath anymore — his lungs were too tired, too full of muck. But he took in as much air as he could.

He'd promised himself that he could save her.

He dove straight down, pushing the icy water with all his strength, and as he did, his hand brushed against something.

He flailed toward it, grabbed hold, and swam for the surface.

CHAPTER 60

Susan's first awareness was of vomiting water.

It splashed onto the pavement beside her like coffee poured out the window of a moving car. Her belly cramped as she gagged, and she had a splitting headache. Her body hurt all over. And she was chilled to the bone, every muscle clenched with cold.

She could hear a noise. The same sound over and over again, and after a while she realized what it was:

"Susan?

"Susan?

"Susan?"

Why was someone saying her name? She was hungover. Or had the flu. Or was having a terrible dream. She needed her rest.

"Can you hear me?" the voice said.

It was Archie's voice.

"Leave me alone," she said.

"Do you know who I am?"

409

She mumbled his name.

"Do you know your name?"

What was his problem? "Susan," she said.

And then it all came back. The river. The flood.

She looked around, her consciousness straining through the fog, grappling for details.

She was on her back on pavement. On a bridge. There were people kneeling around her. Archie. Random, clean-cut National Guard faces. They were all beaming, like they'd baked a pie.

Something felt funny on her chest and she reached her hand for it, and found a giant sticker, some wires. She saw the automatic external defibrillator on the pavement beside her, wires leading to her chest.

They'd resuscitated her.

Holy fuck. She'd been dead.

"You'll be okay," Archie said.

He was soaking wet. He'd done it. He'd found her and pulled her out in time.

Her brain felt like pudding.

"Thanks," she said. And then she vomited all over his feet.

"That's all right," he said. "I'm wet anyway."

She saw the lights of the ambulance before she heard the *whoop-whoop* of its siren. Her senses felt jumbled like that, her brain still struggling to organize information.

"Where's Patrick?" she tried to ask. But it came out more like "Werspatick?"

Somehow, Archie seemed to know what she was talking about. "We haven't found Patrick yet."

The EMTs arrived with a rush of comforting efficiency. They peeled off the AED pads, wrapped Susan in blankets, and strapped her to a gurney.

"Carey's dead," Archie said as they wheeled her away.

"Good," she said.

She turned her head and looked out into the blackness. The EMTs loaded her in the ambulance. She'd been through this routine before, and surrendered to it.

CHAPTER 61

Archie counted twelve helicopters now. The river was abuzz with rescue boats and spotlights. Every bridge, from the Hawthorne to the Steel, was lit up with the flashing red and blue of emergency vehicles. No sirens. Standard procedure in a case like this. They didn't want to muffle the sound of someone yelling for help.

Even with the beating rotors of the choppers, the city felt weirdly silent. The seawall was in shambles. The center of the river still raged from the snowmelt and rain, but the floodwater that had breached the wall had settled into a placid dark lake. The entire landscape of downtown Portland had changed. The Willamette now stretched twice as wide, abutting the facades of the old buildings that fronted the park. It was how Portland had used to look — a hundred years ago, before they had put in the freeway along the west bank and then, decades later, torn it up and replaced it with Waterfront Park, forever separating Portlanders from the river.

Archie had a good view from the top of the Burnside Bridge. The drawbridge had been lowered, and someone had managed to roll the chief's mobile command center up from the east side of the bridge, which, because it didn't have an emergency seawall, had suffered less damage.

Archie was wearing National Guard fatigues with a blanket over his shoulders and nothing but cold, vomit-soaked socks on his feet. There were plenty of patrol cars around he could have climbed into to get warm. But he didn't want comfort. Not until Patrick and Flannigan had been found. He spoke into the walkie-talkie he'd been given. "Anything?"

"Not yet, sir," a voice answered.

Archie looked south into the night, where, miles away, snowmelt and tributaries met near Eugene, and the Willamette River formed, flowing north to Portland, snaking a path through cities and towns and wine country and farmland. Then he turned to the north, downriver where the Willamette took a left, joined the Columbia, and rolled out to the Pacific.

Almost two hundred miles.

And flooding all along it.

Rescue efforts would continue for days. Cleanup for months, maybe years.

They had already pulled a National Guard soldier out of the water and rescued five people from downtown roofs.

But there was no sign of Flannigan or the boy. And no sign of Carey's body.

Archie felt a hand grip his shoulder and Chief Eaton stepped next to him.

"How bad is it?" Archie asked him.

"We won't be able to tell for sure until daylight," Eaton said. "But there's water up to Second Ave, from Burnside down to Market. Governor's asked for federal help. They're sending more Guard soldiers. Washington and California are sending rescue crews. Thank God we got people out of there."

"The flooding is only up to Second?" Archie said carefully.

Eaton gave him a knowing look. "We evacuated the jail hours ago."

Archie had been trying to keep his mind from going to Gretchen. He'd focused on Patrick, and Heil, and Susan. But it had nagged at him. The Justice Center was on Third Avenue downtown. It had been in the flood zone. "Where to?" he asked.

"Down to Salem," Eaton said. "All the

prisoners are accounted for. Including Gretchen Lowell." He looked Archie up and down and raised an eyebrow. "I can't tell if you're disappointed or relieved."

As with everything that had to do with Gretchen, it was a little of both. Archie gripped the blanket a little tighter. "I just want her locked up," he said.

"Go home," Eaton said with a sigh. "It's been an hour. Anyone in that water would have gone hypothermic thirty minutes ago."

Home. Archie had left the Cutlass on First Avenue. He guessed that it wasn't still where he'd parked it. His apartment building probably had a moat around it.

Archie couldn't leave. He raised the walkie-talkie to his mouth. "Anything?" he said.

"Not yet, sir."

Archie gazed over the side of the bridge at the darkened western skyline.

"What do you think Carey knocked up against?" Eaton said.

"Parked car, maybe," Archie said. He had told them Carey was dead. He had left out the part about punching him in the brain. He wondered bleakly if an autopsy would call his account into question if Carey's body ever washed up. Probably. Archie had learned that the more inconvenient a truth,

415

the more likely it would eventually emerge.

Eaton's phone rang and he glanced at it and picked it up. "Yeah?" he said. He listened. "Hold on." He held the phone out to Archie. "It's for you," he said.

Archie took it. "Hello?" he said.

"Jesus," Henry said. "I sound better than you do."

Archie lifted his hand to his forehead. His voice caught. Now that Susan was safe, the rest was hitting him. "Heil's dead."

"I heard."

"I need to call his wife," Archie said.

"Wait until morning," Henry said.

Archie could still feel Susan and Patrick in his arms. Feel them ripped away. "I had the boy, Henry. I had him twice, and I lost him. Susan was underwater. She had to be revived."

"It's not your fault," Henry said. His voice was still hoarse from the respirator tube. "Blame the psycho behind it."

"I have to find this kid," Archie said.

"It's over," Henry said gently. "There's nothing you can do there. Let the professionals do their jobs."

Archie heard a commotion on the bridge and looked over to see a man shouting at a uniformed patrolman. A woman was with him. A pair of headlights suddenly lit the scene and Archie was able to recognize the couple.

They were Patrick Lifton's parents.

"I have to go," Archie mumbled into the phone, and he hung up and handed the phone back to the Eaton.

Eaton saw them, too, and put an arm across Archie's chest. "I can talk to them," he said.

"It's okay," Archie said. "Let them through," he shouted at the officer trying to hold them back.

The officer turned back and saw Archie and then nodded and lifted the tape for Patrick's parents to duck under.

Daniel Lifton's eyes fell on Archie and Lifton ran for him.

His face was twisted with grief, his eyes swollen. He wasn't wearing a coat.

Eaton stepped between then.

"You had him?" Lifton asked Archie, his voice almost a wail.

"I couldn't hold on," Archie said.

Archie thought that Lifton might slug him. He wanted him to. He wanted to feel the pain of his skin splitting, his jaw dislocating. He wanted to taste his own blood.

Lifton turned, trying to hold back sobs. "We almost had him back."

Eaton put an arm around Lifton and led

him away a few steps. "We'll find him."

Find him. They all knew what he really meant — find the body. But even that might not be possible. Corpses could stay hidden a long time in the river.

Patrick's mother shifted close to Archie.

"I was supposed to walk with him, to Simon's house," she said. She stood next to him, so that they were side by side, but she faced the opposite direction, looking out over the railing toward the river. She was wearing a baseball cap, and Archie thought he could hear rain tapping against the bill. "But I was late on a job, a Web site I was building for this little store up in Everett. So I told him he could go on his own. I sat there, writing code, while my son was taken away by some maniac."

"What was the store?" Archie asked.

"The Pet Nook," she said.

Archie tried to keep his expression neutral. "Do they sell fish?"

She turned and looked at him. The bill of her cap shadowed her face. "Yes."

"Did you ever take Patrick there?" Archie asked.

She nodded. He could see her mouth in the light, a small line. "He went with me a few times," she said. "He sat in the back, next to the aquariums, and did homework while I talked to the owner. He loved it back there. Something about the light. He always wanted to come." Her voice trailed off, then she looked at him, her eyes stricken with grief. "That's where the kidnapper found him? He picked him out? Like he was picking out a pet? He just chose him and took him?"

"He must have followed you home."

The walkie-talkie in Archie's hand popped and crackled. "Detective Sheridan?" a voice said.

"I'm here," Archie said, lifting it to his mouth.

"We found your detective. Flannigan. He managed to make it up a fire escape. He's fine."

Archie closed his eyes and exhaled. It made him cough, and he turned his head to his shoulder. His lungs cramped and he fought to catch his breath.

When he'd recovered he looked up to see the Liftons and Eaton staring at him.

"Flannigan's okay," Archie said.

Diana Lifton pointed at the blanket over Archie's shoulder where he'd turned his head when he'd coughed, and where a dark splatter was visible on the gray wool.

"It's blood," she said.

CHAPTER 62

Archie's lung X-ray was displayed brightly on a black flat-screen monitor in the Emanuel emergency room. Dr. Fergus was sitting on a stool. He was tall, and the stool was too short for him, so his knees buckled out at odd, overly acute angles. Fergus typed something up on a keypad with two fingers, stopping every once in a while to hunt for a letter. The stool was on coasters, and Fergus had been rolling it around the same circle since he sat down. Archie wasn't sure he even knew he was doing it.

The Guard fatigues were deemed too damp, and Archie was now back in hospital hand-me-down finest — purple sweatpants, a golf shirt from some tournament in Indiana, and loafers a size too big. Where was the hospital getting all these clothes? From the morgue?

He examined the X-ray. His lungs looked like someone had stuffed cotton in them and the cotton had settled at the bottom.

Fergus was still typing. "We're going to gussy up a suite upstairs and name it after you because of all the business you bring us," he said, not looking up.

"Ha ha," Archie said.

"You should have called me when the fever started."

Fergus hit enter on the keyboard, pulled a pad of paper from his lab coat pocket, and scribbled something on it. Then he ripped the prescription off the pad and wheeled around to face Archie, who was sitting in a chair. "I'm putting you on antibiotics," he said, handing Archie the slip. "These are big league. They'll probably do the trick."

"Probably?" Archie said. A coughing fit overcame him, and Archie buried his face in his elbow. When it was over he looked back up, his face hot, eyes watering. Now that the adrenaline was wearing off, he could feel the full weight of his exhaustion.

Fergus took his reading glasses off and wiped them with the corner of his white lab coat. "You've got bacterial pneumonia," he said. "Early stages, yet. But given your general condition, it's not unserious. If you were anyone else, I tell you to stay in bed at home for a few days, but I know you'd ignore me, so I won't waste my breath."

He opened a cabinet drawer, pulled out a white surgical mask, and held it out to Archie.

"Is that really necessary?" Archie asked.

"When you're around sick people, yes. The pneumonia's not contagious, but the bacteria that's causing it is. You're in a hospital filled with people with compromised immune systems, much like yours. Let's try not to infect all the nice cancer babies, shall we?"

Archie took the mask. "I've seen Detective Sobol since I've been sick," he said.

"I think catching your cold is the least of his problems right now," Fergus said. He leaned forward over his sharp knees and tapped the prescription in Archie's hand. "Now, get this filled right away, at the pharmacy in the atrium."

"Thanks again," Archie said, standing up.

Before he could get out the door, Fergus stopped him. His gruff-doctor demeanor softened. "I'm sorry to hear about the detective you lost tonight," he said.

"Yeah."

Fergus swung back to the monitor. "Do us both a favor," he said. "If you find that you are unable to breathe, or start coughing up more blood, give me a call. And in the meantime don't jump into any more rivers."

"I keep forgetting not to do that," Archie said. He put on his mask and went out the door.

Ngyun was leaning up against the hallway wall waiting for him.

Archie stopped, flustered. He had consoled the family and friends of dozens of victims. Now the words felt cheap. Heil was dead. Archie had been his boss. But Ngyun and Flannigan? They had worked with Heil. Day after day, for over a year. "It was quick," Archie said.

Ngyun nodded and looked at a spot next to Archie's head. Then he reached out and offered something he held in his hand. "I thought you might need this."

It was a cell phone.

"It's a loaner from the office," Ngyun said. "I had your number forwarded. They said it'll take a few hours."

Archie took the phone. "Thanks," he said.

"Do you need me to do anything?" Ngyun asked.

Flannigan was home with his family. Dry and warm in his bed.

"Go home," Archie said.

Ngyun nodded again, still looking at that spot. "Right," he said. He turned after a moment and took off down the hall. Archie watched him go. He had one more thing he wanted to do before he went to the pharmacy.

Susan was lying in a bed, hooked up to all sorts of monitors. A nurse was busy typing up notes on the room's computer. Susan smiled sleepily at Archie.

He stood for a moment in the doorway.

"Flannigan is okay," he said.

Susan's eyes opened wider and she gave him a thumbs-up.

He didn't stay.

"Nice sweatpants," he heard Susan call.

CHAPTER 63

The pills Fergus had given him came in a blister pack. They were oval and white, and if Archie squinted they looked like Vicodin. He slipped his mask aside, took his first dose, and washed it down with a swig of bottled water. Then he punched the rest out and put them in his pocket.

He missed taking pills.

"What are you thinking about?" Henry asked. He was sitting up in bed, propped up on a pillow. His head was freshly shaved and his scalp gleamed under the hospital lights. Claire had pulled her chair close to the bed and held Henry's hand.

Archie coughed. "I should get out of here," he said. He didn't even know when the last time he slept was.

"I'll give you a ride," Claire said.

Anne appeared from the hallway. "I'll do it," she said.

Archie looked up at her. "I don't want to talk."

"I don't want you to cough on me," Anne said. "We both may have to compromise."

Anne had rented a convertible red Mustang.

The rain slapping against the ragtop sounded like a flag snapping in a hard wind.

"It's dark," Anne said.

"It's always dark," said Archie.

The surgical mask was on his lap. They were driving down Martin Luther King, Jr., Boulevard. A news van going too fast passed them at an intersection, heading toward the river.

"Henry looks good," Anne said.

Archie could see the helicopters in the distance, but he couldn't hear them. "Heil's dead."

Anne looked straight ahead out the windshield. "It wasn't a trade," she said.

The glowing towers of the convention center speared the dark sky.

"He liked watching people die," Archie said.

"He liked watching people drown," Anne said, correcting him. "His grandfather drowned at Vanport. The story was probably mythic in his family. The poison provided a way for him to watch people drown

426

on dry land. He justified it as some sort of bent revenge for his grandfather's death. That's why he left the Vanport keys on the bodies. He wanted to make a statement, to be understood. You said he knew who Susan was. He probably slipped that key in her bag, hoping that she'd see the connection and write about it. In the end, his grandfather's story was an excuse. He felt powerless. Killing people made him feel less powerless."

"How does the boy fit in?" Archie asked.

"We may never know," Anne said. "But my guess is that the kidnapping was spontaneous. That Carey recognized something in the kid that was vulnerable. He wanted control. Keeping Patrick Lifton in a basement room was no different to him than keeping a fish in a bowl. It gave him the power that he craved. But after a while it wasn't enough."

"So he sees Susan's story about the skeleton, and gets a bee in his bonnet to go on a killing spree?"

Anne raised an eyebrow and sighed. "I wouldn't be surprised if we found out that he'd been drowning animals since childhood," she said.

They passed the entrance to I-84, north to Vancouver.

Archie couldn't stop thinking about the boy. "If the kid did manage to get out of the river, where would he go?"

Anne thought. "Someplace he felt safe."

Aquarium World was in ruins. The house was cordoned off with crime tape. Patrick's bridge hideout was underwater.

"Oaks Park," Archie said.

"This is ridiculous," Anne muttered from behind Archie as they tromped through the flooded parking lot.

Archie waved to August and Philip Hughes, who stood with flashlights at the main gate up ahead.

"Thanks for coming," Archie said. "How bad is it in there?"

"Two feet, at its deepest," August Hughes said. "She took it pretty well. Most of the rides are above water."

"Is there power?" Archie asked.

"Yes, sir," August Hughes said. "We've got generators as a backup to the main power line." He swung open the gate and walked into the park, his flashlight beam bouncing in front of him.

A few moments later the lights came on. The metal grates and intricate workings of the rides were lit up with fluorescent strips and bright multicolored bulbs. But the park remained still. The rides didn't move.

August Hughes reappeared from around a corner.

"Okay," Archie said to Anne. "Let's look around."

"We can help," Philip Hughes said. "Dad knows the park better than anybody. He knows the kid."

The sooner they got the park searched, the sooner they could determine the boy wasn't there, and the sooner Archie would be able to sleep. "Take the south side," Archie said. "And stick together." He looked at Anne. "You're with me," he said.

"It's the middle of the night," Anne said. "You're ill."

"I just have to make sure he isn't here."

"Patrick?" Archie called.

"This place gives me the creeps," Anne said.

Archie called Patrick's name again. "It's Detective Sheridan," he called.

"There," Anne said.

"What?"

"I saw something move," Anne said, pointing.

"What?" Archie asked.

"A shadow," Anne said.

"Was it him?"

"I don't know," Anne said. "It was something."

"Patrick?" Archie called again.

He saw something then, too. A flash of movement. Someone disappearing through a door into one of the rides.

Archie jogged through the water toward the ride, calling the boy's name.

He stopped at the door.

It wasn't really a ride. It was some sort of building. Something you walked through. A haunted house.

A shadowy figure lurked just inside the door.

"It's safe," Archie said. "You can come out."

The boy stepped into the light. He was wet and dirty, his face scratched.

"Jesus Christ," Anne said.

Patrick took a tentative step toward them and then flung himself into Archie's arms, all cold, wet elbows and knees.

Archie glanced up at the side of the attraction the boy had emerged from. The door was a mouth. Framed by a pair of huge red open lips.

Garishly painted letters spelled out BEAUTY KILLER HOUSE OF HORRORS.

Archie held Patrick Lifton very tightly for a very long time before he pulled out his phone and called the chief. "It's Archie," he said. "Call the Liftons. I've got him. I've got him."

Archie was sitting with Patrick in the back of an open ambulance. EMTs had checked the boy's vitals and put Band-Aids on his scratches. He would still need to go to the hospital, but the EMTs had agreed to wait. Archie saw the patrol car cruise in, lights flashing, going too fast, its tires throwing up water on the pavement. It came to a stop alongside another patrol unit, about five yards from the ambulance. The back door flew open and Diana Lifton exploded from the car. She was wearing pajamas and sneakers and a coat, her hair knotted in a quick ponytail. Daniel Lifton slid out behind her from the same door, dressed in sweat shorts, a worn T-shirt, and slip-on velour slippers worn over white tube socks. They held each other as they approached the ambulance. The rain had slowed to a spit. Lights from the surrounding emergency vehicles split the darkness with flashes of red and blue.

Patrick didn't see them at first. Archie held him on his lap, wrapped in a blanket, the boy's head against Archie's shoulder, his arms hooked around Archie's neck.

Archie could smell his hair, the sweat of his scalp, the mulch of river muck. "Your family's here," Archie whispered.

He felt Patrick lift his head, and heard the boy's mother make a sound somewhere between a laugh and a cry.

"Mama?" Patrick said.

The boy's arms pulled away from Archie's neck and the blanket fell aside as Patrick Lifton dove from Archie's lap into his mother's arms. There was no hesitation. No moment of confusion or fear. His parents embraced him.

"You're safe," Diana Lifton said. She kept repeating it.

Archie got up and walked slowly away, leaving the Liftons to their reunion. The generators were still on and the park below blinked with bright colored lights. The dark cloud cover above had finally split, revealing a slice of stars in the night sky.

"I could hear you wheezing from all the way over there," Anne said, motioning to where she'd been standing several yards away, on the telephone.

"Calling home?" Archie asked, nodding at the phone in her hand.

"One of my boys totaled the minivan," Anne said.

"You have a minivan?"

Anne smiled. "Used to."

"Your boy okay?" Archie asked.

"Until my husband gets done with him," Anne said.

Archie's gaze fell on Patrick Lifton. His parents were still on either side of him and were helping to get him back into the ambulance. When he was secure, they got in behind him.

"Will he ever be okay?" Archie asked Anne.

The ambulance doors closed. A patrol unit got in place to escort it. And then the two vehicles pulled away into the rain. "Better than most of us," Anne said.

CHAPTER 64

Susan had been moved upstairs to a hospital room with a view of the parking garage. The blinds were open and flat winter morning light filled the room.

There was a rose-colored plastic chair in her room, an old-fashioned real live landline, and a bedside table with a plastic cup and a water pitcher that matched the chair. A picture of Mount Hood hung on the wall. She wondered if people who had views of Mount Hood had pictures of parking garages hanging on their walls.

She counted to ten and then picked up the phone and dialed the number she had written on a hospital pad in front of her. She followed the prompts, entered the credit card information, and was connected to the cruise ship her mother was on.

When the ship's operator picked up, Susan asked to speak to Bliss Mountain, stressing that it was important, just in case

434

her mother was in the middle of sun salutations when they found her and refused to come to the phone.

Susan imagined a purser walking the ship's decks carrying a silver tray with a cordless telephone on it.

It didn't take as long as she thought it would.

"Hello?" her mother's voice said uncertainly.

"Bliss? It's me," Susan said. And then she felt the need to add, "Susan." She paused, wishing she had prepared more. "I just wanted to let you know what's going on." *I was clinically dead? I was kidnapped by a serial killer? Again.* She settled on: "The river's flooded."

"Is Sally okay?" Bliss asked.

"The goat's fine," Susan said. "I'm calling to let you know that I drowned."

Her mother sucked in a breath. "What?"

"I mean, I'm all right now," Susan said. "I was a hostage. There were these octopuses. And this kid. I tried to save him. And I got caught in the river when the seawall broke, and I went under. My heart stopped. They had to reboot me."

"A kid with an octopus?"

Was she listening? "Mom, I had to be resuscitated."

"Where are you?" Bliss asked.

"I'm in the hospital." Susan fought the urge to add *obviously.*

"I can't get off the ship right now," Bliss said. "The next port is St. Thomas. I can arrange a flight back from there."

"No, Bliss," Susan said. "Seriously. You'd never make it." Her mother was notorious for getting lost in airports. Half the time she got in line for the wrong flight. "And you know you can't fly through Miami."

"That was years ago. I'm sure they've forgotten about it."

"They found four joints in your purse, Bliss." The two times Bliss had flown through Miami since, she'd been subjected to a body-cavity search while Susan waited in the hall for four hours.

"That was for personal use," Bliss said. "And it was Jamaican." As if that made a difference.

"Don't come," Susan said. "I'm fine. They say I'm going to make a full recovery. But it may take a few days to get my purse released from the crime scene." They'd been hassling her for her health insurance card. "When you get fired, do you still have health insurance for a while?"

Bliss paused. "I think so. Why?" Her mother sighed. "Oh, Susan. You didn't."

Susan didn't want to get into it. "I should go," she said quickly. "This is costing me six-ninety-five a minute. I love you. Go meditate or something."

"I love you, too, sweetie."

Susan hung up the phone and handed the credit card back to Archie.

He took the card and tucked it back in his wallet.

"Tell me again about his parents," she said.

Archie sat back in the rose plastic chair and folded his hands over his chest. He looked better than he had in days — like he'd actually gotten some sleep. "They cried," he said. "They came right to the park, before we even got him out of there. They held on to him. I'm not sure they'll ever let him go."

"What about Carey? Are you sure he's dead?"

"Yes," Archie said.

"I was right about McBee."

"You and Gloria Larson."

"Do you think she'll ever be able to tell us the whole story?"

"Maybe. On a lucid day." He stood up, one hand pressed against his chest, like it hurt. "There's still a lot to do," he said. "I'll come by later." He looked around the room,

437

at the roses and lilies that sat on every surface. "Leo Reynolds?" he asked.

Susan glanced over at the small bouquet that Archie had brought, clearly purchased in the hospital gift store. Dyed-pink carnations and baby's breath in a weird little plastic vase.

"I like yours more," she said.

Archie did an awkward shuffle with his feet. Then he took a step toward the door, paused, coughed once, and turned back.

"Do you want me to go by and check on the goat?" he asked.

Archie had left Susan's room and was headed down the hall to make his way up to the ICU when who should appear but Leo Reynolds himself. He was wearing a dark suit, perfectly pressed and clearly not off-the-rack. Archie had never had anything tailored to his specifications in his life. But he appreciated it when he saw it — the cut of the shoulders, the length of the arms. Archie had first met Leo when Leo was in college, and Archie was investigating his sister's murder. He'd dressed like that even then.

Leo could afford it. His father had made a fortune importing massive amounts of heroin and coke.

Leo walked over to Archie, carrying a bouquet of plump pink roses. Archie wondered where the hell he was getting all these fancy flowers in the middle of a natural disaster.

"How did you know she was here?" Archie asked him.

"She called me," Leo said.

Archie hadn't considered that.

Leo looked around, and then took a small step closer to Archie. "You haven't told her," he said. "About me?"

"No."

"I wouldn't want to ruin my bad-boy reputation," he said. He rubbed his jaw with his hand, and Archie thought he detected a hint of disappointment. Leo wanted Archie to tell Susan he was DEA. He wanted her to know. Leo was one of the agency's most valuable assets. An insider who'd wanted out of his family by the time he was in college, who'd come to Archie for help, and whom Archie had sent to the DEA, which had in turn talked Leo into staying. Archie always suspected that Leo hated him a little for that.

"Your bad-boy reputation is intact," Archie said. Susan could never find out. They both knew that. There was too much at stake.

"I heard you saved her life."

"We trade off," Archie said.

"I'm serious about her." Leo looked down at the bouquet in his hands. "I feel like I should ask your permission."

Archie liked Leo. It complicated things. Deep cover came with a cost. Leo hated his father, but he didn't seem to mind the drugs and women and expensive suits. "You have a dangerous life," Archie said.

Leo met Archie's gaze. "So do you."

Archie could feel the weight of something pass between them. "I'm not sleeping with her," Archie said.

Leo raised his eyebrow.

Archie felt flustered. "I have to get going," he said.

"Me, too," Leo said.

They headed in separate directions — Archie to the ICU, Leo toward Susan's room, the roses tucked under his arm.

CHAPTER 65

One week later

Gloria Larson opened her apartment door wearing a dark blue fleece robe over a light blue flannel nightgown, white socks, and slippers that looked hand-knit.

"It's good to see you again," Archie said.

"Wipe your feet," Gloria said.

It had stopped raining three days before. The floodwater downtown had receded, leaving billions in damage. Archie's Cutlass had been found four blocks from where he had left it. Patrick Lifton was back in Aberdeen, sleeping in his own bed, playing with his dog, and embarking on what would probably be a lifetime of therapy.

Archie's and Susan's shoes were dry. But they wiped them anyway.

"Sit down," she said. And they took a seat on the couch.

The TV was off. Archie was grateful. He'd had enough local news. Enough aerial shots of floating cars. Enough of reporters wading through water to show how deep it was. Enough hypothesizing about Elroy Carey's motives.

Gloria set a cup of tea in front of him. "Chamomile," she said. "Your favorite. Let it steep," she said. Then she went back for a cup for Susan and set it down in front of her. "Peppermint," she said.

"McBee's first name," Susan said. "Was it Elroy?"

"Elroy McBee," Gloria said slowly, as if she were trying it out. She brought her gaze back to Susan and patted her on the knee. "You know about the Vanport flood?"

"We know some," Susan said with a glance at Archie. "But why don't you fill us in?"

"I was a lot younger then. Twenty-six." Gloria smiled slyly. "And I was an independent woman, like a lot of us during the war. I worked at the stockyards as a secretary to the president, a man named Williams. It was a big operation back then. Just south of Vanport." She stopped and gave Archie a careful look. "You said you had an affair?" she asked.

Archie coughed.

She waited.

"Yes," he said after a moment. He glanced at Susan. "When I was married, I cheated on my wife."

Gloria patted him on the knee, seemingly satisfied.

Archie pulled the tea bag out of his teacup and laid it on the side of the saucer.

"I was involved with two men," she continued. "One of them — Elroy McBee — was married." She nodded to herself. "I was the other woman." She looked at Archie. "Like your other woman, I suppose."

Not exactly, thought Archie.

"After a time I broke it off with McBee," Gloria said. "The other gentleman and I were going to move to California together." She blinked rapidly. "McBee was angry. And they fought. Ugly things were said. I wanted them to settle down, so I told McBee that I'd meet him the next morning to talk things out. Have you heard of the Vanport Theater?"

Archie shook his head no, and took a sip of tea.

"It sat seven hundred and fifty people, and showed three double features a week," she said. "We were supposed to meet behind it." She leaned forward and lowered her voice to a whisper. "But when I got there, he was dead. I found him slumped against the wall, head down, legs splayed out. Someone had shot and killed him."

Archie looked up from his tea.

"I knew that my gentleman friend had to be responsible. He knew where and when McBee and I were meeting, and he knew that McBee would do everything in his power to stop us from going away together."

"He was a fireman?" Archie asked.

"Yes," she said, smoothing the robe on her lap. "The gun was on the ground. I thought my friend's fingerprints would be on it, so I picked it up and I threw it in the storm drain. And I got in my car and I drove to work. I waited all day to hear news that the body had been found. I could barely think straight."

Her eyes filled with amazement. "But the day passed, it was almost four o'clock and he hadn't been discovered. Can you imagine? And then I remembered what day it was."

"Memorial Day," Archie said softly. "The theater was closed."

"I didn't have the day off," Gloria said. "The stockyards depended a lot on train service, and the dike that protected Vanport also happened to be a railroad bed. We knew there was snowmelt. My boss, Mr. Williams, had men out in cars patrolling the tracks. At four o'clock one of the men came running back to Mr. Williams's office. He said that the dike had a sixty-foot breach. We all ran to the window, and we could see the railroad bed from there, giving way, water gushing out."

She reached for her tea.

Susan scooted forward. "You were his secretary," she said. "You were in there on a holiday. He must not have been able to function without you."

"That man couldn't have signed his name by himself."

Gloria had said that Williams had made two calls that day. But Williams was the president of the company. Used to giving orders.

"Your boss didn't make the first call," Archie said.

Gloria smiled to herself. "Of course he didn't. A man like that, back then? He told me to do it. I had a desk outside his office and I went to it and I picked up the phone. He had told me to call the Housing Authority, which ran Vanport. But then I thought, what if I don't?" Her hands were fists. "What if Vanport gets washed away, and McBee with it?"

Archie took another sip of tea.

Gloria was sitting perfectly still. "My gentleman friend, you see, he was a porter. And I knew that he was in Seattle by then, not due back until evening. He would be safe." Her shoulders raised and fell. "I returned to Mr. Williams's office and told him that I had made the call," she said. "And we watched for five or six minutes as the dike gave way. Until the breach was a hundred and fifty feet wide. And still we didn't hear the evacuation siren. And Mr. Williams, he was turning red in the face. He was a good man, you see, and he knew that those people were in danger. And he picked up the phone himself." She raised her white eyebrows. "I had never seen him do that before. I had never seen him make a call himself. And he called the Housing Authority and he screamed at them. He told them, in very colorful language, that they needed to sound the alarm."

"What happened to your friend?" Archie asked.

"I never saw him again. I was too afraid of what he'd done, and ashamed of what I'd done. Three children drowned that day. But it worked. McBee was never found. Until last week."

"Your friend, he was black?" Susan asked.

"Yes."

"That's why you wanted to move to California?" Susan said.

"They had just made mixed marriage

legal. There had been a big case. Lots of stories in the newspapers. And when it was settled, my friend asked me to marry him. We used to take the trolley to Oaks Park, and that's where he asked me. On the carousel."

Archie's mouth felt dry. "What was his name?"

"I'm sure he's dead now, Detective. It was a hundred years ago."

"We still need his name," Susan said.

"Hughes. August Albert Hughes."

"I think there's something you should know," Archie said.

CHAPTER 66

The picnic table at Oaks Park was crooked, lifted by floodwater and resettled at a slight angle. The grassy area under the elms was a field of mud. Across the river, the west side looked scarred where the river had carved away at its bank. But the clouds had cleared. The sky was blue. And the wooden top of the picnic table felt warm in the sun.

Archie watched his son and daughter play nearby, laughing as the mud sucked at their sneakers.

Ben looked up and waved, and Archie waved back at him.

It had been weeks since Archie had seen them. It had been too easy to make excuses.

He had let Susan do the talking, watching his children as she rattled off Gloria Larson's story to August Hughes. Hughes sat quietly next to her on the picnic table bench until she was done.

"I didn't kill Elroy McBee," August

Hughes said finally when she was done. "I figured he drowned, like everybody else. I figured it broke Gloria's heart. That she still loved him."

Susan's brow furrowed and she glanced at Archie. "That's why you never tried to see Gloria again," she said.

"I didn't kill him," Hughes said again. "So who did?"

They both waited for Archie to say something.

"She said she threw the gun down the sewer," Archie said. "Some of the sewer system is still there. When they built the golf course they reused it for irrigation. I've got people looking for it."

"And if you find it?"

"It will have your fingerprints on it," Archie said. "Or it won't."

It was a bluff. The odds of them finding the gun were next to none, the odds of there being any prints after sixty years were even slimmer.

But Hughes didn't back down. "Will you tell her I didn't do it?" he asked.

Susan looked up, behind Archie, toward the parking lot. "Tell her yourself."

Archie turned and saw Gloria Larson and her daughter stepping out of a car. Another car pulled up beside it and Debbie got out and waved at him. He stood up. His kids ran to their mother.

"I have to go," Archie said to Susan. "I've got something across the river."

"The hearing, right?" Susan said.

"Today's the day."

"Good luck," she said. She glanced back and forth between August Hughes and Gloria Larson and grinned from ear to ear. "It's like fate," she said.

CHAPTER 67

Archie sat on the hard bench in the court house hall, his feet on the marble floor, his back against the plaster wall. He emptied his pocket of pills. There were four left. They had worked. His lungs were clear.

Henry had been released from the hospital in time to attend Heil's funeral. Heil had been cremated, so there hadn't been a casket. Archie felt relieved. He hadn't wanted to see him again.

The bench was making Archie's back hurt and he checked his watch. But it had stopped. He held it against one ear and shook it. It wasn't ticking. The water damage had finally taken its toll.

The crowd outside filled the park across the street. News vans lined the street. Archie could hear the distant chanting of the crowd, but he couldn't make out the words. The media had been banned from the court house, but there'd be no escaping them outside.

The courtroom doors opened and Archie looked up to see the assistant district attorney. She was wearing a skirt and suit jacket and heels. It was a big day. Archie's phone rang. He glanced at the ID and held up a finger for her to wait.

It was Robbins.

"Hey," Archie said, slipping the pills back in his right pocket. "Make it quick."

"We found the gun," Robbins said. "It was in an unused portion of the pipe, so it's been dry for most of the time it's been down there. There was a partial print. It's kind of amazing. It wouldn't have lasted all these years if it hadn't have been so oily."

"Was it Hughes?" Archie asked.

"McBee. He shot himself. I matched the print to the fire department records. Through the mouth, I'd guess. Bullet lodged in his brain. That's why we didn't see evidence of bullet damage to the skeleton. He died instantly. Hand spasmed. Gun landed a few feet away."

Carey had killed five people in some sort of bent revenge because of a mistaken belief that McBee had drowned. And Gloria Larson had lived with the heavy guilt that she'd cost lives by delaying the alarm.

452

"Can't prove it," Archie said.

"Can't prove anything," Robbins said.

Archie paused. "You think Carey's body will surface?"

"Sure," Robbins said. "Give it a few months. Someone will fish him out."

"Maybe in sixty years," Archie said. He glanced up at the ADA.

You're almost up, she mouthed.

"I've got to go," Archie said, hanging up.

The ADA smiled. "Beautiful day, isn't it?"

"I didn't wear a tie," Archie said.

"It's okay," she said. "Follow me."

He stood up and followed her to the courtroom entrance. A bailiff nodded at them and opened the doors to Gretchen Lowell's sanity hearing.

The sun streamed through the tall windows and glimmered on the hardwood moldings and benches.

Archie stopped.

He could see Gretchen sitting at the defendant's table, her back to him, her blond hair golden in the light. She slowly turned her head and looked at him. She still hadn't spoken since her second arrest. Not a single word. Her face was unmarred by incarceration. Her skin glowed. She reached up with her manacled hands, brushed her hair behind her ear, and smiled at him.

"You can sit here," the ADA whispered, ushering him to slide onto a back bench. "Just a few minutes."

Archie took a seat, and the ADA slid in next to him.

It was a closed hearing, so attendance was limited to witnesses and court personnel.

The judge shuffled some paperwork on his desk. "Ms. Lowell. The court has been notified that you've decided not to testify on your own behalf, is that correct?"

Gretchen leaned close to her attorney. Her hair fell like a curtain between their faces and Archie couldn't tell if she was telling him something or just tilting her head. After a moment, her attorney stood. "Actually," he said, "if it pleases the court, Ms. Lowell would like to make a brief statement."

Even with so few people in the courtroom, the murmur of surprise was audible.

"Go right ahead," the judge said.

Gretchen pushed her chair back from the defendant's table and rose to her feet. She moved languidly, relaxed but purposeful, as if she were excusing herself after just paying the tab for lunch at a restaurant.

She walked to the witness box and sat down. She was wearing prison-issue orange cotton pants, an orange cotton shirt over a T-shirt, and flip-flops. The male and female inmates all wore the same clothes. The T-shirts, along with the underwear, were dyed pink, after years of attrition from inmates filching underwear when they were released.

Gretchen looked right at Archie. The pink collar of the undershirt made her look girl-ish. Her skin glowed. Her perfect, pretty features still made his gut hurt.

"I just wanted to make it clear that I don't regret anything," she said. Her blue eyes left Archie and skirted around the court, find-ing everyone, making each person shift in his or her seat as her gaze settled and then lifted. "You can justify killing anyone, really," she said. "You just need to give yourself permission. Everything I've done, I've done for a reason." She looked back at Archie and smiled that beauty queen smile. "I knew you'd come, darling," she said.

He'd been subpoenaed.

Archie didn't look away. He reached into his left pocket and rolled a pill between his fingers.

It was smaller than the antibiotics. A single Vicodin. He'd been saving it.

"You ready to do this?" the ADA whis-pered.

Archie met Gretchen's stare. The sunlight through the window flattered her, the shirt was small and hugged the curve of her breasts. He showed her nothing. No emotion. No reaction.

Until her smile faded, and her perfect lips fell slightly open.

Then he grinned.

"Absolutely," Archie said.

EPILOGUE

Heather Jadot was out of shape. Baby bulge. Dylan was six months old, but the pregnancy fat was still there, an extra inch of flesh around her thighs, hips, and belly. All the Spanx in the world couldn't hide it. Most of the Eastbank Esplanade had reopened. It wasn't raining. So she didn't have any more excuses. Dylan was snug in the baby jogger and Vixen was on her leash tumbling alongside them.

She could see the bulldozers on the west side, still working to clear debris. Barges pushing along rafts of detritus had become a common sight in the Willamette. Waterfront Park had been completely destroyed. A capital campaign was already under way to fund a redevelopment effort. Heather had joined the Facebook page.

Her Reeboks hit the pavement as she headed north, alongside the freeway. The concrete pathway had been underwater, like everything else. When the water receded it had left a layer of silt on everything, which had to be pressure-washed with fire hoses. The riverbank, which had never been pretty, was now a mush of dead plants and mud. Garbage came to the surface and clotted the weeds faster than the volunteers could get to it.

Vixen hopped off the path into the grass and skittered down the bank a few feet.

Heather stopped the stroller and pulled on the leash, but Vixen wouldn't budge.

She was into something. Snuffling around.

Heather could smell something rank. Vixen had already rolled in the remains of a drowned squirrel in the parking lot.

Heather tugged hard and Vixen's face popped up above the foliage.

"Leave it," Heather commanded.

Vixen hesitated.

Dylan whined.

"Leave it," Heather said louder.

Vixen disappeared for a moment and then came bounding up to the path with something in her mouth. Heather drew back in disgust and Vixen dropped it on the pavement.

Heather looked down. It was only a piece of elastic. Like a portion of a man's suspenders. That was a relief.

Heather nudged the elastic back into the weeds with the tip of her Reebok. She wasn't going to touch it. Someone else would pick it up.

Everything ended up in the river anyway.

She adjusted her pink baseball cap over her ponytail, set her eyes on the next bridge, and started jogging.

She wanted to get away from that smell.

ACKNOWLEDGMENTS

This book would not exist without the Herculean efforts, persistence, and patience of my editor, Kelley Ragland. You were right about the kid, Kelley. Joy Harris is simply the best literary agent ever. Thank you, Joy. And thank you to Adam Reed and Sarah Twonbly at the Joy Harris Literary Agency. (I am always careful to include the full name of Joy's agency, because when I was a struggling writer, someone told me that a good way to find an agent was to look in the acknowledgments of books I liked and see who was thanked.) My writing group still meets once a week. They are: Lidia Yuknavitch, Chuck Palahniuk, Monica Drake, Mary Wysong, Diana Jordan, Erin Leonard, Suzy Vitello, and Cheryl Strayed. The writing I've read in that room is some of the best I've ever read anywhere ever. You guys each inspire me. A big thanks to my film-rights wrangler, Nick Harris at Mosaic.

Keep working on that fake British accent, Nick — I think people are really starting to buy it. I launched two new Web sites this past year: chelseacain.com and iheart gretchenlowell.com. It was hard. And it took a lot of people. Thank you to the fabulous Storm Large (always my Gretchen Lowell), Lia Miternique of Avive Design, the team at Dorey Design Group, project manager Karissa Cain, photographer extraordinaire Laura Domela, make-up artist Crystal Slonecker, writer Courtenay Hameister, and copy editor Rob Simpson. Ryan O'Neil and Jake Kelly wrote Gretchen Lowell murder ballads and performed them at readings with me. You can check out audio clips on iheartgretchenlowell.com.

Much love to my husband, Marc Mohan, and our daughter, Eliza Fantastic. And hello to my nephews Jacob Duwa and Luke Duwa, just because I think they'll get a kick out of seeing their names in this book. (Though they're not allowed to read it.)

For the big finish, I am thankful every day to have a publisher like St. Martin's Press, which is populated by so very many smart, lovely people. Special thanks to Andrew Martin, George Witte, Sally Richardson, Matthew Shear, Matt Baldacci, Matt Martz, Hector DeJean, Nancy Trypuc and Tara Cibelli. Also, I'd like to apologize to Talia Sherer, Macmillan's Library Marketing Manager. I know this book isn't gory enough for you, Talia. I promise to make up for it next time.